THE STONE OF KUROMORI

The Kuromori trilogy

The Sword of Kuromori

The Shield of Kuromori

The Stone of Kuromori

JASON ROHAN

THE STONE OF KUROMORI

Kane Miller
A DIVISION OF EDC PUBLISHING

First American Edition 2017
Kane Miller, A Division of EDC Publishing

Original English language edition first published in 2017 under the title
The Stone of Kuromori by Egmont UK Limited, The Yellow Building,
I Nicholas Road, London, WII 4AN

For information contact:
Kane Miller, A Division of EDC Publishing
P.O. Box 470663
Tulsa, OK 74147-0663
www.kanemiller.com
www.edcpub.com
www.usbornebooksandmore.com

Library of Congress Control Number: 2015954166

Printed and bound in the United States of America
I 2 3 4 5 6 7 8 9 I0

ISBN: 978-1-61067-357-0

To Anoop, who was there at the beginning

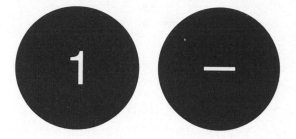

"**K**enny! Over here!"

Kenny Blackwood pushed the café door shut and wove his way between crowded tables to where his classmate Stacey Turner sat, ensconced in a booth by the mirrored wall.

"You're late," she said, narrowing her eyes before Kenny had even slid into the seat opposite. "And don't tell me the train was delayed – trains are never late in Japan. Let me guess, you missed the stop. No? Forgot something? How many times –"

"I came out of the wrong exit, that's all," Kenny said. "It took me a while to realize and I had to double back. You should have told me it was the south exit."

"And you should have checked first." Stacey blew a rubbery pink bubble and ran her finger down the coffee shop menu. "What are you having? My treat."

Kenny leaned back and laced his hands behind his head. "You're being unusually nice. What do you want?"

"Kenny Blackwood, I am shocked that you would

think such a thing," Stacey said in mock horror. "I'll tell you in a minute."

She raised a finger to summon the waitress, who glided over to take their order.

"I'll have an American coffee and a slice of green-tea cheesecake," Stacey said. "And a royal milk tea for him."

"So what's the big mystery?" Kenny asked, once the waitress had gone. "We could have had coffee at school. Why here?"

Stacey picked up the menu again and pretended to read it more closely. "It's haunted."

"Huh?" Kenny's eyes swept the coffee shop. It was bustling with college kids and high school students.

"It's true," Stacey said, lowering her menu shield. "You know me. When have I been wrong?"

"Well, there was that time –"

"It's a rhetorical question. Anyway, check this out." Stacey delved into her backpack and extracted a slim folder, which she handed to Kenny.

"I can't read this," he said, flipping through the newspaper cuttings inside. "My Japanese is still preschool level."

"I know. That's why I translated it for you. Look in the back."

Kenny knew better than to argue with Stacey. His classmate was top of their year in everything, including self-esteem.

By the time he had finished reading the dossier, Stacey had drained her coffee and was demolishing the cheesecake. "Well?" she said, chasing an escaped chunk around her plate. "What do you think?"

"I'm thinking you have some weird reading habits. Two guys commit suicide in the restroom of a bar. Why is that something you want me to . . .? Wait. You think this is the same place? It's not." Kenny opened the folder to a crime-scene snapshot. "The layout is totally different."

Stacey sighed. "Kenny, Kenny, Kenny. When will you learn not to doubt me?" She leaned forward and lowered her voice. "After the first guy killed himself, things went quiet for a while, but then business started to come back. When the second death happened, people stayed away and the bar eventually closed. Then these guys bought it, remodeled it and relaunched under a new name. It's the same place all right. I checked the address and the deeds of sale."

"You did? You're even more nuts than I thought."

A pink bubble popped in reply. "Here's what I think is happening: two years ago, on this same day, at 4:44 p.m., Mr. Kishibe went to the bathroom. Farthest stall on the end. Six hours later, at closing time, the owner saw that the door was still locked and forced it open. He found Mr. Kishibe."

"I read that, yeah." Kenny sipped his tea and tried not to picture the grisly scene.

"Last year, same day, same time, a Mr. Moteki went to use the bathroom. He also went into the same end stall, locked the door and was later found dead."

"And the police said both cases were suicides. So why are we here?"

"Kenny, who kills themselves in a bar bathroom? Besides, they didn't find a blade . . . either time, so how could they have done it?"

Kenny tilted his head. "You think there's a rogue *yokai* in there?"

"I know there is. Now, since you're one of the few people who can see these things, are you going to do your stuff and deal with it, or do I have to call in your friend Sato?"

"Shh." Kenny looked around and leaned in close enough to touch foreheads. "You know you're not supposed to talk about that," he whispered.

"Oh, please. Like anyone's paying attention to us. Listen, it's your job, isn't it, to stop these things? You're like a one-man *yokai* police force."

"It's not only me –"

"We don't talk about *her*."

Kenny fumbled for his phone. "I should check with Kiyomi first."

"Can we just leave your psycho girlfriend out of this?"

"She's not my girlfriend."

"At least you didn't say she isn't psycho." Stacey tapped her watch. "It's 4:38. You've got six minutes, so get in there and hold that stall. If any monster comes in, you can teach it a lesson."

"No way." Kenny finished his tea and stood up.

"Thanks for the drink, Stace. If I knew this was what you had in mind, I wouldn't have come. You have no right getting involved in this stuff."

"Kenny, people have died. Think about it. If I'm wrong, then nothing happens: no harm, no foul. But if I'm right and you walk away, then anything that goes down is on you. You want to read about some dead guy tomorrow, knowing you could have stopped it?"

"All right, all right," Kenny grumbled. "I'll go have a look."

Stacey smiled her approval. "I've saved you a bite of my cheesecake. That'll be your reward."

Kenny took a deep breath and stepped into the narrow stall which housed a traditional squat toilet.

This is so stupid, he thought, closing his eyes and shaking his head. *I can't believe I let Stacey talk me into this.*

Ever since she had uncovered Kenny's secret life as the bearer of a divine sword and a warrior sworn to keep monsters in check, Stacey had been itching to find ways to get involved, searching for unusual news stories and trawling the Internet for urban myths, much to Kenny's annoyance. He checked his watch: 4:43. A minute to go.

Even though he was pretty sure this was a waste of time, he could at least take advantage of where he was. Kenny unzipped his fly – and an ice-cold hand clutched his shoulder while a voice breathed in his ear.

"Will sir be wanting the blue or the red option?" it purred, its breath as foul as an open sewer.

"YAAH!" Kenny jumped, splashing one shoe into the toilet and spraying his jeans. He hastily zipped up and whirled around, to see nothing but a blank wall.

Two hands grasped his shoulders and the voice asked again, "I repeat, which option will sir be having, the red or the blue?" There was a harder edge now, clearly demanding an answer.

Kenny staggered around in a circle, but the thing, whatever it was, remained unseen. "What are you?" he said. "Show yourself."

The air seemed to condense into a vaguely human form, outlined by the drape of a long red cloak with a thick hood covering the face. It floated, without legs.

"Last time," it insisted. "Blue or red?"

"How about dead?" Kusanagi, the sacred sword, materialized in Kenny's hands and he lashed out, striking cleanly to slice the spectral creature in half. It shimmered as the sword edge penetrated, but the *katana* passed harmlessly through and bit into the tiled floor with a clang.

The thing resolidified and dead hands clawed outward from the folds of its cape, the fingers flattening and elongating into gleaming, razor-sharp blades.

Kenny pivoted backward and struck again, before slipping in the confined space and dropping to one knee. The creature flickered again, shifting its density around the blade, and closed in, slashing the air with its deadly claws.

"May I observe that sir has neither the space nor the speed to harm me in here?" Red Cape said. "I, on the other hand, have both."

Kenny instinctively raised his arms as a furious whirl of flashing blades ripped towards his face. Head down, with eyes closed, he heard the scream of metal, like a buzz saw grinding against steel, and felt a tingling in his arms.

Opening one eye, Kenny saw Red Cape backing away, its clawlike fingers mangled and bent. His own arms were gleaming chrome, with the ragged shreds of his shirtsleeves dangling from his elbows. Without thinking, he had channeled the element of metal to transform his arms.

"Sir has some tricks," Red Cape said. "But so do I." It flickered again, fading like a shadow, before re-forming with its ruined blades restored.

Kenny jumped up and swung the sword in a wild arc, missing the creature completely. Kusanagi sliced through the tiled wall, severing the copper pipes that ran across the divide. Water hissed into the stall, spraying the air.

"That was careless," Red Cape said, wagging a scalpel-like finger.

"Let it go," Kenny said, raising his voice over the fizz of escaping water. "You can't hurt me and I can't hurt you. Call it quits and get lost. Leave these people alone."

"Oh, no. The guilty come to me for punishment. No one is innocent – not even you." It thrust its dagger hand towards Kenny's chest and he jumped back, slamming against the door. "Besides, I don't take orders from *gaijin*."

"Don't say I didn't warn you." Kenny coughed, wiping water from his eyes. "If you had a nose, you'd know something was wrong by now. Hear that hissing sound? It's not just water. Let's see if you can dodge – this!" He snapped his fingers, producing a single spark.

WHOOMPH! An explosion ripped through the stall as the pocket of leaking gas ignited. The blast smashed Kenny through the door, still protected by his metallic form. He glimpsed shredded fragments of Red Cape burn into nothing.

With his eyes streaming and his ears ringing, Kenny staggered back into the coffee shop, shouldering open the door which was now hanging by one hinge. Everyone stared, openmouthed. His clothes were in tatters and flames filled the corridor behind him.

"Wooh! You do *not* want to go in there!" Kenny said, fanning his hands to clear the air.

Before anyone could respond, Stacey ran forward, grabbed him and steered him straight out of the front door.

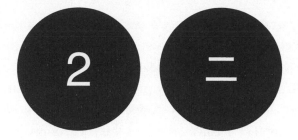

2 二

BANG-BANG-BANG-BANG!

"*Hnh? Whuzzah?*" Kenny pushed himself up on one elbow, his mind lurching towards wakefulness. Blinking his eyes and pinching the bridge of his nose, he fumbled for his watch.

4:09. In the morning.

He sat up. Stifling a yawn, he wavered between flopping back down to sleep or investigating the source of the noise. Drowsiness won and he slumped back onto his warm *futon*.

BANG-BANG-BANG! The front door rattled with the urgent pounding.

Fully awake now, Kenny jumped up and threw off the duvet. A strip of light blinked on at the base of his bedroom door and he heard his father, Charles, trudging along the hallway.

Scrubbing his hairline with his fingers, Charles unlatched the door. It slammed inward, catching him on the ankle, and a Japanese girl in biker leathers stormed past him.

"Oww! Kiyomi, what's with all the hammering?" Charles muttered, hopping and clutching his bruised bone. "Do you have any idea what time –"

"Where's Kenny?" Kiyomi's clenched jaw and the flash of anger in her eyes stopped Charles mid hop.

"Kiyomi?" Kenny stood in his bedroom doorway. "What's happened?"

"Why don't *you* tell me?" She put her hands on her hips and glared at him.

"Uh, Dad. It's OK," Kenny said, catching his father's look of concern. "I've got this."

"Really?" Charles said. "Not from where I'm standing."

"We need to talk," Kiyomi hissed at Kenny. "In private."

"Fine, but I don't see why this couldn't wait until the morning," Charles grumbled, pointing to the living room. Kiyomi marched past, with her boots still on.

Charles dipped his head closer to Kenny's. "You two aren't going to fight, are you? I mean, literally fight, as opposed to just arguing?"

"Dad!" Kenny said, throwing up his hands.

"OK, just asking. I don't need the place trashed." Charles stifled a yawn. "I'm going back to bed, so try to fight quietly."

Kenny padded into the living room where Kiyomi was pacing like a caged tiger. She rounded on him, stabbing a finger at his nose. "What have you done?"

"*Wha-?*"

"Don't act stupid with me."

"It's not an act." Kenny jerked his head away from the accusing finger and ran through the hundreds of reasons Kiyomi might be angry with him. Had she heard about him tackling Red Cape alone? Did he forget to text her? Had he left the toilet seat up again? He had no idea.

Kiyomi grabbed a handful of his T-shirt, marched him backward towards the sofa and pushed him onto it. "Sit down, shut up and hear what we have to say."

"We?" Kenny looked around in bewilderment until he spied a fat, furry, raccoon-like animal waddling in from the kitchen area, an open package of roasted-squid-flavored potato chips in its paws.

"Hey, I was saving those," Kenny objected.

Poyo spat a mouthful of chewed potato onto his paw and offered it to Kenny.

"Ugh. No thanks."

"Do you mind?" Kiyomi snapped at the *tanuki*, who retreated back into the kitchen.

Kiyomi strode over to the balcony windows and stared out into the dark Tokyo night. "I just had a dream," she said, "or nightmare more like." A shudder ran through her slender frame and she wrapped her arms around herself.

Kenny sat up at once, fully awake. Dreams were not to be taken lightly; he had learned that the hard way.

Kiyomi continued, her voice flat and emotionless. "I've been to *Yomi* once, if only for a few minutes, so trust me,

11

I know Hell when I see it." She shuddered again. "It's a dark, desolate, empty wasteland infested with every kind of filth and vermin."

"This was your dream?" Kenny asked, eyes wide with concern.

"I said to shut up and listen." The city lights beyond the window sparkled in Kiyomi's dark eyes. "In my dream, I was flying through the Land of the Dead, zipping over the earth until I came to this palace made of bone. It's the only building of any size, so it's obvious who it belongs to: the Lord of the Underworld. Do you know who that is?"

Kenny swallowed hard. He sensed that something bad was thundering towards him and there was nothing he could do to avoid it.

"You can answer," Kiyomi said.

"No, um, never heard of him," Kenny lied, hoping to protect her.

Kiyomi spun on one boot heel. "Well, he knows who you are! In fact, he's on first-name terms!"

Kenny's heart sank. This was rapidly going from bad to worse. "Uh, was there any more to your dream?"

Kiyomi's jaw tightened and her eyes drifted into the middle distance, while she replayed the vision. "The palace doors go up a mile. They're so high that I can't see the top. Anyway, I stand at the entrance, with this freezing-cold wind howling. And there's this ... this moaning and wailing sound, of dead people – and guess what happens?"

"A pizza delivery guy shows up?"

Kiyomi grabbed an eraser from the desk and hurled it at Kenny, bouncing it off his forehead.

"Oww," he protested. "Sorry, I can't help it."

Kiyomi took a deep breath. "So the doors swing open and this . . . rotting thing . . . ushers me in, like some kind of zombie butler, and says that his lord is expecting me." She held her hands out in Kenny's direction, as if pleading for help. "Don't you get it? I've been summoned . . . invited. Me personally."

Kenny absently wiped a cold sheen of sweat from his brow.

"Inside, the palace is a crumbling ruin," Kiyomi said, "all decaying glory. I'm taken through this maze of corridors to the throne room, high up, and there's like a thousand *oni* standing there, all waiting for me."

Kenny scowled, trying to picture the scene.

"And you know what they do?" Kiyomi's voice went up almost an octave and a grimace of horror twisted her face. "They *bow*. All of them. They bow – to me, like I'm one of them."

Kenny's head spun and he felt dizzy. "But . . . I thought –"

"No, Ken-*chan*, you didn't think. You never think through the consequences of your actions."

"What actions? What exactly am I supposed to have done?" Kenny shrugged. "Uh, back to the *oni* . . .?"

"Yeah, the *oni*. Half of those guys should be lining

up to tear me apart, after I sent their sorry butts back to Hell, but no. Now they're treating me like long-lost family. Then the doors open and in comes the Storm God himself, ruler of the underworld."

"Susie?" Kenny breathed, firing a glance in Poyo's direction.

"Susano-wo himself. He comes over, takes my chin in his hand and kisses the top of my head. Ugh! It's so disgusting. A centipede is crawling through his hair and a cockroach plops onto my shoulder." Kiyomi closed her eyes tightly and grimaced at the memory.

"Does he say anything?" Kenny asked, dreading the answer.

Kiyomi nodded. "You bet he does. He says, 'Welcome, child. Any friend of Kuromori is a friend of mine. How is young Kenny? Has he forgotten me and our arrangement?'"

A cold chill ran through Kenny. "But this is a dream, right? From your imagination? Maybe it's post-traumatic stress –"

"Shut up," Kiyomi said. "After the dreams you've had, you think I don't know when the gods are sending a message?"

"But . . ."

"I haven't finished," Kiyomi warned. "So then he takes out a bronze mirror, about this big." She held her palms out, marking a space roughly as wide as her shoulders. "And he shines a beam of light on it."

"Let me guess," Kenny interjected. "He says, 'Mirror, mirror, on the wall, who's the fairest of them all?'"

"Close," Kiyomi said, her voice cold. "He says, 'Show me the resting place of the *Yasakani no Magatama*.'"

"The what?"

"It's the Jewel of Life. The image in the reflection changes to show the surface of the ocean, then it shifts to the seabed."

"The bottom of the sea?"

"Uh-huh," Kiyomi said. "And then Susano-wo looks at me and says, 'Tell Kuromori he has four days to bring me the precious Stone of Life or our bargain is at an end. My patience grows thin.' He holds up his hand and shows me this white jade ring on his finger. It's the twin to that ring you gave me – the red jade one. 'Tell him to remember our agreement and honor it,' he says, 'or I will reclaim my prize.' And then . . ." Kiyomi stopped, her breath catching in ragged gasps. "And then . . . he punches his claws into my stomach and rips out this . . . white, glowing mist."

"Your soul," Kenny gasped.

"My *ki*," Kiyomi corrected. "That's when I woke up."

Kenny rubbed his face with both hands. "That's some nightmare all right."

Kiyomi remained by the window, shaking. "It wasn't a dream, Ken-*chan*. It was a message – from a god."

"How can you be so sure?" Kenny asked.

"Because . . ." Kiyomi pulled out her phone and

15

scrolled through the photo gallery. "When I woke up, I found this . . ." She handed Kenny the phone.

He stared for a few seconds, uncomprehending, before his mind finally made sense of what he was seeing. The picture showed a bedroom wall and scrawled in mucky red fingerprints to form large marks and symbols was:

二十四.二十五.五十五.二北,
百二十三.〇〇.三十九.六東

Kenny zoomed in on the photograph and his stomach lurched as he recognized the sticky drips and spatters that formed the writing. The message was written in blood.

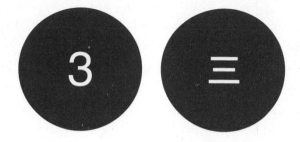

Kenny felt the acid tang of bile in the back of his throat. "Whose blood?" he croaked.

"Not mine, if that's what you're asking," Kiyomi said, snatching back her phone, "although it was all over my hands. Took ages to clean off and I had to wipe the walls down with bleach. Nice way to leave a message."

Kenny blanched, unable to clear the image from his mind. "If it's not your blood, then . . ."

"Don't be such a baby. I checked the fridge and there was a packet of *wagyu* steak missing."

"*You* wrote that?"

"Duh. Hello, Sherlock. Looks like someone can make me write in my sleep as well as walk. Aren't I talented?"

Kenny rubbed his eyes. "Am I allowed to get up now?"

Kiyomi gave a curt nod. Kenny stood and went over to the workstation by the window. He picked up a notepad and jotted down the symbols.

"These numbers," he said. "What do they mean? Is it some kind of code? A puzzle? Some ancient language?"

Kiyomi rolled her eyes. "You're such an idiot

sometimes. Give me that." Kenny handed her the pad and for a moment the only sounds were the scratching of the pen and a quiet crunching from the kitchen. "Here." Kiyomi held out the pad.

Kenny took it and read:

$$24°2'55.2'N \; 123°00'39.6'E$$

"Oh, man. This is some kind of mathematics problem? Am I supposed to draw it?" He scratched his head.

"They're coordinates. You know, as in finding things on a map." Kiyomi took the pad back and drew a circle on a fresh page. "This is Earth, right?" She drew a horizontal line through the middle and a vertical one, cutting it in quarters. "This is the equator. Sideways lines are latitude. Down through the poles is longitude. Zero is Greenwich in London. Got it?"

"Yeah. And because it's a globe, it's three hundred and sixty degrees in any direction, right?"

"No. That works for longitude, but you count one hundred and eighty degrees east or west of Greenwich to make a complete circle." She drew arrows pointing to the left and right. "For latitude, it's ninety degrees north or south of the equator. OK?"

Kenny furrowed his brow and closed his eyes to visualize the planet. "So, twenty-four degrees north of the equator is about a quarter of the way up . . . and a hundred and twenty degrees east of London is about two-thirds of the way to the International Date Line . . ."

"Why don't you use that big shiny box called a computer, before your brain has a meltdown?" Kiyomi flicked her head in the direction of the monitor.

"Fine," Kenny grumbled, powering up his dad's clunky desktop. He called up a browser window, found a mapping site and keyed in the coordinates. The cursor flashed on a page of blue.

"Zoom out," Kiyomi advised.

Kenny clicked on the scale and a gray, clam-shaped blob appeared at the top of the screen. He clicked again, shrinking the island, and continued zooming out until the state of Taiwan filled the page to the left.

"Keep going," Kiyomi said.

Kenny waited until Japan appeared, on the top right, then sat back and whistled through his teeth. "Wow. That's on the doorstep of China. It's closer to Korea than it is to here." He hit the print button. "So why were these coordinates given to you? Where is this?"

Kiyomi crossed her arms. "I'm not telling you anything until you explain what is going on."

Kenny sighed, taking the map from the printer.

"Well?" Kiyomi glared again.

Kenny hesitated. He was sworn to secrecy, unable to tell a soul about the deal he had made with Susano-wo, the Lord of the Underworld. On the other hand, what was he supposed to do now that Susano-wo had shown himself to Kiyomi? Not only had he dropped Kenny in it, he had also given Kiyomi important information to deliver.

"OK," Kenny sighed. "You're right. Susano-wo offered me a deal."

"I knew it!" Kiyomi said, her face twisting in fury. "To do what?"

Kenny looked away. "It was for you. For your soul."

Kiyomi froze. "Wh-What?"

Kenny's rubbed his stinging eyes again. "Back in July, when you . . . died – not all of you came back. The missing part was made up by Taro, and his *oni* soul began taking over, gaining control."

"Oh!" Kiyomi gasped in horror. "The red jade ring – it was from Susano-wo, wasn't it?"

Kenny nodded. "It was half of your missing soul. That's why you've been feeling better, why the *oni* part has been weaker this past month."

"And what did you have to do?" Kiyomi said, her voice a horrified whisper. "What did he demand in return?"

Kenny shrugged, but it was stiff and awkward, the complete opposite of the nonchalance he was trying to project. "He wanted some trinket, that was all."

Kiyomi's hand went to her mouth. "You gave him the Mirror of Amaterasu? Please, no. Tell me you didn't."

"I did it for you," Kenny said, reaching out to take her hands. "To save your life. I had to do something."

Kiyomi jerked her hands out of reach, shrinking from Kenny's touch. "We have to go to Inari," she said, turning towards the door. "Right now."

"What? No way!" Kenny declared.

"Why not?" Kiyomi paused in the hallway.

"Because she'll try to stop me."

"Good. Someone has to."

"And then what happens to you?" Kenny blinked, trying to stem the tears suddenly brimming in his eyes. "And me? I won't be able to survive here without you."

Kiyomi bit her lip and stepped back into the living room. She placed a hand on Kenny's arm. "It's for the best."

He pulled back. "Says who? What's the big deal anyway?"

"Kenny . . ." Kiyomi's voice was low, the warning tone unmistakable. "You have no idea who you are messing with, or how much trouble we're all in."

"No, I don't, so tell me." Kenny stared at her defiantly.

"That mirror isn't just any old relic, like the ones your grandad used to recover. It's *sacred*. It holds some of the essence of the Sun Goddess herself, but – more importantly than that – it's also one of the Three Sacred Treasures, the Imperial Regalia."

"Which means what?"

Kiyomi grabbed Kenny's shoulders and fought the urge to throttle him. "Do you have any idea how dangerous, cunning, unpredictable, manipulative and plain old psycho Susano-wo is? He was crazy enough to start with, but thousands of years in Hell have hardly helped. He'll trick you, first chance he gets."

21

"No, he won't," Kenny said. "He's kept his word so far – including healing you, I should add – and, if he does try anything . . . then me and Kusanagi will be ready for him."

"Yeah, right." Kiyomi released her grip and lowered her head, a curtain of black hair surrounding her face. "So, you did a deal to restore my soul? You went to the Lord of the Underworld . . . just for me?"

Kenny smiled. "Yeah."

Kiyomi stroked his cheek. "Aw. That was *sooo* sweet –" Kenny closed his eyes and relaxed a little "– and so stupid!"

WHACK! The slap was so hard it rattled Kenny's teeth and made his ears ring. Spots flickered before his eyes.

"Don't you know I'd be better off dead than have you help that filthy, treacherous, lying, slimy piece of –"

"No, you wouldn't!" Kenny fired back, rubbing his jaw. "You can't fool me. I remember how you were before . . . You didn't want to die. You wanted to *live*. To be normal, to hang out, to have friends, to laugh and play. You even wanted to be kissed." He wiped his swelling lip with the back of his hand. "Somehow, I don't think being stuck in *Yomi* with a thousand *oni* lining up to torture you forever is a better option."

Tears glittered in Kiyomi's eyes and her voice was little more than a murmur. "But still . . . you should never have done this."

Kenny slipped his arms over Kiyomi's shoulders and

drew her closer. "It was worth it," he whispered.

BRRAAPPP!

Startled by the sudden noise, they glanced around to see Poyo squatting on top of the counter. He waved a paw to clear the pungent air, then held out two steaming mugs of hot chocolate.

"Great. Talk about a mood killer," Kenny grumbled, taking one of the cups.

Kiyomi joined Kenny at the counter and they sipped their drinks.

"I didn't figure everything out," Kiyomi said. "I made Poyo tell me the rest, about your little trip to Matsue."

Kenny glowered at the *tanuki*. "Thanks for nothing. Some partner you turned out to be."

Poyo ignored him, rolled onto his back and aimed the nozzle of a can of whipped cream into his open muzzle. *FW-AAAWSH!* A cloud of surplus cream clung to Poyo's whiskers, making him look like Santa Claus.

"Well, I am *not* going to see Inari, I can tell you that," Kenny said, eyeing Kiyomi. "Besides, you heard what Susie said in your dream. He's giving me four days to find this precious stone for him, or you're going full *oni*."

Kiyomi flinched and stared down into her Newcastle United mug.

Kenny leaned closer. "Kiyomi, I need your help. That's why Susie summoned you in the dream. He knows I can't fetch this jewel on my own, so he's brought you in to help me."

23

"This is wrong," Kiyomi insisted.

Kenny's grip tightened on his mug, his knuckles whitening. "What choice do we have? Go to Inari? Beg for forgiveness?"

"You can do your duty, as she commands."

"Not if it means losing you."

He slid off the stool and went to the desk, where he scooped up the map printout. After studying it, he returned to the computer screen and adjusted the map scale.

"According to your dream," Kenny said, "the mirror showed that this stone he's after is at the bottom of the East China Sea. If I'm reading this correctly, it's somewhere off the coast of Taiwan, about sixty miles east. Man, why is this never easy?"

"Because if it was, Susano-wo wouldn't need us," Kiyomi said, coming over to examine the map.

"Does anyone mind if I have a look?" Kenny's father said from the hall. He yawned and closed his bedroom door. "I was trying not to listen, but you two hardly keep the noise down. As for you . . ." He fixed Poyo with a glare. "You'd better clean up this mess. I'm tired of picking *tanuki* hair out of my food. Got it?"

Poyo straightened up, snapped a salute and fell into the sink.

"Dad . . ." Kenny began.

"I know, I know," Charles said. "I've heard it all before. Not my concern. It's for my own good. Blah-blah-blah." He held out his hand for the map. "Well, not this time. Last month, you pulled that routine on me and look where it got you. Lost in the mountains before ending up in orbit of all places. If not for me, you'd both be space dust by now, so I think I've earned the right to know what's happening. Besides, if there's any treasure hunting going on, I don't see why you and my father get to have all the fun." He winked.

Kiyomi plucked the map from Kenny's grasp and handed it to Charles with a winning smile and a small bow. Charles collected his reading glasses from the desk and scanned the map.

"This isn't so bad," he said. "Technically, these are still Japanese waters. The tiny island is Yonaguni. It's the westernmost of the Ryukyu Islands and it's accessible by plane. I can make the arrangements."

"Whoa," said Kenny. "Just like that? No arguing? No telling me I can't go without an escort?"

"There's no need," Charles said, taking off his glasses. "I'm going with you. If you don't like it, I'll phone Harashima-*san* right now and the trip is off."

Kiyomi's face fell at the mention of her father.

"Dad!" Kenny protested. "We have to do this."

"Good," Charles said. "Then you won't mind me coming along."

4 四

The twin-propeller plane touched down with a bump at the tiny Yonaguni Airport at 1:15 p.m. the next day. Compared to other airports Kenny had seen, it hardly merited the name, being little more than a mile-long runway with a flat, single-story white building to one side that served as the terminal.

Stepping out of the Ryukyu Air Commuter plane, Kenny felt like he was walking into an oven. After the chilly air-conditioning of the pressurized cabin, the warm tropical breeze was a wonderful welcome to the island.

"I hope you packed your deodorant," Kiyomi said, skipping down the steps. "It's nearly ninety degrees here."

"That's because the latitude is not dissimilar to Hawaii," Charles added, bringing up the rear. He shielded his eyes from the dazzling sunshine and looked out over the sapphire sea to the north.

"Is that where we have to go?" Kenny asked, following his gaze.

"No. The coordinates you were given are to the south

of the island. Let's get settled first before we discuss that. Follow me."

Kenny's father led the way through the baggage claim area and out into the arrivals lobby where they were met by a white-gloved taxi driver holding a placard. He escorted them to a waiting car and they all piled in.

"Lucky I called ahead," Charles said, once the taxi started moving. "There are only three taxis on the whole island and I didn't fancy walking." The narrow gray ribbon of road followed the coastline, bordered by parched fields of yellowing grass.

Looking out of the window, Kenny noted that the island was relatively flat, with some steep hills and outcrops rumpling the wooded interior. There were few tall trees – testament to the scouring power of the typhoons that wound their way through during the summer months.

"Oh, look," Kiyomi said with delight, her nose pressed against the window. "Cute little horses."

The taxi slowed to allow them a better look at a small herd of chestnut ponies grazing by the road, each about three feet tall at the withers.

"They're like Shetland ponies," Kenny said, "only not as hairy."

"Yonaguni horses," Charles said. "They're a native breed, found only on this island."

The road curved to the left and skirted the tops of steep black cliffs before descending to the little port of Kubura.

"This is us," Charles announced as the taxi pulled up outside a white-walled, seafront bungalow.

Stepping out, Kenny paused to sound out the Japanese writing above the entrance. "Ta . . . ka . . ."

"*Takahashi Minshuku*," Kiyomi read for him. "Looks cozy."

Charles shrugged. "We're on a budget. This will be fine. We'll be ready to set out first thing and it means we can keep a low profile."

Kenny raised his eyebrows. "That'll be a first."

The *minshuku* was a bright, cheery bed and breakfast and it took minutes to check in, stow luggage and grab a table outside on the terrace shaded by ornamental palms.

"This isn't so bad, is it?" Kenny said to Kiyomi, looking up at the sunlight sparkling through the palm fronds. "I mean, compared to our usual sewers or quarries."

"No," Kiyomi agreed. "It could be worse."

Charles returned with a tray of cold drinks. "We're in luck," he said. "Takahashi-*san*, the owner, knows a good diving school that can take us out to the south side tomorrow morning."

"Diving school?" Kenny asked.

"This jewel you're looking for – isn't it on the seabed? How else did you expect to reach it?" Charles took a long glug of ice-cold beer and closed his eyes in satisfaction.

"Are you guys heading out to the ruins tomorrow?" A male voice resounded across the deck.

Kenny turned to see a pair of bronzed torsos. Two

muscular men in swim shorts, with closely-cropped hair and several Celtic tattoos, had approached their table. Charles reached over to shake hands and the new arrivals pulled up seats.

"I'm Matt and this is Dwayne," the first one said, flashing a gleaming set of pearly white teeth.

Kiyomi edged closer to the newcomers and ran her hand through her hair.

"We're US Navy," Dwayne added in a rumbling baritone. "On R & R from Okinawa. What brings you guys down here?"

"Uh, my son's learning to scuba dive," Charles said, thinking quickly.

"I'm his instructor," Kiyomi added with a wink.

"What? No, you're – OWW!" Kenny rubbed his ankle as Kiyomi caught him with her boot.

"Did I hear you say something about ruins?" Charles said, ignoring Kenny's outburst.

"Yeah, I thought that's why everyone came down here," Dwayne said.

"They're something special, man," Matt said. "You know these islands, right? They're all part of the Ryukyu Island chain. Well, I googled all this stuff on Ryukyu, yeah, and you know what? *Ryu* means 'precious stone,' as in archipelago of jewels. That's what Ryukyu means."

"That's a fair interpretation," Charles conceded.

"But you know what *ryu* also means?"

Charles slipped into professor mode. "There are a

number of meanings, depending on the *kanji* and the context in which –"

"It means 'dragon,'" Matt interrupted. "The original name for these islands is Ryugu-jo – 'Palace of the Dragon God.' Isn't that nuts?"

"Nuts I'd agree with," Charles said, sipping his beer and wondering how much the sailors had drunk already.

"And this is where the ruins come in," Dwayne said, leaning closer. "There's like this whole underwater city out there, bro, with walls, stairs, doorways, statues, temples – totally crazy. Some folks say it's Atlantis, but I don't buy that. It's more like some kind of ancient civilization that got swallowed up by the waves. Isn't that, like, totally awesome?"

Charles sat back, his fingers linked behind his head. "I do seem to recall reading something . . ."

"Dad, are you serious?" Kenny said. "This has to be some kind of scam. How can you believe this stuff?"

"Because we've seen it," Dwayne said, as though this was the most obvious thing in the world. "Me and Matt here have dived the site over fifty times."

"You don't strike me as amateur archaeologists," Charles said, scrutinizing them closely. "What's so interesting about these ruins?"

"Ah, that would be telling," Matt said, finishing his beer. "Heard you guys are going out tomorrow, right? Maybe we could hitch a ride in your boat – if you don't mind, that is."

"And why would we agree to that?"

"On account of we know the site. It's about a hundred feet down, which is no good for a beginner."

"There are dangerous currents too," Dwayne said. "It's all open water with no reefs."

"And did we mention the sharks?" Matt said. "Thousands of hammerheads at this time of year. Breeding season."

"Well," Charles said, draining his glass, "that's a very generous offer and I thank you for the warnings. I'll tell you what. Let me go have a chat with some people and, depending on what they say, we'll see if we can work something out."

"*Da-ad!*" Kenny said, stretching it to two syllables. "How do you know we can even –?"

"Sweet," Matt said, crushing Charles's hand in his as he stood up. "Sounds like a plan to me."

Kenny followed his father out to the lobby before he realized Kiyomi was still on the terrace. He strode back, hooked an arm through her elbow and tugged her away.

"Did you see the arms on that Dwayne dude?" she said, looking back. "I think his bicep is bigger than my thigh."

"Who cares?" Kenny grumbled. "It's probably all steroids anyway."

"I have an idea," Charles said, when they caught up with him at the entrance. "Why don't you two go burn off some steam with a hike up to Cape Irizaki, while I go

31

talk to the guys at the diving shop?" He pointed uphill, across the bay. "It's only a mile. It marks the westernmost point of Japan, like Land's End does back in England. You can use that lighthouse as a marker."

"OK," Kenny said, eager to put some distance between himself and the Americans. He stomped off, heading up the road.

Kiyomi caught up with him and grabbed his hand. "Ken-*chan*, you don't have to be jealous of those meatheads."

Kenny reddened. "Why would I be jealous of them?"

"Exactly. There's a big difference between admiring muscles and liking the owner. Do you think either of those two would pull someone out of a burning building? Or suffocate a shark? Or bargain with a god?"

"No . . . I guess . . . not if you put it like that." Kenny looked at Kiyomi's smile and felt his annoyance melt away.

"Or save millions of lives, including mine?" Kiyomi took both his hands in hers and pulled him closer.

Kenny smiled and his pulse quickened. He brought his lips closer to hers, when *THWAPPP!* Something cold and heavy walloped the side of his head, knocking him to one knee.

"Uh-uh, big fella. Stay right where ye are, if ye knows what's good for ye," commanded a squeaky voice.

Peering around as he rubbed his head, Kenny saw five child-sized humanoids emerging from the tall grass. Naked, apart from grass skirts, they had shocks of bright-red, waist-length hair and long pointed ears. Two carried short spears, two had arrows nocked against bowstrings and one was absently plucking the eye from a large fish.

"Ken-*chan*, it's OK, don't hurt them," Kiyomi said, raising her hands and backing away. "*Kijimunaa* are harmless."

Kenny stood up and almost tripped on a gleaming sea bream at his feet. "Did you just hit me with a fish?" he accused the nearest creature.

"We's got no quarrels with ye, boy, but it's the girly's got to go," said the fish thrower. He popped the freshly extracted eyeball into his mouth and chewed.

Kiyomi took another step back from the advancing creatures and felt the soil slip away from under her heel; she was at the cliff edge.

"What's she done?" Kenny said, weighing his options.

"Girly's not clean," the *kijimunaa* said. "No *oni* on this island. Must get off – *now*!"

At this, the grass parted at Kiyomi's side and two more creatures sprang up. One flung a length of rope with a stone tied at each end, while the other leapt into the air.

Kenny watched in horror as the cord spiraled around Kiyomi's legs, ensnaring her long enough for the second creature to land a drop kick, launching her headfirst over the side of the cliff and down towards the rocks far below.

5 五

With no time to think, Kiyomi's training kicked in. Her reflexes, honed by years of practice, made her tuck her knees into her chest and close her hand on the dagger in her boot as she fell. With a single upward stroke, she slashed the binding around her legs, grabbed the loose rope in her left hand and straightened her body.

Blue sky swam far below her feet and the rocky shore was three hundred feet overhead. The lapping waves were too far away for a splash landing – but she caught sight of a stubby, thick-trunked pine clinging to the face of the cliff.

Kiyomi slung out the weighted end of the rope. The stone glanced off the trunk, rebounded and snagged on a branch, looping over it. She braced herself for the sudden, wrenching stop. The rope snapped tight, a shooting pain lanced through her arms from wrist to elbow to shoulder, and her body jerked upright, whipping towards the craggy surface of the cliff. Twisting around to face it, Kiyomi drew her legs up, slamming both soles hard against the rock. She grimaced in pain before yelling, "Kenny! I'm OK. Don't do anything stupid!"

"What? Are ye deaf?" squeaked the *kijimunaa*, squirming under Kenny's shoe. Its eyes were crossed from staring at the sword Kenny had pressed against its throat. At the top of the cliff, the other *kijimunaa* stood like statues, no one daring to move.

"See? Girly's fine," said one of the spear holders. "Heh-heh. No harm done."

"We's just playing," added one of the archers.

"Then help her back up," Kenny ordered. "And no tricks. This sword's getting very heavy."

The two creatures that had originally ambushed Kiyomi scurried away and returned seconds later, tugging at the sleeves of her jacket as she crested the brow of the cliff.

"Friends now?" the lead *kijimunaa* said, motioning for the others to lower their weapons.

"Ken-*chan*, I'm fine," Kiyomi said, tipping her head from side to side and rotating her shoulder joints. "Arms are going to kill me in the morning, but I'll live."

Kenny took his foot off the little man's chest and squatted for a better look, leaning on the sword for support. "Has anyone ever told you you look just like a troll doll?"

The *kijimunaa* clambered to his feet and bowed to Kenny. "Me Tomba," he said, smacking his chest and gesturing for the others to bow too, which they did, their long hair fanning out on the ground.

"You guys can stop that now," Kenny said. "I get it.

You're sorry. It's all a big misunderstanding, right?"

"Oh, yes. Big mistake," Tomba agreed. He pointed at the blade in Kenny's hand. "Me know this sword. Who are ye, big fella?"

"Kenny. Uh, Kuromori."

"Ahhhhh," the *kijimunaa* all said together, bobbing their heads as if this explained everything.

"Ye're the one bring back the sun, yes?" Tomba said.

"Something like that," Kenny said. He shrugged and the sword shimmered in his hand, melting away to nothing.

"So, why ye bring *oni*-girly to island?"

"Will you stop calling me that?" Kiyomi said, hands on hips.

"We're here to find a missing object," Kenny said. "Maybe you can help."

The *kijimunaa* drew closer, their long ears twitching. "Ye seek treasure?"

"Yes. Well, no. Maybe. I don't know," Kenny replied.

"Ye should stay well clear of the drowned city," Tomba said.

"So, it's true? There really is a city out there, under the water?"

"Very bad place," Tomba said, shaking his head in warning. "Great danger. Kuromori not go there."

"Sorry, I have to," Kenny said. "Otherwise, *oni*-girl's going to –"

"Hey!" Kiyomi interrupted. "I said don't call me that."

"Sorry," everyone else said.

"Going to what?" Tomba prompted, his nose twitching with curiosity.

"Slowly go insane as this *oni* spirit inside of me takes control and turns me into a mindless killing machine," Kiyomi said, her voice flat.

"Which, you'll probably agree, is a bit of a bummer," Kenny said.

"Ah, me know," Tomba said, brightening. "We's kill ye now and fix problem. Yes?"

"Actually, we're hoping to find a cure," Kenny said. "Down in that underwater city."

"Ohhh," Tomba said, stroking his chin. "Me know who ye's looking for."

"You do? Who?"

Tomba's wide eyes searched the tall grass all around, as if fearful of someone watching. "Will not say, but me'll warn ye. Don't trust him one bit. He will trick ye if he can."

PHEEEP! One of the spear-carrying *kijimunaa* let out a short sharp whistle and the group scattered like rabbits, vanishing into the long grass. Kenny cast an uneasy look around, wondering what had startled them, only to see his father approaching.

"There you are," Charles said. "I thought you'd be farther up the hill by now. Come on, slowpokes, we can still make it to the monument in time for the sunset. You might even see Taiwan." He stopped to examine something silvery by his foot. "What's a fish doing up here?"

*

At 5:30 the next morning, Charles, Kiyomi and Kenny crept out of the *minshuku* and trotted downhill, following the coastal road north towards the harbor. Overhead, the starry veil of the Milky Way laced the glittering sky.

Whispering waves washed the beach and the full moon dusted the horizon with silver while it slipped into the sea. Beautiful as it was, Kenny was secretly glad the moon was setting. After recent events, he was grateful for moonless nights.

Leading the way, Charles scrambled down a bank, across a small parking lot and onto a concrete jetty.

"Here we are," he said, approaching a small diving boat with a covered cabin. A stocky Japanese man with a leathery tan and closely cropped salt-and-pepper hair was strapping a dozen steel air tanks into position.

"Kids, this is Captain Mike," Charles said, climbing aboard.

"Yo, dude! Wait up!" barked a voice from the quay.

"Oh, great," Kenny grumbled, seeing Matt and Dwayne sprinting towards the boat. "I thought we'd ditched these guys."

"They must have been sleeping outside," Charles said, "to make sure they caught us."

"You guys heading out?" Dwayne asked, his breathing normal despite sprinting a hundred yards with a heavy backpack.

"Yes, we are," Charles answered.

"Mind if we hitch a ride? It'd sure be nice to get a last

couple of dives in before we head back to base."

Charles removed his glasses for a quick wipe. "Well, we're on a very relaxed schedule here. It might not work out if you chaps need to catch a flight back."

"No problem," Matt said. "If that's the case, we'll just swim back to shore."

"With all your gear?" Charles looked doubtful.

"Sure. Besides, your boy's never been scuba diving before. Strictly speaking, he shouldn't be anywhere near open water."

"I'll manage," Kenny said, his jaw jutting.

Matt grinned. "I'm sure you will, kid, but that's not what the rules say. It'd be a shame if someone blabbed and the captain here lost his license over something as silly as that. What say Dwayne and I come along? That way, you've got two expert buddy divers in case anything goes wrong."

"*Three* expert divers," Kiyomi added with a wink. Kenny scowled at her.

"OK," Charles said, after chewing it over. "You can come with us."

Captain Mike opened up the throttle and the small boat set off, kicking up foam in its wake as it headed west to circumnavigate Cape Irizaki.

"We've got about fifty minutes to equip you," Kiyomi said to Kenny. "Come here and I'll measure you."

Kiyomi went through the equipment box, finding Kenny a face mask to cover his eyes and nose, a neoprene wet suit, buoyancy regulator and flippers.

"Normally, you'd get some classroom study, a dip in a shallow pool to get used to all the gear and then an accompanied dive in open water," Kiyomi said, adjusting the straps on the mask. "In this case, we're just going to have to fast-track you."

"You know I don't need all this stuff," Kenny smirked. He lowered his voice. "After all, I can breathe underwater."

"Don't get cocky," Kiyomi warned. "That was a pond and a water tank. This is the open sea and we're going down to about a hundred feet. You've got currents, sharks, coral, limited visibility . . . Here, try this." She held out the mouthpiece of the breathing regulator; the other end was attached to a steel tank. "It's compressed air. Put the rubber flange inside your mouth and breathe through your mouth only. Breathe in and out steadily until you get used to it."

Kenny did as he was told and felt the dry air push into his lungs. He forced the breath out and inhaled again. It was a weird sensation and it made his throat burn, but with Kiyomi counting time on her fingers, he soon relaxed into a regular pattern.

At Kiyomi's signal, he pulled out the mouthpiece and worked his tongue around his teeth. "Urgh. I sound like Darth Vader with that thing."

Kiyomi nodded. "OK, that's a good start. Remember, when you're in the water, always breathe like that, slow and steady. Don't hold your breath, ever, and if your ears start to fill up, or hurt, you need to pop them like this." She pinched her nose, closed her mouth and pushed air out. "You can also swallow, waggle your jaw, whatever works."

"Like going up in an airplane?"

"Same principle, only you're going down where there's greater pressure."

It was daunting, having so much to remember, but Kenny wasn't going to let on. "What else?"

For the next twenty minutes, Kiyomi walked Kenny through the basics of scuba diving: hand signals, use of the buoyancy control device, how to clear the mask of water, one-handed weight belt release, where to find the backup air supply.

"It all looks so easy on TV," Kenny grumbled.

"Do you two know what you're looking for?" Charles asked, coming over to the rear of the deck. He aimed a finger downward.

"No." Kiyomi shook her head. "But Susano-wo wasn't being subtle. The stone is down there somewhere. Who knows? Maybe it'll find us."

Dawn painted the sky with pastel fingers of lemon, rose and lavender by the time Captain Mike powered down the engine and chugged to a stop.

"This is us," Kiyomi said, looking north over the gentle waves towards the soaring cliffs of Yonaguni Island.

Kenny lay on his back, grunting and wriggling to pull

on his wet suit. He had both legs in, but despite all his stretching and squeezing, he was struggling to pull it up past his waist. "This . . . thing . . . is impossible," he complained.

"Let me help," Kiyomi said.

"No, I can do this," a red-faced Kenny declared.

Five minutes later, he stopped to catch his breath, one loose sleeve flapping behind like an elephant's trunk.

"Shoulda let the girl help," Dwayne said, resting his foot on the gunwale. He was in his diving gear, unlike Matt who was still in shorts.

"Oh, wait," Matt said, from beside him. "He's trying to impress her." He laughed. "Real smooth, dude." He began to unzip his duffel bag.

Kiyomi glared at them both, reached over and, with one firm tug, snapped the wet suit up to Kenny's neck.

"Ow." He squirmed. "You've given me an almighty wedgie."

"Here." Kiyomi helped him pull the scuba-tank harness on over the buoyancy jacket and then fitted on the weight belt.

"This stuff weighs a ton," Kenny said, holding on to the railing for support.

Kiyomi slipped into her harness, positioned the breathing regulator and checked the instrument panel.

"What's the plan?" Dwayne said. "Are you kids just going for a swim around the ruins or is there anything else you want to do?"

"Just a dive," Kiyomi said, reaching for a knife to strap onto her leg.

"Nuh-uh," Matt said, with an unmistakable tone of menace. "No knives down there. You might get hurt."

"What?" Kiyomi rounded on him. "Every diver carries a knife, in case they get tangled –" She broke off as she saw the speargun in his hand aimed directly at her chest.

"But not you. Hand over the knife, real slow, and nobody gets hurt," he ordered.

6 六

"**N**o move!"

Kiyomi looked up to see Captain Mike pointing a flare gun at Matt.

"My boat," he barked. "I boss."

"Not anymore," Dwayne said, pulling out a heavy knife and brandishing the tip in the captain's direction.

"Kenny, don't do anything stupid!" Kiyomi warned.

"As if," Kenny said, his body straining under the weight of the dive equipment.

Charles rounded on Matt. "What's going on? If this is a hijack, we have nothing of value. I let you have a ride as a favor and –"

"Cool it, Gramps!" Matt yelled back. "Or should I say 'Professor'?"

Charles flinched. "How do you –?"

"Oh, please. Just cos I pump iron doesn't mean I'm stupid. There aren't that many *gaijin* in Japan. First thing I did was check the hotel register to find your name. A quick Google search and I knew exactly who you were."

"A history professor coming all the way down here

to check out the ruins only means one thing," Dwayne chimed in. "Treasure."

"Oh, don't be absurd," Charles started.

"Then why did we hear you talking about a jewel on the bottom of the sea, huh?" Matt challenged.

Charles raised his hands in a calming gesture. "Kiyomi, put your knife on the deck and kick it over to Dwayne. Matt, take your finger *off* the trigger. We don't want any accidents, do we?"

Kiyomi glowered at Matt. "You're lucky," she said. "This time last month, I'd have been mad enough to see how good you are with that thing." She stooped and sent the sheathed knife skittering across the planks. Dwayne stopped it with his foot.

Matt lowered the speargun. "You'd be dead then. I never miss."

Captain Mike muttered in Japanese and put the flare gun back in its case.

"Here's how it's gonna be," Dwayne said. "Me and the kids are going for a swim. They're going to show me where this treasure is and in return I'll make sure they get back up here safely."

"And I'm going to stay on deck with Britney here – " Matt patted the speargun " – to make sure no one tries anything cute."

"But what if there's no treasure?" Kenny asked, sweat plastering his hair to his head.

"Let's just say we'll cross that bridge when we get to it."

"I told you we couldn't trust those meatheads," Kenny griped while Kiyomi gave his equipment a final check.

"Really? You think now is a good time for I told you so?" she fumed. "Put your regulator in and start breathing." Kenny pulled down his mask and waddled to the edge of the dive platform. "Here's where normally you take a big stride into the water, but in this case . . . Eyes on the horizon!" Kiyomi planted a foot firmly against Kenny's backside and pushed.

"AAAAGH!" Kenny grabbed his mask and regulator to hold them in place before plunging into the sapphire sea amid a cloud of white bubbles. Water flooded into his mask and he kicked upward, thrashing to the surface before he remembered he could breathe.

Kiyomi splashed down beside him, rose and gave a thumbs-up signal in the direction of the boat. Captain Mike waved in acknowledgement and raised a red flag with a diagonal white stripe to signal to other vessels that divers were down.

Dwayne jumped in and bobbed alongside, while Kiyomi showed Kenny how to clear his mask by blowing air into it. She adjusted the air in his buoyancy jacket until he barely floated, and then gave the thumbs-down sign to descend.

Taking Kenny's hand, Kiyomi released some air from her own jacket and then lowered her head to swim downward. Kenny copied her movements and the divers kicked gently through the clear water.

Kenny forced himself to relax. It took all of his effort not to sweep his arms and kick his legs as he would for normal swimming. Here, he was weightless, gliding beneath the tropical sea. The only sound was the hypnotic rhythm of his breathing. Shafts of sunlight lanced down from above, illuminating sparkling shoals of fish. A huge leatherback sea turtle labored upward, close enough for Kenny to see the barnacles growing on its shell, and a glittering curtain of glassfish exploded into mirrorlike fragments as the divers approached, re-forming after they had passed.

As they descended farther, Kenny felt an uncomfortable feeling building in his ears. Remembering his training, he pushed air into his pinched nose and waggled his jaw. His ears popped just as a shadow fell across his back. Twisting his head upward, Kenny saw the unmistakable bullet shape of a large shark.

Dwayne continued to lead the way, glancing back from time to time to make sure that Kiyomi and Kenny were keeping up. He pointed and, in the distance, Kenny could see a dark, angular form rising up from the seabed. Even from here he could discern stone blocks and massive terraced steps, like the sides of a truncated Mayan pyramid.

As they drew closer, the features of the underwater ruin became more distinct. Kenny could make out a standing pillar, narrow channels, a road of sorts, platforms, stairs –

and more sharks. Thousands of adult hammerhead sharks were circling lazily around the edifice like a slow-motion tornado, funneling upward. Everywhere Kenny looked, he saw stubby, twig-like shark silhouettes revolving as if on guard.

Dwayne released more air from his buoyancy jacket and cruised down to the seabed, gesturing for Kiyomi and Kenny to follow. He glided along the bottom, kicking up sand with each stroke of his flippers, and led the way beneath the sharks to the south side where a crude staircase appeared to have been cut into the rock.

He motioned for Kiyomi to take the lead and in reply she circled a finger to indicate a loop around the ruins. Still holding Kenny's hand, Kiyomi led them in a counterclockwise circuit of the city. They passed a huge star-shaped slab which resembled a turtle, a small triangular pool, twin pillars that looked as if they had come from Stonehenge and a partly eroded stone face.

By now, Kenny had forgotten everything except the scene around him. He turned his head in every direction, drinking in the wonder of the underwater world. Questions crowded into his mind. Who or what could have built such a structure? Did it sink or was it always underwater? Was it part of an ancient civilization or just an odd natural formation?

He could see why it would be fascinating for treasure hunters, but was there any actual treasure? If so, what hope did they have of finding it? Yet why else would

Susano-wo have sent them here?

Kiyomi gave his hand a sharp tug and pointed upward. Kenny looked. All he saw was the silhouette of the giant turtle still cruising above, a black shadow against the bright surface. And then it hit him: he could *only* see the turtle. Where had all the sharks gone? Kenny's stomach lurched. What could scare off a thousand sharks?

The answer came from the middle distance: a cluster of silvery dots growing larger with each passing second. Kiyomi looped her fingers into Kenny's weight belt and hauled him backward. She pointed to a narrow chasm behind a rectangular boulder and kicked towards it.

Dwayne glided away to take a better look at the rapidly closing objects. Not liking the look of them, he unsheathed two wicked-looking combat knives and held them ready.

The approaching objects sharpened into fifteen-foot-long metallic-blue cylinders with stabilizing fins, dead black eyes and gaping mouths crammed with hooked teeth: mako sharks.

Kenny took a last look and gasped, almost ejecting his breathing regulator, as Kiyomi yanked him into the fissure. As if a hunting pack of mako sharks wasn't terrifying enough, each predator was carrying some kind of humanoid creature on its back. It was only a split-second glimpse, but Kenny saw gray skin, pointed heads and jagged spears in hands, all bearing down on the hapless Dwayne.

Kiyomi wriggled her way as deep as she could into the dark crevice. Kenny followed blindly, bumping his face into Kiyomi's shoulder and dislodging his mask. Salt water flooded in. He was about to clear his mask when he felt Kiyomi's steely grip on his hand. Squinting through the seawater stinging his eyes, he saw Kiyomi holding her breath and stabbing a finger upward. A cloud of silvery air bubbles was rising from his exhaust valve, as obvious as a smoke signal.

Kenny concentrated for a moment, summoning his *ki,* and imagined one large bubble. The rising cluster of individual globules shivered and coalesced into a single sphere. Maintaining his focus, Kenny directed the bubble downward, into the depths of the channel they were hiding in. Now all they needed to do was wait it out until the shark pack lost interest and moved on.

Something brushed against Kenny's head and he reached up to catch a hard, flat object. Peering at it in the near dark, he recognized the blade of one of Dwayne's knives. He turned it in a semicircle, to grasp the handle – and was confronted by a severed hand, still gripping tightly.

"YAAAAGH!" Kenny yelled, losing his mouthpiece and his concentration. The bubbles shot upward once more.

He fumbled for his regulator and exhaled to empty the water from his mask. As his vision cleared, he saw Kiyomi shaking her fist at him and backing away along the crevice, while shooting fearful glances upward.

Shadows converged overhead and one of the shark riders dismounted to stand astride the chasm. It peered down into the gloom and Kenny felt its eyes bore into him. He shrank back, pressing himself against the rock to blend into the shadows. He knew he had nowhere to run.

In its webbed hands, the creature clutched a long spear with twin serrated blades. It steadied itself and took aim.

7 七

"Something's wrong!" Matt said, staring out at the placid sea from the stern of the boat.

"What do you mean?" Charles asked, stepping out of the shade of the small cabin. "In what way?"

"Just give me that aquascope over there." Matt pointed to a fat tube stowed beside the scuba tanks.

Charles fetched the instrument, but didn't hand it over immediately. "That's my son down there. I need to know if he's in danger."

"Fine," Matt grumbled, holding his hand out. "I just saw a bunch of hammerheads jump out of the water."

"Is that unusual?"

"Uh, yeah. It's one of those things that's possible in theory, but no one's ever seen it happen. Question is, why are they doing it now?"

Matt took the aquascope. He flattened himself on the diving platform, pressing his face against the tube's cushioned viewing pane, and plunged the other end into the sea. He evidently didn't like what he saw. Muttering, he jumped up and went for his speargun.

"What's going on?" Charles asked, a knot of worry growing in his stomach.

"Mako sharks," Matt said. "Big suckers. I've never seen anything like it before. They're hunting in groups and sweeping like in a search pattern."

"Searching? For what?"

"Give you three guesses. Whoa! There goes one of them now." Matt's outstretched finger followed the silvery dorsal fin of a shark gliding by the boat. He stood on the edge of the platform, leveled the speargun and took aim.

"I wouldn't stand there if I were you," Charles warned.

"Chill out, Prof," Matt said. "I know what I'm doing. If I can bag this one, the blood will draw the others and they'll eat him alive. That'll buy time for our guys down there."

The triangular fin disappeared, leaving only bubbles on the surf. Matt groaned.

"Are you sure this is a good idea?" Charles asked, holding on to the rail. "I mean, we need to get our swimmers back up. How is sending the sharks into a feeding frenzy going to help?"

Matt's eyes danced over the sparkling sea. "Sharks don't eat a lot. Once they've had a bellyful, they're done. The quicker they feed, the quicker they leave." Another fin broke the surface, slicing through the waves. "Ooh, right there. Hold that pose, you ugly . . ."

He swung the tip of the speargun in a wide arc,

tracking the shark, then *KRAKK!* pulled the trigger. The stainless-steel shaft discharged and buried itself deep into the flesh below the shark's dorsal fin.

"Hah! Told you I never miss!" Matt crowed as a bloom of crimson stained the sea. He reached for a second spear to reload the gun, watching in keen anticipation. "Any second now . . . Hmm. That's weird. They're not eating it."

The fin sailed away, trailing blood in the water. Another fin sliced past, heading towards the boat, before it dived straight down.

"Hey, where'd my shark go?" Matt said, readying the speargun for a second shot.

"I don't know," Charles said, "but wasn't the other one coming this way?"

WHAM! Without warning, the vessel lurched as if it had struck a rock; the hull groaned and the bow rose six feet into the air. Charles hooked an elbow through the railing as his feet slipped out from under him and the deck tilted at a forty-five-degree angle.

Matt, standing at the edge of the platform, was pitched headlong into the water where the wounded shark was waiting. "*YEE-AAGH!*" Treading water, he tried desperately to bring the speargun on target, but the giant mako took him down with a single bite.

Charles's stomach heaved as the boat righted itself again, throwing up a huge bow wave. Captain Mike staggered from the bridge. "*Nandayo?*" he growled, looking for Matt. "*Sono bakayaro wa dokoda?*"

"He's gone," Charles murmured. "One shark tips the boat, the other gets revenge. This is bad."

One hundred feet straight down, Kenny was thinking exactly the same thing. The shark-rider stabbed the spear into the crevice where it struck the stone wall by his head, making a tiny spark and chipping off a splinter of rock. Not satisfied, the creature repositioned itself and aimed again. Kenny squirmed and this time the blade scraped against the lead weight of his belt, scoring a groove in it. The rider raised its arm for a third attempt.

Kiyomi watched in dread while the creature tracked the rising bubbles from Kenny's exhaust valve and readied another spear thrust to skewer him. Knowing he was trapped and it was only a matter of time before his luck ran out, Kiyomi grabbed hold of the sides of the chasm and launched herself upward, into the open.

Gathered around the crevice were a dozen mako sharks, each with a handler; some were still sitting on top of their rides, holding on to the dorsal fin. Others had dismounted and were directing their attention to the jagged crack. The creatures' heads were large, seeming to grow from their shoulders with no discernible neck; large round eyes stared from each side where ears should be; wide mouths filled with pointed teeth gaped open; and brawny limbs sprang from powerful torsos. Despite being human-shaped, they were definitely creatures of the sea.

Kiyomi recognized them as *gyojin*. She waved to attract their attention and then bolted, thrusting hard with her arms and kicking out with her flippers. Two spears fizzed past and she ducked down towards a square boulder for cover.

Half of the *gyojin* mounted their steeds and charged after her. The others made way for a newcomer gliding in from the depths. Three giant moray eels churned through the water in undulating coils, each wearing a harness with a seaweed rope attached; a fish-man held the ropes in its hands like reins. He planted his webbed feet in the sandy seabed and gave two sharp tugs on the cords. The eels dropped low and waited, mouths open, gulping water, their fins rippling.

The eel handler peered into the narrow ravine and signaled to his living weapons, a proud smile on his face. At this command, the three eels surged forward and arrowed into the blackness.

Kiyomi hauled herself over the stone block and weighed her options: the breakaway pack was now hunting her and Kenny was still trapped. Being unarmed, with limited air and no time to return to the surface safely, it wasn't looking good. She crouched down, pressing her back against the rock, as the mako sharks circled.

Kenny watched the spear-carrying *gyojin* back away from the edge and exhaled in relief. Unable to dislodge him, the creatures seemed to be giving up. He craned his neck towards Kiyomi, to give her a thumbs-up, but she had disappeared.

Scanning for any sign of her, Kenny saw three long sinewy shadows swim into view. He stared in horror at the nightmarish, prehistoric heads with their tiny eyes, gaping maws and long, sharp, backward-facing teeth. The moray eels honed in on their target.

The mako sharks continued to circle until they had completed three loops each, at which point one of the riders dismounted and pointed in Kiyomi's direction. His shark immediately surged towards her. Kiyomi reached for her knife out of habit and groaned when she remembered that Dwayne had taken it. She wondered if she could poke the creature in the eye, but it was a slim hope. She watched the pointed nose lift and the yawning tunnel mouth open wide.

Without warning, a large shadow glided into the space between girl and shark. Instinctively, Kiyomi jabbed out a hand, latched on to the turtle's shell and flattened herself against its back. The shark's teeth clamped down hard on seawater and it wheeled away, returning to its master, baffled as to how its meal had vanished.

At the same time, Kenny took one look at the savage teeth closing in and hurled himself upward, out of the chasm, and into the trap. The waiting shark riders pounced on him, spears at the ready.

8 八

Kusanagi, the Sword of Heaven, flashed into Kenny's hand and, with one stroke, spearheads tumbled towards the seabed. The pursuing eels scattered before attacking from three different directions. The sword moved to protect its master, slashing first downward, then flipping Kenny upside down to deliver a reverse sweep before slicing horizontally. Swirls of blood stained the water pink and chunks of eel floated downward.

The sharks and their riders hesitated, while the giant leatherback cruised past. Kenny glimpsed the yellow blur of a scuba tank on its back and kicked off, chasing after the turtle. It was surprisingly fast and Kenny, worried he wouldn't catch up, wondered if he could summon a current of water to push him along. Kusanagi bucked in his hands, spinning him around to take off the nose and lower jaw of a mako that had closed in.

With a flick of its enormous flippers, the leatherback changed direction, heading for the ruins of the city. With Kiyomi holding on, Kenny followed. Behind him, at a safe distance, came the sharks and their riders.

The turtle skimmed the surface of the top terraces and dropped sharply over the edge, gliding towards a narrow gap in the rocks. A stone slab rested on top of two monolithic blocks, forming a Stonehenge-like rectangular arch. The space was tight and Kenny, swimming as fast as he could, wondered what the great sea reptile was doing. It was easily six feet long from head to tail, with flippers of the same length; there was no way it could fit through the opening.

Looking up past the turtle's head, he saw Kiyomi release her grip as the turtle rolled onto its side and soared towards the passage. Kusanagi jerked in Kenny's hand, deflecting another spear, while the pursuing shark pack spread out to encircle him. He beckoned for Kiyomi to join him, but she was staring at the leatherback heading for the rocks.

The shadow of the arch fell across the turtle and it ducked its head, folded its flippers like a pair of wings and sailed into the gap, where it flickered and vanished.

Kiyomi looked from the archway to Kenny and to the sharks around him. Silvery shapes in the distance signaled that reinforcements were on the way. She furiously gesticulated for Kenny to follow and struck out for the archway. Seeing this, two shark riders broke formation to stop her.

Kenny had seen enough. Screwing his eyes shut, he concentrated, imagining an underwater tsunami rolling over the seabed. A roaring sound filled his ears and the nearest sharks were flipped tail over head, then slammed into the sides of the ruins. The surging current struck Kenny like a wall, flinging him towards the rocks.

Swimming hard, Kiyomi glanced over her shoulder; her eyes widened and Kenny plowed into her, grabbing her by the scuba harness and holding on. The archway loomed larger and Kenny barely had time to direct the wave through the narrow entry. He twisted around, shielding Kiyomi with his body, and the surging tide carried them both through the gap.

Kenny had a moment of weightlessness before crashing down to land on something hard. "OWW!" he yelled and the regulator popped out of his mouth. In a panic, he scrabbled for his alternate air source, then stopped. He could breathe.

Kiyomi was sprawled at his feet in the damp sand. Kenny struggled to sit up, but his whole body felt leaden. He released the catch on his weight belt and shrugged out of the scuba-tank harness, rising to his knees. Kiyomi had done the same and was staring in rapt wonder at the scene around them.

They were on the seabed, but no longer in the water. A quicksilver membrane billowed above, enclosing them in a spacious bubble of air. Outside, beyond the pulsing walls, sea creatures were watching them as if they were interesting zoo exhibits. Fish of all shapes and sizes pressed close to the glistening surface and peered in: giant groupers, majestic rays, globular puffers, domed jellyfish, bluefin tuna, fluttering sea horses.

"Kenny, is this your doing?" Kiyomi whispered, removing her face mask.

"No. No way. At least . . . I don't think so," Kenny answered, also pushing up his mask.

"Then who –?"

A bassoon-style drone reverberated through the air pocket, abruptly changing pitch to an echoing squeal. Kenny glanced upward to see the source of the noise, and gaped at the immense bulk of a whale passing overhead like a jumbo jet.

"Is this some kind of welcoming party?" he wondered aloud.

"You wish," Kiyomi muttered. "More like a buffet line and we're on the menu."

The bubble wall quivered behind Kenny and crept inward.

"Uh-oh," he said. "Is this thing shrinking? Are we using up the air?"

"No," Kiyomi said, kneeling to examine the perimeter. "Carbon dioxide would replace the oxygen; it wouldn't shrink. It's changing shape. See for yourself. This end is contracting, but the opposite side, over there, is expanding. It's elongating."

As Kenny watched, the bubble stretched out a wide, tunnel-sized, amoeboid limb. The shrinking end of the air pocket was almost by his feet now. He kicked off his flippers and started walking along the extended arm.

"What are you doing?" Kiyomi asked.

"This bubble is moving," Kenny said. "If we don't move with it, we'll be left on the bottom of the sea, surrounded by all those hungry mouths. If we go with it, at least we stay alive a bit longer."

"But what about our gear?" Kiyomi said, pointing at their scuba tanks on the sand. "We can't just leave our stuff behind. How are we going to get back up to the surface?"

"This thing isn't going to wait for us." As if to emphasize the point, the bubble wall slid over Kenny's flipper, which was snatched up and carried away by a red sea bream.

Kiyomi stood her ground, fuming, until the membrane wall touched the back of her head and she felt the sting of ice-cold water against her scalp. "OK, you win!" she yelled, slipping out of her scuba equipment and scurrying beside Kenny. She clasped his hand and together they walked along the seabed, directed by the air tunnel that rolled ahead of them.

Before long, the sand underfoot changed to a finer pinkish material, which formed a wide strip.

"Is this a road?" Kenny said.

Kiyomi nodded. "Ground coral. Looks like it goes through that rock wall."

The bubble bounced up against a cave-like entrance in a low cliff, shuddered and squeezed itself inside. Kenny prepared to call up a ball of light, but there was no need; the inside of the tunnel was lined with bioluminescent plankton and glowed a starry blue. A reddish gleam marked the end of the passage and, when they reached it, the rock walls opened out onto a scene that left both Kiyomi and Kenny openmouthed.

Towering above them was a vast structure of white and red coral forming ridges and corners, spires and turrets, windows and arches, walls and battlements. Crystal inlays sparkled in the sunlight, piercing the ocean depths, and the surface of the stronghold crawled with teeming sea creatures.

"Oh," Kiyomi whispered, her voice hushed in awe. "It's Ryugu-jo."

"Ryu-what?" Kenny repeated. "You know this place?"

"It's his palace; it has to be."

Kenny scowled in irritation. "I can see it's a palace. Whose did you say it was?"

"Ryujin. He's the Ruler of the Sea."

"That doesn't sound so bad."

"He's also the King of the Dragons."

Kenny flashed back to his previous encounter with a dragon: Namazu, the bringer of earthquakes, destroyer of worlds. Kenny had managed, barely, to stop it from destroying America's West Coast.

And now it looked like they were about to meet Namazu's boss.

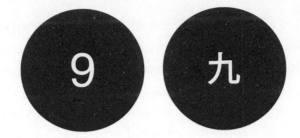

The road ended at a broad set of steps, leading up to a grand coral arch, each side guarded by an armed *gyojin* sitting astride a giant sea horse. Kenny and Kiyomi stopped at the foot of the stairs.

TAN-TAH-TAH-TAH-TAH-TA-RAAH! blasted a fanfare played on different-shaped conch shells by more of the human-shaped fish creatures. A shadow loomed from the top of the stairs; all around, fish, whales, mollusks and crustaceans bowed their heads in reverence.

Kiyomi bowed too and tugged at Kenny's wrist. "Quick, bow," she hissed. "We're in enough trouble already without being disrespectful."

Kenny folded awkwardly at the waist, hating the wet suit as it rode up at the back.

"Greetings and salutations, my most honored guests!" came a voice from above. "Please arise that I may address you properly."

Kenny straightened, looked up and was surprised to see a tall, slim Japanese man, who looked to be in his fifties, standing on the top step. His long red hair fell over his shoulders and the ends of his moustache drooped to his chest. He wore an iridescent green kimono, richly embroidered with seashells, and the gold circlet upon his head was shaped like a dragon biting its own tail.

"Come, please," he said, gesturing for them to join him. "I receive visitors so rarely that you must forgive my poor manners. I am Ryujin. Mortals call me the Dragon King." The air bubble expanded and stretched up the steps. Kenny looked to Kiyomi, who shrugged, and they ascended together.

Ryujin allowed the air bubble to encase him, held out his hands for his guests to take and led the way into his palace.

Kenny gazed at the magnificence around him. Huge glowing jellyfish hovered by the ceilings, serving as living chandeliers; rainbow streaks of mother-of-pearl lined the floor; ornate coral sculptures grew out from the walls; crystal skylights allowed sunlight to filter in from above; and fish servants, some wearing robes, swept aside to allow their king to pass.

Kenny made an attempt at small talk. "Dragon King, huh? So that's like a cool nickname, right?"

"Do not be fooled by this human form," Ryujin said, with a playful smile.

Kenny's face fell. "You mean, you're really . . . a dragon?"

"And Ruler of the Sea."

"Ohh."

"I have heard many things about you, Kuromori."

"You have? Oh, you shouldn't believe everything you hear," Kenny stammered.

"I heard it from Namazu – from the dragon's mouth itself, you might say. He says you are a formidable adversary, and that it would be a grave mistake to underestimate you."

"Uh, yeah, sorry about that. How is he these days?"

"He still suffers headaches and his left eye is not so good. Other than that, he'd love to meet you again."

A long hallway led from the entrance to a grand atrium, which Kenny took to be some kind of throne room. On a dais at the back of the hall sat a huge coral chair with fish of all kinds assembled before it, filling the floor.

Ryujin took his seat on the throne and positioned his guests on either side.

"My loyal subjects," he said, gazing over the crowd with a benign expression. "As you can see, the hour of our salvation is at hand."

A quiet ripple of applause came back as fish slapped their fins together in approval.

"We have pleaded with the gods for help and they have answered our prayers."

Kenny exchanged a puzzled look with Kiyomi. Alarm bells were ringing in his head.

"I have decreed a feast in honor of our esteemed guests," the king continued. "They are to be afforded every care and respect, for tomorrow they will venture forth to deliver us from the great evil which has beset our realm."

More applause churned the sea until, at a signal from the king, the assembled creatures whooshed away with flicks of their tails.

Ryujin beamed at his visitors, and expanded the air bubble to fill the hall with a sweep of his arms.

"Uh, your highness," Kenny began, "can I ask what you meant by 'salvation' and a 'great evil'?"

Ryujin chuckled. "Oh, come now. Surely you know why you are here?"

"Not really . . ." Kenny said, eyeing Kiyomi for a clue as to how he should play this. "The, uh, gods didn't really fill us in."

"That's right, Oh Great One," Kiyomi added. "We came to Ryugu-jo by accident."

"There is no such thing," Ryujin said. "Your arrival was foretold."

"Oh, no, not that again," Kenny muttered under his breath.

"You are Kuromori, yes, chosen one of Inari? And this is Harashima, the future mother of your children?"

"Hah!" Kiyomi guffawed. "Which idiot made that prediction?"

Kenny blushed as red as coral. "Yeah, I think that's getting a bit ahead of things."

Ryujin ignored the dissent. "The fact remains that you are here, yes, whether by accident or design?"

"I suppose," Kenny conceded.

"You were never in any real danger from my *gyojin* guards," the king said. "They were under strict orders to direct you here, once you ventured close enough to the gateway between realms. As long as you did not attack them, they would not harm you."

"Try telling that to the guy who was with us," Kiyomi said.

Ryujin shrugged. "He was of no consequence. A true warrior would have proved his worth, as you did. I have no place for ineffectual fools."

"Wow, that's cold," Kenny couldn't help remarking.

"Let's get back to the 'great evil' thing," Kiyomi said, shooting a warning look in Kenny's direction. "Why have the gods sent us here?"

"Father! You mustn't monopolize our guests like this," a female voice gently chided.

Gliding up to the dais was a Japanese girl. She looked to be about sixteen and her slate-gray kimono shimmered with rows of silvery flecks.

"My honored guests," Ryujin said, beaming at the newcomer, "allow me to introduce you to my most treasured daughter, Otohime."

The princess bowed before Kiyomi and Kenny, who returned the greeting.

"It has been such a long time since we had visitors from the surface world," Otohime said, "and never one so handsome." She smiled at Kenny, looking up coyly at him, while a smile danced on her lips and a crescent dimple shadowed her cheek.

Kenny blushed furiously. The princess was so beautiful that he had to concentrate hard on not looking at her, even though he wanted to, to check that he wasn't imagining it.

Kiyomi rolled her eyes and dug an elbow in his ribs. "Give me a break," she muttered.

"Heh. It's, uh, warm in here," Kenny said, wiping his moist forehead with the back of his hand.

"That would be from your strange garments," Otohime said, gesturing towards the wet suit.

"My child is right," Ryujin said, clapping his hands together. "You need to be correctly attired before the feast. We cannot leave you two looking like seals. My servants will show you to your rooms and provide clothes for you to change into."

"I'll go with you," Otohime said, reaching for Kenny's hand. "I can help you out of those wet things."

"Not necessary," Kiyomi said firmly, inserting herself between them. She linked her arm with Kenny's and smiled sweetly. "Ready when you are."

The bubble contracted once more, allowing seawater back into the atrium, along with two haughty-looking sea bass, who led the way along flooded hallways and corridors until coming to a stop by a huge scallop-shell door.

Otohime waved her hand and the door slid aside, revealing the silvery wall of another air pocket. "This room has been made habitable for you," she said, directing them inside. "Please." She led the way, moving effortlessly between water and air.

The room was larger than Kenny's apartment with passages leading off from the main chamber. It was richly furnished with silk-covered divans, low stools, large vases, cushions, tapestries, rugs.

"Come this way," Otohime said. She guided them into an adjoining bedroom and pulled back a curtain to reveal an extensive wardrobe of sumptuous gowns, robes and kimonos. "Choose anything you like," she said to Kiyomi. "And for you, Kuromori-*san* . . ."

She beckoned for Kenny to follow, taking him through another opening to a guest room. Laid out on the bed was a navy-blue silk *kamishimo* ensemble, embroidered with silver and gold bamboo patterns.

"I had this made for you especially," the princess said. "Do you need help to get dressed?"

"Ken-*chan* will manage just fine," Kiyomi said from the doorway. "Won't he?"

"You know how much trouble I had getting into this thing," Kenny grumbled, pulling at his wet suit. "Yeah, I'll manage."

Otohime bowed. "I will wait for you outside, Kuromori-*san*. When you are ready, I will take you for a tour of the palace."

"Ahem." Kiyomi cleared her throat.

"And I will send a physician to attend to your cold, Harashima-*san*."

*

"Are you decent?" Kiyomi called out twenty minutes later.

"Er, I think so."

She went into his room, took one look and burst out laughing. Kenny had managed to slip into the kimono and the upper waistcoat, but the baggy pleated trousers with long straps had defeated him. "These things are impossible to put on," he complained. "It's worse than an apron."

"Allow me." Kiyomi's crimson kimono swished as she moved. She expertly tied, folded and knotted the *hakama* cords around Kenny's waist. "There, much better. Now you're ready for your date."

"That's not funny," Kenny scowled.

Kiyomi looked up from under her brow. "Do you think she's pretty?"

"Huh?" Kenny stalled, unsure if he should lie. "She's all right, I suppose."

Kiyomi smiled. "Poor thing probably hasn't seen a human male in years. She's obviously not picky."

"Hey!"

"Just don't get carried away, that's all I'm saying. I think it's sweet; probably a good idea for you to get to know her better and find out what they want from us. Ask her about the jewel if you get a chance."

Kenny went to tuck his hands into his pockets, only to find there weren't any. "Is that it? Aren't you . . . jealous or anything?"

"Of a *turtle*?" Kiyomi laughed at the shock registering on Kenny's face. "What, you didn't recognize the markings on her kimono? She's the one who brought us here, dummy."

Kenny decided a change of subject was in order. "What about you? What are you going to do while I'm gone?"

Kiyomi knelt to pick up the dive computer and instrument panel from on top of Kenny's wet suit. "I'm going to see if I can work out an escape route."

"Escape? You make it sound like we're prisoners."

"Duh. Don't be fooled by all that 'honored guest' nonsense. Ken-*chan,* we're surrounded by guards and, without our gear, we have no way of getting back to the surface. You may not have noticed it, but we're trapped down here and the clock is ticking."

10 +

Princess Otohime held Kenny's hand. She had an amazingly strong grip and Kenny wasn't sure he could make her let go even if he wanted to. In spite of himself, he was enjoying her company. She was vibrant and bubbly with a contagious laugh and a quick wit.

She drew him away from a balcony offering views of verdant lawns and vivid flower beds. "Keep your eyes shut," Otohime said, leading the way down a long corridor. The air bubble moved with them, causing palace staff, mainly fish, to turn tail or hide in nooks until they had passed. "I said no looking!"

"All right." Kenny closed his eyes, but images of the palace tour played on his eyelids. He had already seen countless staterooms, halls, galleries, a library, dining rooms, trophy cabinets, a music room, museum, council chamber – all exquisitely arranged.

The palace was built as a large square surrounding an immense inner courtyard. Composed of coral, it seemed to have emerged organically from the seabed. Life teemed everywhere, from tiny anemones to giant crabs. Outside, expansive gardens stretched out to reach fortified walls and mountains towered beyond.

"You can open your eyes now."

Kenny did as instructed and blinked in disbelief. They were on another balcony overlooking the grounds. Trees of every variety flourished, some waving in the currents, others Kenny recognized from dry land, growing in cocoons of air. What staggered him, though, were the crystals of ice sifting down.

"It's . . . snowing?"

"Yes. Isn't it beautiful? And so romantic."

"But . . . I thought it was summer back there." Kenny pointed in the direction they had come.

"That's right. Each side of the palace faces out onto a different season. If you look east, it's spring. We have *sakura* all year round."

"And it's autumn to the west? Wow."

"You can have any fruit you want, at any time, freshly picked from the tree. I have spent many days wandering through the gardens and palace." Her voice trailed off and she looked at the floor.

"You sound . . . sad about it. I thought you'd love it here."

Otohime laid her soft hand against Kenny's cheek. "Kuromori-*san*, it is kind of you to express concern over me. I am happy here, except . . ."

Something moved at the periphery of Kenny's vision.

"I have no one to share it with."

Kenny leaned forward for a better view. Clouds of disturbed silt billowed from the slopes of one of the mountains, far beyond the garden walls.

"Is that an avalanche?" He pointed.

But then he saw the glitter of a hard, shiny surface, moving within the landslide. He couldn't be sure, because of all the debris, but it appeared to be heading towards the palace.

"What *is* that?"

"That is why you have come to us, Kuromori-*san*." Otohime's eyes shone with hope. "That is the evil which you have come to defeat."

Even from this distance, Kenny could see the creature was gargantuan. "You've got to be kidding me."

Kiyomi knelt on her bed and switched off the dive computer. Normally, it was used to monitor the time and depth of a dive, tracking air consumption to avoid decompression sickness on the way back up, but none of the rules seemed to apply down here.

They were on the seabed, but any adverse effects from pressure were countered by the air pocket. However, if they attempted to escape and dash for the surface, the rapid change in depth would be fatal. Ryujin had them right where he wanted them.

A heavy knock on the door interrupted Kiyomi's musing. "Ken-*chan*, you're back quick." She padded over to the entrance and slid the shell aside.

Crouched in the doorway was a towering shape with black eyes, savage jaws and a pointed snout.

Kiyomi somersaulted backward, kicked over a chaise lounge for a barrier and armed herself with a fruit bowl, all the while hating the kimono for hampering her movements.

"Wait! Mistress, me mean no harm!" growled the shark-*oni* in the corridor. It dropped to its knees and bowed, touching its head to the floor.

"Hold on a minute," Kiyomi said, setting down the bowl. "I know you."

"Yes," the monster said. "We meet before. Me try kill you, but Kuromori spare my life. Me owe him."

Kiyomi drew closer and watched the shark-*oni*, who stayed behind the wall of water. "I thought you said they'd kill you for failing."

"Yes. That why me come to Ryugu-jo, to hide."

"Then what do you want with me?"

The shark-*oni* raised its head to look from side to side. "Kuromori in great danger," it said in hushed tones. "Me come warn him."

"He isn't here. But I can pass on a message."

The creature's gill slits rippled in agitation. "Me speak to Kuromori only."

"As you wish." Kiyomi moved to slide the door shut.

"Wait! Me tell you." It shook its head sadly. "Ryujin not good king. No honor. Mood changes like sea. One day calm, next day storm. Not trust him. Will betray you."

"That's hardly news, but thank you," Kiyomi said, before a thought occurred to her. "You've been here a while. Do you know any way out? Any shortcut, or secret passage? A palace this size must have more than one entrance."

"Me not know, but will find out." The shark-*oni* rose to its feet and bowed in farewell.

"Wait," Kiyomi said. "Do you have a name?"

"Kakichi," it said and, with a flick of its tail, it was gone.

Otohime escorted Kenny back to his room and explained that the feast would commence shortly. As soon as she had bowed and left, Kiyomi recounted the shark-*oni*'s message.

"Can we trust him?" was Kenny's first response.

"As much as we can trust anyone around here," Kiyomi said. "He's an outsider, like us, and he owes you his life. That counts for something."

"I guess." Kenny paced, trampling a path in the thick rug.

"So, how was your date? What did you find out?"

Kenny made a sour face. "That this place is massive. There're so many amazing things in here, you could spend a lifetime and not see them all."

Kiyomi shrugged. "That makes sense. Seventy percent of the planet is covered with sea. Count up all the ships that have sunk and all the stuff that gets washed away, it's no wonder. Where did you think all these furnishings came from?" Kiyomi ran her hands over the silk divan where she perched.

"I also learned that Ryujin loves gems: emeralds, rubies, diamonds, sapphires – you name it. Can't get enough of them."

Kiyomi's eyes lit up. "Did you see them?"

"That wasn't part of the tour."

"What else?" Kiyomi could tell that something was bothering Kenny. His constant pacing was out of character.

"I know why we were brought here."

"You do?" Kiyomi sat up.

"Some kind of giant creature has been attacking the kingdom. Every day it's getting closer to the palace. Ryujin's been sending his armies out to fight it, but they've only slowed it down. By tomorrow, it'll be here. I've seen it – it's big."

Kiyomi stood up and put her hands on Kenny's shoulders. "How big is big?"

Kenny gave a queasy smile. "Remember Namazu?"

Disbelief clouded Kiyomi's face. "What? But . . . he was over half a mile long."

"Exactly. This thing's even bigger."

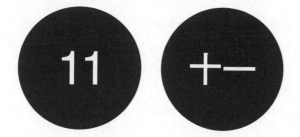

"**I** thought this was supposed to be a party," Kenny grumbled as he and Kiyomi followed their sea bass escort to the throne room. Strains of otherworldly but decidedly gloomy music were filtering into the air bubble. They stopped at a brightly lit archway.

"My lords, ladies and others," announced a grand-looking gurnard, "it is my deepest honor to present to you our most welcome and esteemed guests – nay, our impending saviors no less – from the surface world, sent to us by the gods themselves, the living legend that is Kuromori Ken and his, er, assistant!"

"Hey!" Kiyomi protested, but she was cut short by the burst of applause and cheering that greeted the announcement.

Princess Otohime bowed, took Kenny's hand and led him onto the dais to kneel on a cushion beside her. The acclaim grew louder. Ryujin beckoned to Kiyomi and patted a seat to his right. She joined him, her lips fixed in a tight smile.

The hall was packed with a wide variety of excited

sea life, jostling and joggling to catch sight of the visitors. Gradually, the crowd nudged closer and the hubbub grew louder until fish were poking their snouts into the air-filled enclosure.

"Enough!" Ryujin barked and every fish instantly returned to its assigned place. It was an impressive sight as sea creatures were arranged in rows and columns, like a huge cubic grid stretching away to the far end of the hall.

The music resumed, played by a small band. An octopus comprised the percussion section, whacking drumsticks on different-sized clamshells while wielding shakers and maracas in its other arms. A quintet of puffer fish clasped conches to their lips and blew long brassy notes. Behind them, a choir of toadfish was arranged by size, the large ones droning like didgeridoos and the smaller ones chirping like synthesizers.

Kenny started to laugh.

"Does something amuse you?" Otohime asked, placing her hand on his.

"It's just . . . this reminds me of a Disney movie."

Otohime smiled politely, having no idea what Kenny was talking about.

The feast commenced in earnest when a school of manta rays glided in, each bearing seashell plates of delicacies on their backs. A servant set a tray down before Kenny and he was surprised to see *sashimi* served alongside roe and seaweed dishes.

Ryujin beamed and waited, his chopsticks poised.

Kenny looked up and saw that all eyes were on him.

"Kuromori-*san*," Otohime whispered, "it is customary for the guest to eat first. No one will eat until you do."

"But it's *fish*," Kenny sputtered. "I can't eat this with all of them watching me. What if it's someone's cousin?"

"Kuromori-*san*, do surface dwellers not eat their own cousins too?"

"No! What do you . . .?"

"Mammals are one family, like fish. Yet humans eat mammals and fish eat other fish."

"Well, since you put it like that." Kenny swallowed hard. "*Itadakimasu*." He picked up a wobbly pink square of *sashimi* and popped it into his mouth.

A cheer went up and the hall was soon filled with the sounds of everyone eating.

"Your Majesty, I have a question," Kenny said to Ryujin, lowering his voice. "This creature that threatens your kingdom. What is it? Why can't you . . .? I mean, you're a dragon and King of the Sea. Surely . . .?"

Ryujin set down his chopsticks and sighed. "The tales of your legendary wisdom are indeed true, Kuromori-*san*."

Kiyomi snorted, then covered her face with a napkin to stifle her guffaw.

"The gods are clever indeed," Ryujin continued. "Always, there is balance. Light and dark, water and fire, *yin* and *yang*. So they could not allow dragons to be all-powerful, lest we ruled the world in their stead, and they created for us a balance, a monster too terrible for us to fight."

81

"What does it do?"

"Its armor is impossible to breach, its jaws are strong enough to crush rock and it spits a venom so deadly that no creature can stand against it."

"Once it breaks through the outer wall, it will destroy everything," Otohime said.

"My *gyojin* elite warriors have been battling it every day, to slow its progress, but their numbers have thinned," Ryujin said. "The few remaining will join forces with you."

"But it has a weakness too?" Kiyomi asked, recovering her composure. "Because everything is balanced."

"Yes, that is so," Ryujin agreed. "This dreadful monster has its own enemy, to keep it in check."

"Which is . . .?"

"Humans, of course."

"How did I know you were going to say that?" Kenny grumbled.

"How long do we have?" Kiyomi asked.

"It will be at the palace walls come morning. We shall ride out to meet it." Ryujin stroked his moustache.

"If we succeed, if we stop this thing for you . . ." Kiyomi began.

"Then I will give Kuromori-*san* my most valued treasure."

"And what do I get?"

Ryujin looked at her, surprised. "You have the honor of carrying Kuromori's banner. Is there anything greater?"

"Hah! Nice try, but no," Kiyomi said. "Listen up,

without me, Ken-*chan* will be lucky to tie his own laces."

Kenny nodded. "It's true."

"So, if we do this, I want my own reward: the *Yasakani no Magatama*, the Jewel of Life. I know you have it."

Ryujin's nostrils flared with anger. "Out of the question," he snapped.

"Then we don't help you. You're on your own and we'll take our chances."

"Why, I could have you put to death first." The air bubble trembled and bucked, threatening to collapse.

"Father!" Otohime said. "It is a small price to pay for our kingdom." She put a calming hand over his fist. "What is one stone against everything we have?"

"Very well," Ryujin said, his voice as cold and hard as ice. "I agree."

The feast ended with a dessert course: a fabulous array of fruit, fresh from the gardens.

When Kenny got to his feet, Otohime took his hands in hers and gazed into his eyes.

"Kuromori-*san*, I composed a poem for you, a *haiku*. Do you wish to hear it, before you go into battle?"

"I, uh . . . sure. Why not?"

Otohime pulled a tiny scroll from the sleeve of her kimono and read:

> *"Hair like seashore sand;*
> *Eyes as blue as coral seas –*
> *His smile steals my heart."*

Kiyomi's eyes widened and she turned red as she tried to suppress her laughter.

"Wow. Thank you," Kenny said. "That's . . . nice."

Otohime beamed at him, while Kenny cringed inside.

Back in their guest quarters, Kiyomi cracked up again, remembering Kenny's mortified face.

"This isn't funny!" Kenny fumed, pacing again.

"Yes, it is. You're worse than James Bond, with women falling at your feet wherever you go."

"It's not like I've led her on or anything," Kenny protested. "Anyway, how did you know Ryujin has the jewel?"

"It's obvious. We've already seen how he hoards anything that ends up in the sea, right? You said he loves precious stones and the mirror showed us the gateway on the seabed. It led us here."

"He'll try to trick us. Shark boy was right: we can't trust him."

"Of course. But Ken-*chan*, there's no point worrying about that now. We have to figure out how to stop that thing."

"Yeah, right. The Dragon King and all his armies can't do anything yet somehow it falls to us. We are *so* dead."

12 十二

Early the next morning, the palace was bustling with preparations for battle.

One of the many large halls had been converted into a makeshift armory and, all around, armored *gyojin* warriors were selecting weapons from racks, crates and trunks.

"Is this it?" Kiyomi asked, from inside her air bubble. "Not even a Stinger missile that fell off a ship?"

"These traditional weapons have always served us well," grunted a nearby soldier, hefting an ax. "What use are guns underwater?"

"Have you got a torpedo?" Kiyomi asked hopefully.

"Harashima-*sama*, are you sure you don't wish to wear armor?" another *gyojin* asked, eyeing Kiyomi's wet suit with suspicion.

"No," she said, strapping on a pair of *katana*. "We need to move freely and quickly. Besides, I don't think armor is going to help much."

The troop of warriors snapped to attention as Ryujin

entered. He too was dressed for war, albeit in ceremonial armor.

"How are your preparations, Kuromori-*san*?" he asked, stepping into the air pocket. "Do you have everything you need?"

Kenny scratched his head. "I've got Kusanagi, but I'll need transportation."

"It has been arranged and is waiting for you. My scouts are standing watch; when the beast draws near once more, we will know."

Princess Otohime came in by a different entrance; she, too, was wearing armor, although hers looked worn. "Harashima-*san*, I found this, as you requested." She held out a small wooden box.

"Thank you," Kiyomi said, opening it. She removed the packaging and took out two blocks wrapped in brown paper, each stamped *C-4 High Explosive*. "Perfect."

"And here is the *yumi*," a voice rumbled. Kakichi, the shark-*oni*, held out a curved bow, over six feet long, and a quiver of arrows.

Kiyomi took the bow and felt the weight, giving a few pulls on the hemp string. She nodded her approval.

"There is something else I must do for you," Otohime said. She gestured and the life-support bubbles shrank down to become form-fitting cocoons around the humans' physiques.

"So, what do we have?" Kenny said to Kiyomi. "A

handful of troops . . . me with Kusanagi . . . you with bow and arrows . . ."

"Me go with you," Kakichi said, striking his chest. "Me have debt to repay."

"And I too will fight at Kuromori's side to defend my realm," added Otohime.

"No!" said Ryujin. "I forbid it. It's too dangerous."

"But Father, we're all going to die anyway if –"

"Sire, it's here! The beast is upon us!" panted a sailfish at the door. "You must get to safety."

"Lead the way!" cried the *gyojin* leader and the warriors fell in line, swimming after the messenger.

Kakichi wrapped his arms around Kiyomi and Kenny and swept them along. "Faster this way," he explained, zipping through corridors and hallways until he reached the main entrance, where he set them down again, on the top of the steps.

"Oh," Kiyomi said, looking upward.

Rising in front of them to obscure the horizon was an enormous cloud of sediment gouged up from the seabed. It hung in the water like a volcanic ash cloud, rippling and billowing. Something moved inside the murky depths and emitted a piercing shriek of rage. It was still twelve miles away, but approaching fast.

"Ken-*chan*, what else have we got?" Kiyomi yelled. "Have you learned anything new from Genkuro-*sensei*?"

"I can do fire, water, earth, metal and air," Kenny said, counting them off.

"None of which is much use down here." She turned to Otohime, who had joined them on the steps. "That thing – does it breathe air?"

"Yes," the princess answered. "It climbed out of the seabed a week ago and nothing we have tried has hurt it."

"Your mounts," Kakichi said, as two sleek silvery gray shapes swooped down to them, with pointed noses and mouths shaped like smiles. Each dolphin had been fitted with a crude saddle behind its dorsal fin and makeshift reins of kelp.

"This is Shachi and the other is Iruka," Otohime said, petting them. "They volunteered to help you."

Kenny took one last look around the palace. It seemed like every denizen of the undersea kingdom had assembled at the front and all their lives now hung in the balance. Kiyomi gave his hand a squeeze and the *gyojin* mounted their sharks for the final assault.

"Are we ready to meet our ancestors?" shouted the squad leader. "To die, protecting our home? Then go!" The shark-riding fish-men stormed through an archway, out towards the oncoming monster.

His stomach churning, Kenny sat astride his dolphin and tapped it with his heel. Shachi sped forward, dropping down the angled steps and out into the ocean. Clinging on to the kelp reins for dear life, Kenny watched the cluster of dots in front advance towards the menacing cloud. He had Kiyomi to his right, Kakichi to his left and an armored turtle that could only be Otohime behind.

Ripples within the plume and another heart-stopping shriek told Kenny that the battle was already under way.

"Look out!" Kiyomi yelled. "Bank right!"

Kenny jerked the reins just as a huge shadow toppled from the murky cloud and barreled towards him. It was a massive gray block, the size of a submarine. Shachi ducked and swooped, whistling and clicking to avoid the object which thudded onto the sea floor.

Glancing back, Kenny shuddered when he realized the slab was the lower jaw of a sperm whale. What sort of monster could bite a whale in half?

The answer came a split second later when a head burst out of the cloud. Two long horns grew from the center and curved backward while pairs of giant crescent fangs formed its lower jaws. Tiny eyes blazed with hate as its armored, segmented body reared up.

Shachi twisted away and the beast fell upon the dead whale to tear into it with its mandibles. Kenny directed his dolphin in a wide circle to better judge the size of the monster. Section after section of it stretched for over half a mile, like an enormous train with pairs of powerful spiny legs instead of wheels.

"It's a *mukade*!" Kiyomi said. "A giant centipede."

The *gyojin* attacked, striking the monster from all sides. Shark riders went to hack at the front legs, while others soared above the shielded head, hurling spears. The sharpened points bounced off, but the creature rose up to snap its jaws, exposing its underside.

"Fall back!" Kenny yelled, swooping by. "Fall back!"

But it was no use. In their eagerness to strike a telling blow, the *gyojin* concentrated their assault on the neck area, only to find that their weapons were useless against the thick carapace. With its antennae tracking their movements and jaws snapping, the centipede was making short work of the warriors.

"We've got to get them out of there!" Kenny cried, summoning Kusanagi and directing Shachi down towards the powerful legs. Otohime kept pace alongside, but Kiyomi and Kakichi cruised upward, towards the head.

The gigantic body surged past at dizzying speed, but Kenny was only interested in the forest of legs churning the seabed. At his urging, Shachi slipped under the beast, skirted the limbs and Kenny lashed out with the sword.

KLAK-KLAK-KLAK-KLAK-KLAK! To his horror, the sacred blade bounced off the tree-trunk legs.

Two hundred yards above, Kiyomi directed Iruka up the creature's back, towards the nightmarish head. Nocking an arrow in the longbow, she waited until she was directly over the flat face at the point where the antennae emerged, and took aim. Just behind on each side was a pair of tiny black eye spots. She loosed the arrow – but the steel point bounced harmlessly away.

The *mukade* spat out the shark it was feasting on and turned its attention to the fleeing dolphin. Its long antennae twitched and it honed in.

Kenny emerged from beneath the final pair of hooked legs and hung on while Shachi made a sharp turn in search of Iruka.

Kiyomi glanced back to see the awful fangs closing in. "No!" She dragged on the reins and twisted, pulling her dolphin to one side as a raking mandible slashed through the currents. The centipede was adjusting its footing for another assault when a dark shape slammed into its head. It staggered from the impact of the armored leatherback, but only for a second. Lashing its head backward, it swatted Otohime away and opened its fangs wide.

"Look out!" cried Kakichi, lunging towards Kiyomi.

Two purple jets of thick venom streaked from the centipede's mouth towards the hapless Iruka. The shark-*oni* shouldered Kiyomi aside and grabbed her leg, dragging her away from the poison sizzling in the water. Iruka wasn't as lucky.

Kenny pulled hard on the reins to stop Shachi getting too close and watched in horror as the stricken dolphin disintegrated before his eyes.

With a squeal of triumph, the *mukade* resumed its relentless charge towards the palace.

13 十三

"This is nuts!" Kenny exploded, fighting back tears of anger and frustration. "There's no way we can stop that thing."

He stood in the deep trough the centipede's legs had scored into the seabed. All around lay the bodies of Ryugu-jo's defenders: sharks, whales, giant squid, *gyojin*.

Kiyomi, Shachi, Kakichi and a bruised Otohime, now in human form, huddled in a small group, thrown into shadow by the looming cloud of silt marking the *mukade*'s onslaught.

"There must be a way," Kiyomi said. "You heard Ryujin; the gods aren't stupid. There's a balance at work. We just have to figure out –"

"And you call *me* stubborn?" Kenny railed. "We just got our butts kicked, in case you hadn't noticed. Nothing works. The sword can't hurt it. You put an arrow in its eye. It spits acid. What have we got left?"

"I don't know, but there has to be something," Kiyomi insisted.

"Harashima-*san* right," Kakichi rumbled. "Cannot give up. Many die."

"Kuromori-*san*," Otohime said, "you were sent here for a reason. I know you can defeat this monster. The lives of my people depend on you."

Kenny let out a deep sigh. "Well, it's not like I've got anything else to do right now. Does anyone have a plan that isn't suicide?"

Shachi let out a low whistle followed by a buzzing series of clicks.

"He say you get angry. Fight duel. One-on-one," Kakichi translated.

"Hah! Like that's going to happen." Kenny paused; the germ of an idea was taking hold in his brain. "Wait a minute. I'm faster than you guys if I use the currents. Maybe I can slow it down long enough for you to evacuate the palace. Would that work?"

"I'm going with you," Kiyomi said. "You'll need my help."

"OK, and you two, go back and warn everyone to get out of there. The best I can do is try and draw it away," Kenny said. "And no arguing. That's an order."

Otohime and Kakichi both bowed and took off, racing back to the palace.

Ryujin watched the approaching cloud from the top of the palace steps, stone-faced.

"Your Majesty, we have to leave. It will be here in minutes," pleaded an attendant.

"It's true, sire. The humans have failed. We saw it. Your army is gone. There is no one left to defend us," added another.

"Father!" Otohime called, gliding up the stairs, with Kakichi following. "It's over. You need to find safety."

"No," the Dragon King said firmly. "I know this Kuromori. While he breathes, we have hope. I will not surrender until he does."

"Ken-*chan*, I've got an idea," Kiyomi called to Kenny.

"What is it?"

They were shoulder to shoulder, hanging on to Shachi's dorsal fin while the young bottlenose powered through the water.

"Don't think."

"What?"

"I mean it. I just realized something. In the aquarium when the glass blew, and the lake when we were falling – both those times you acted without thinking. It's like your spirit knows what to do, even if your mind doesn't."

"You want me to empty my head?"

"Yes. Trust your instincts, not your brain."

The centipede loomed larger and Kenny could hear the grinding of its feet.

"So, you want me to be even more stupid than I usually am? Well, considering what I'm about to do, that shouldn't be too hard."

Sensing incoming movement, the *mukade* stopped and

reared up into an attacking posture, baring its claws and fangs. It was less than a hundred yards from the outer walls of the palace. Shachi swooped in low and dropped Kenny off.

"You!" he said, drifting down and pointing at the giant creature. "Why don't you pick on someone your own size?"

The antennae twitched and the monster cocked its head.

"That's right, I'm talking to you. I'm going to give you three seconds to turn around and go home and we'll forget all about this. Otherwise, I'm going to have to kick your . . . your, uh, rear segment. You hear me?"

Kiyomi let go of the dolphin and took up position in the shadow of the wall.

"One . . ."

"Has he lost his mind?" wondered the watching Ryujin.

"Two . . ."

Each one of the *mukade*'s legs took a step back.

"Three!" Kenny finished. "Well? Go on, clear off!"

Emitting a thunderous bellow of rage, the gigantic head plunged downward to crush the annoying human.

Kenny was ready. A blast of current slammed him backward and the centipede's head crashed against the ground, embedding its fangs into the dirt.

"Yeah! How did you like that?" Kenny exulted.

The *mukade* wriggled its head to work it free and,

when it came back up, half a fang had broken off.

"I'm still here, on the menu!" Kenny called. "Come and get it . . . uh-oh!"

This time the centipede attacked low, its body scraping the seabed and its synchronized legs levering forward with the force of a bullet train. Kenny summoned a gush of water to launch him upward, but the *mukade* anticipated and, moving with blinding speed, it flicked out an antenna, catching him and hurling him back to the ground.

"Kenny!" Kiyomi screamed, watching him bounce once before the centipede rammed him with its head and trampled him into the seabed.

14 十四

Otohime covered her mouth with her hand and stared in horror, while Kakichi bowed his head in silent prayer.

Ryujin swallowed hard – and then his eyes widened as the seabed began to judder. "*Shinji rarenai*," he croaked.

Kenny felt his feet sink deeper and deeper into the silt until he was up to his knees, but he remained upright with his hands high to fend off the crushing weight of a thousand tons of monster.

"Oh!" Kiyomi said. A shimmering spherical force field was emanating from Kenny's outstretched hands, aimed into the jaws of the *mukade*. It continued to press forward, pushing Kenny back until he bumped up against the wall.

"Hey, you can't eat me now that you've only got half a mouth!" Kenny goaded.

The centipede made one last attempt to crush the boy before rising up again, like a cobra preparing to strike.

"Is that it? The best you can do? Bring it on, you overgrown maggot!"

With a low hiss, the creature opened its fangs and mandibles to their fullest extent, took aim and the poison glands pumped again, spewing purple venom over Kenny.

"Urggh!" he grunted. He was trapped, with the palace wall to his back, the beast in front and his legs stuck in the murky sand. Thick, gloppy poison flowed over the force field, obscuring his view. He had to focus, to not lose concentration or to overthink, otherwise he was a goner.

Kenny heard the *mukade* spitting on him, again and again, until finally he snapped.

"You know what? That's really disgusting! In fact, I've had enough of you and your garbage. You think you're so tough? Let's see how *you* like it!" Kenny collected saliva in his parched mouth and spat a glob of foam in the centipede's direction.

The effect was immediate. A shriek of panic rang out and the pounding legs started up again. Where flecks of spit had touched the inside of the energy field, the poison shrank away. Peering through the emerging gaps, Kenny saw the creature backing off.

"You're kidding me," he said to himself, dropping the force field and pulling his legs out of the mud. He whistled for Shachi.

The dolphin swooped in, extended a flipper and pulled Kenny along, after the departing centipede. "Kiyomi!" Kenny yelled as he soared by. "It's afraid of spit!"

"It's afraid of *what*?"

"Shachi, take me to where it bit the dirt," Kenny said to his ride. "I need to check something."

The dolphin sliced its way to the crater on the sea floor. Kenny dismounted and scrambled to the center where a shiny blade of chitin was embedded.

Concentrating for a second, Kenny created a wider air bubble around his hand. He cupped it under his mouth and spat out a blob of saliva, then knelt and daubed it on the broken fang. Bubbles instantly appeared, along with a fizzing sound, and the tough exterior melted away. Shachi bobbed his head in approval.

Kenny nodded in grim determination. He summoned Kusanagi, extended the bubble and spat on the blade, sliding his thumb and forefinger over it to smear on as much saliva as he could muster.

"Shachi, it's not getting away," he said. "I need a repeat of our earlier maneuver, got it?"

The dolphin settled low so that Kenny could climb aboard and took off, closing the gap on the fleeing *mukade*.

From the palace steps, a huge cheer erupted. Otohime danced with excitement and Ryujin grinned.

"Hey, you guys!" Kiyomi yelled, swimming upward to emerge from the shadows of the wall. "It's not over yet. Kakichi, can you give me a lift? Whoa!"

Her words were lost as the shark-*oni* bulleted towards

her, flung out a huge arm to grab hold and charged over the wall towards the receding cloud.

Shachi flexed his powerful tail and honed in on the monstrous centipede like a torpedo. Hugging the seabed, he zeroed in low, ducked under the tail and skirted the inside of the legs on the right. Kenny clung to the dorsal fin with one hand and leaned out, slashing with his sword in the other. This time, Kusanagi sliced through the massive legs with ease and the *mukade*'s body collapsed.

The monster shrieked and twisted around, trying to snap at its attacker. Its underside slammed into the ground and it dropped limply, rolling so as to maximize its spread.

Kenny glanced up at the dwindling light, saw the gigantic body bearing down and jerked Shachi to the right, directing the dolphin into the narrowing gap between two legs. The centipede sprawled, half of its legs missing on one side, and swiped a fang at the tiny dolphin emerging from the displaced silt.

"Hah! How'd you like that?" Kenny cried.

The *mukade* roared in defiance and struggled to right itself with its remaining legs.

"Ken-*chan*, it's my turn!" Kiyomi yelled, as Kakichi swam into view. She pulled a saliva-coated arrowhead out of her mouth, nocked it against the longbow and drew back, taking careful aim. The centipede shrieked and opened its fangs, ready to fire a volley of poison in her direction.

"Smile!" Kiyomi released the bowstring.

Arcing through the water in its bubble of air, the arrow thudded into the monster's mouth, embedding in its throat, and detonated the block of C-4 plastic explosive tied to the shaft.

KRA-KA-BOOM! The creature's head flew apart amid a flash of light and a roiling haze of white froth.

"*Yatta!*" Kiyomi's celebration was short-lived as the shock wave buffeted her aside.

Like a slowly falling redwood, the huge body of the *mukade* crashed to the seabed and lay still, while ragged chunks of carapace floated down.

"Yes!" Kenny cried in triumph, before he slumped, drained from the exertion.

Kakichi set Kiyomi on his shoulders and Kenny directed Shachi back to the palace.

15 十五

The victory feast was even more lavish than the welcoming one, with many more speeches. It seemed that every mollusk, fish and crustacean that had witnessed the battle wished to express personal gratitude on behalf of all of its many individually named family members.

Kenny lost count of the number of courses he was served before the floor was given over to dancing. It was fascinating to watch the sea creatures frolic, since their concept of space was entirely different. Dance moves went up to the ceiling, spiraled down backward, flipped head over tail and involved synchronized color changes and fin clapping. Despite their protests, Kenny and Kiyomi, dressed once again in their finery, were dragged onto the dance floor.

Kakichi revealed a hidden talent for break dancing, spinning on his head and doing the worm, while Otohime held Kenny close for a slow number. Ryujin kept time graciously before finally bringing the celebration to a close. He stood and motioned for everyone to return to their places.

"The gods have indeed favored us by sending us these warriors who have vanquished the vile *mukade* and saved our kingdom," he said, to raucous applause. "It is only right that we reward them accordingly to show our appreciation. Step forward, Kuromori-*san*."

Kenny stood, embarrassed, before the king. Ryujin placed both hands on the boy's shoulders and beamed at him. "Kuromori, you have performed a deed befitting only the greatest of heroes. You have proved yourself worthy to receive my most valued treasure . . ." He took Kenny's hand in his. "The hand of my daughter, Otohime, in marriage."

The color drained from Kenny's face. Ryujin placed Otohime's hand in Kenny's and a huge cheer went up from the onlookers. "One day, when I am gone, Otohime will rule this land. Only a true hero like you is worthy to govern by her side."

Kiyomi caught the look of panic in Kenny's eyes and bowed before the king. "Your Majesty," she said, "Kuromori-*san* is, uh, already betrothed to me."

"He is?" Ryujin raised an eyebrow. "I see no ring on your finger. In this realm, my word is law, so I absolve you of any former alliance you may have made."

Otohime looked up at Kenny with an adoring gaze.

"Well, what about my reward?" Kiyomi asked. "I killed your monster and you promised me the *Yasakani no Magatama* in return."

"Did I?" Ryujin scratched at his moustache. "I do not

recall making such a promise."

"Why you – Everyone heard you! That's why I made sure to ask you in front of your people," Kiyomi raged.

Ryujin addressed the crowd. "Did anyone hear me say such a thing?"

As one, every sea creature shuffled its fins and looked away, shaking its head.

"Father!" Otohime cried. "You must not act this way. It ill befits a great king. I heard you make the promise. Harashima-*san* fought with honor to save your throne. It's the least you can do."

Ryujin chewed his lip, thought for a moment and sighed. "Very well. I shall give the girl the jewel she wants. Consider it a wedding present." He beckoned two *gyojin* guards. "Show the girl to my treasure chamber. You know what to do."

"I'll go with her," Kenny said. "To, uh, make sure she doesn't steal anything else."

"That will not be necessary," Ryujin said.

"But I want to. It'll be . . . a last good-bye."

"Father, I shall accompany them," Otohime said, ending the discussion.

Ten minutes later, after winding down water-filled corridors, tunnels and shafts, they arrived at a solid granite wall. One of the guards slotted a crystal into the rock and a section melted away, revealing a long passage with a cavernous, air-filled chamber at the end.

"Wow. This place must be well below the seabed," Kenny observed.

"Yes. It is the most secure vault my father could build," Otohime said. "There is no other way in or out and it is encased in solid rock."

"And the jewel's in there?" Kiyomi said. "Who's going to fetch it?"

The guard leader grunted.

"My father's orders are you can have the jewel, but you must find it for yourself," Otohime translated, giving the guard a dirty look.

Kenny sighed. "Let's go then." He traipsed down the tunnel, with Kiyomi close behind, before he realized that they were unattended. "Wait. Isn't the princess coming?"

"No!" Otohime yelled from the entrance. "Unhand me, you oaf!"

Kenny spun around, to see a guard pull the princess away and the passage vanish back into solid stone, leaving him and Kiyomi trapped under thousands of tons of rock.

16 十六

"A light would be a good idea," Kiyomi said. The surrounding darkness was absolute, fitting for a tomb.

"I'm on it." Kenny conjured up a small glowing sphere which floated aloft, causing thousands of sparkling points of light to reflect back like a miniature galaxy.

He let out a long low whistle. "You weren't kidding about all the world's treasures washing up here."

The entire cavern was crammed with gold, silver, jewelry, gems, goblets, plates, ornaments, rugs, crystals and other precious objects.

"He's clever, I'll give him that," Kiyomi said. "Filling this chamber with air not only preserves this stuff, but also stops any of his subjects sneaking in."

"So, now what? I could probably try cutting a way out, but if there's miles of rock all around . . ." Kenny turned in a circle, wondering where to begin.

"Let's start with the jewel," Kiyomi said. "That's what we came for."

"You want to find one jewel, in here?" Kenny dropped

to his knees and scooped up a handful of Spanish doubloons.

"I know. It'd be easier to find a needle in a haystack," Kiyomi said, opening a wooden chest packed with opals.

"I did that once," Kenny said, sitting back. "My grandad made me scatter all this hay and then go over it with a powerful magnet. It worked."

"Well, that's not much use here." Kiyomi kicked out, scattering a pile of silver coins.

"What does this *tamagata* thing look like anyway?"

"It's *magatama*. It's like a big comma of green jade, the size of your hand, with a hole at the top."

"That's it? A lump of jade?"

Kiyomi nodded. "Better start looking."

Two hours later, Kenny slumped on a hill of coins.

"This is hopeless," he moaned. "We could be here for a month and still only get through a tenth of this."

Kiyomi sat heavily on a chest, elbows on knees and chin on palms. "I know. Stupid, eh? After everything we've been through, we get to starve or suffocate down here."

After a minute of brooding, Kenny asked, "Tell me again. What's the big deal with this stone? Why does Susie want it?"

"I don't know why he wants it, but it's a powerful object. You remember the story of the mirror?"

"When the Sun Goddess shut herself away in a cave

and they had to trick her to come out?"

"Yeah. Well, the gods hung a necklace in the tree along with the mirror, to entice her out. This jewel was on that necklace."

"And Susie called it the Jewel of Life, right?"

Kiyomi nodded.

Kenny's mind was churning. "You said something before, back at my place, about Three Sacred Treasures. What are they?"

"There's the sword, the mirror and the jewel. Together they symbolize the power of Japan."

"Hm. Like we have the crown, the orb and the scepter, for the British royal family?"

"Yep, they go together. Like a boxed set."

Kenny sprang to his feet, a wild gleam in his eye. "Hey, wait a minute . . ."

"Uh-oh. What are you thinking now?"

The sword Kusanagi shimmered into Kenny's hand. "This is one of the Three Treasures, right?"

Kiyomi stood up. "What about it?"

"It's our magnet!" Kenny said, holding the sword out in front of him and waving it from side to side.

"Have you flipped?"

"No, think about it. I know Kusanagi has its own mind; it spoke to me once. It also fights for me and it can open doorways. So maybe it can find its teammates." He stumbled forward, brandishing the sword like a metal detector. "Come on, you. What did Susie say about the mirror? That one leads to the other. Show me where this precious stone is hiding. Come on. I know you want to . . ."

Kiyomi picked up a fist-sized emerald and gazed into it, seeing multiple reflections staring back. "Ryujin won't let you die in here," she said.

"Huh? Why not?"

"Because you're his future son-in-law."

"Oh, don't start that," Kenny said, wading through a dune of silver. "It's not going to happen."

"Why not? You'd be king one day and all this would be yours. Not a bad deal for staying alive. And you like her."

"Will you shut up? I'm trying to concentrate here."

"I'm serious."

"So am I. She's nice and all that, but . . . she's not you."

"Not some crazy, monster-hating mess you mean?"

"There's a lot more to you than that. Look, she's very sweet and all, but I couldn't rely on her to cover my back in a fight. You, on the other hand . . . I trust you with my life. So what if we're both messed up? Thing is, we're a good team. We balance out each other's – whoa! Did you see that?" Kusanagi bucked in Kenny's hand, swinging him around in a half circle.

"I'm not falling for that!" Kiyomi scoffed. "You just twisted it."

"Shh! I'm serious." Kenny crept forward, sweeping the sword from side to side. "There!" It locked in position again, this time to his left. "It's definitely sensing something."

Kiyomi scrambled closer. "Under that pile of coins,"

she said, scooping aside handfuls of gold. Her knuckles scraped on wood and she unearthed a small oak chest. "Locked, of course."

With one cut, Kenny sliced off the padlock and watched Kiyomi open the box. It was stuffed with jade jewelry, including dozens of comma-shaped jewels.

"Is it any of these?" she asked, holding up a selection.

Kenny passed the sword over each one, but it made no response. "That's weird."

"Now what?" Kiyomi said, tipping out the contents and slumping down.

"I'm not giving up that easily," Kenny muttered, continuing to sweep the blade. It stopped over the empty chest. "Hmm . . ." Kneeling beside it, Kenny measured the depth inside then turned it over. He tapped the base which gave a hollow thud. "This thing's got a false bottom." Using the sword handle, he smashed in a corner and lifted off a panel. Inside was a circular marble block, half-black and half-white, in the classic *yin yang* design. "Is that it?" he said, holding it up. "All this trouble for a piece of junk like this?"

"Ken-*chan*, wait," Kiyomi said, but it was too late.

Annoyed, Kenny threw the thick disk against the wall. "What's the point? It's not like we can eat gold, is it?" He dismissed the sword and stomped away, kicking coins.

Kiyomi picked her way over to the broken halves of the ornament and grinned. "Ken-*chan*, you're an idiot," she said. "Look."

110

Kenny trudged over and Kiyomi held up the two pieces.

"*Yin* and *yang*," she said. "Representing harmony and balance."

"So?"

"Each is shaped like a comma, just like the *magatama*." She fitted the two pieces together. "Where better to hide it?" She gently struck the white half on the rock floor and it crumbled to reveal a polished green stone inside. "Very clever. Someone encased it in calcite and shaped it like marble. There's no way we'd have found this without your brainwave." She held it out for Kenny to inspect.

"You mean this is it?" he said, turning it over. "The Jewel of Life? We found it?"

Kiyomi shrugged. "Check it with the sword."

Kenny called Kusanagi back to his hand and waved it over the stone. It jumped and the blade clinked against the curved jewel.

"That settles it," Kenny said. He reached into a mound of jewelry, selected a heavy gold necklace and threaded it through the hole in the stone. "Who gets the bling?"

"You keep it," Kiyomi said. "It's your job to deliver it."

"Don't remind me." Kenny draped the chain around his neck and tucked the heavy pendant inside his clothes. "Susie gave us four days. How long have we been down here?"

"No idea, but I don't think we've got long. I've been craving raw meat like you wouldn't believe."

"Then we need to find a way out of here fast."

"You know, I've been hanging around with you for too long," Kiyomi said with a sly smile.

"Uh-oh. Why's that?"

"Because I've got a plan. It's dumb, it'll probably get us killed, but it's all I've got. Want to hear it?"

17 十七

"You're going to blow us up?" Kenny's voice bounced off the walls of the treasure chamber. "Are you nuts?"

"No, think about it. We're under the sea, encased in a tomb of rock. It's a one-way door and only they can open it, so we have to give them a reason."

"And because Ryujin is so utterly obsessed with all this wealth, you reckon he'll come running if we destroy it?"

Kiyomi grinned. "Wouldn't you? And if that doesn't work, what better way to get back at him?"

"Yeah, that's stupid enough to be one of my ideas. How do we make an explosion?"

Kiyomi turned her back, reached into the folds of her kimono and withdrew a squished lump of C-4. "Never leave home without it," she said. "There were two blocks and I used one on the centipede, so . . ."

"Wait. I've seen what that stuff can do. Surely, if you set it off in an enclosed space like this, the blast will kill us?"

Kiyomi patted Kenny's cheek. "And this is the clever bit. Why do you think it's called the Jewel of Life?"

"Uh, because it's a cool name?"

"Because whoever holds it can't die – at least that's what the legend says. And it heals any wound."

"For real?" Kenny took out the precious stone and inspected it.

"That's what it says."

"It's too risky."

"What? You have a better plan? I know, let's test it." Kiyomi picked up a heavy porcelain vase and advanced on Kenny.

"I'm not sure – hey!" Kenny tried to duck as Kiyomi smashed the vase over his head, knocking him to the ground.

He collapsed and sprawled on the floor. "Urggh," he groaned. "I think . . . you cracked . . . my skull . . ." He lay unmoving and his chest fell still.

Kiyomi watched him, her fists on her hips. "Kenny, stop messing around. This isn't funny." She faltered. "I mean it . . . Oh, no. No. Kenny!" She dropped to her knees and cradled him, feeling for a pulse. "Kenny! I'm sorry. I didn't mean –"

"Gotcha!" Kenny snorted with laughter. "I owed you that one."

"You – *bakayaro*!" Kiyomi dropped him. "I ought to punch your stupid head off for that."

"Go ahead." Kenny grinned, rubbing his head. "I wouldn't feel it. Was I going to get the kiss of life?"

Kiyomi scrambled to her feet. "Get lost. We're on the clock here."

Kenny carried the block of plastic explosive over to where the entry passageway had been. Taking Kusanagi, he stabbed the sword into the rock face, all the way to the hilt, and twisted it in a tight circle to cut out a long cylinder. He extracted the core and Kiyomi handed him a small coil of gold thread she had picked from a cloak.

Kenny pressed one end of the metal fiber firmly into the explosive, stuffed the C-4 into the hole and rammed it home with the shaft of rock. Backing away, he unspooled the gold, coming to a stop beside Kiyomi who was crouching behind a makeshift barricade of chests, statues and rugs.

"You know, we could always just wait it out," Kenny said. "We won't die of hunger or suffocation now that we have the jewel." He held it up.

"Sure. I bet you'd love being trapped in here with an *onibaba*." Kiyomi clasped her hand over Kenny's, wrapping it around the stone. "I suppose if I was to rip off your head for supper, you'd just grow it back."

"Good point," Kenny said, and he snapped his fingers to produce an electric spark. It crackled down the gold wire, hit the detonator packed into the C-4 and – *KRA-KA-BOOOMM!*

Far above the vault, Otohime paced the empty hall while her father sat stubbornly on his coral throne.

"Father, no good will come of this," Otohime pleaded. "You will anger the gods."

Ryujin leaned back and steepled his fingers. "And I have told you many times that my treasures are too precious to be shared with humans. It will only corrupt them. It is better this way."

"To starve them into submission and then to enslave them? After they saved your kingdom? Father . . . you act without honor."

"Enough of your insolence! Try my patience no more lest I –"

A subsonic rumble radiated through the floor, shaking it from side to side, and a deep fissure splintered through it and up the walls, scaring the jellyfish chandeliers.

"The *mukade*! It's not dead!" Ryujin shrieked, jumping up from his throne. He stared around in bewilderment. "An earthquake?"

"Sire!" called out a *gyojin* guard. "It came from your vault."

Otohime shot a defiant glance in her father's direction. "I tried to warn you. It's Kuromori."

"Oww!" Kenny heaved the shattered chest of coins off his back and crawled upright, pulling Kiyomi to her feet. "I guess we're alive then."

"That was awesome!" Kiyomi said. "Like being in the heart of the sun!"

All around was destruction. Chests and statues alike

had been blown apart by the shock wave and piles of coins were now melted slag. A huge crack split the ceiling and seawater was cascading down.

"Here they come!" Kiyomi warned, watching the stone wall melt away to reveal the exit tunnel with dark shapes moving inside.

"I got this!" Kenny cried, and stood in front of the passage, hands held up in surrender, while salt water gushed towards him.

The first *gyojin* through the portal hefted a two-pronged spear and stabbed it through the boy's chest.

"That tickles," Kenny said, stepping back. He reached for the shaft, pulled it free and tossed it to Kiyomi. "Thanks," he said to the gawping fish-man. "My turn now." Kusanagi appeared in his hands. "The name's Kuromori. You might have heard of me."

The *gyojin* turned to run, shoving its way past its comrades who were spilling through the opening.

"*Ki-aii!*" Kiyomi launched herself at the group, striking out with the butt of the spear in an arc. She pivoted on the ball of her foot and landed a spinning roundhouse kick, followed by an elbow smash. The *gyojin* scattered in disarray, giving Kiyomi time to snap the spear over her knee and to then whale on them with the two short staves.

Kenny grimaced at the sound of breaking bones and edged his way around the mayhem towards the exit. More guards were coming his way. Concentrating hard, with hands outstretched, he pictured a powerful gale pushing back waves. The water in the tunnel retreated as the air in the chamber forced its way outward.

"Kiyomi, time to go!" Kenny said.

"Be right with you," Kiyomi answered, walloping the last *gyojin*.

With the air bubble extending towards them, the fish-men in the passage hastily backed away.

"We need reinforcements!" one of them yelled before a large shadow silenced him.

Emerging from the tunnel, Kenny looked up to see a hulking shape blocking his way. "Kakichi!"

"Me know way out. Must hurry! King angry. Send guards."

"We need to get back to the gateway," Kiyomi said, stepping from the passage. "To get home."

"Me know where it is, but cannot open."

"Let's deal with one problem at a time," Kenny said, forming an air bubble around his head.

The shark-*oni* nodded, grabbed Kenny and Kiyomi in each arm and took off, his powerful tail churning the water. He careened through the warren of flooded hallways and corridors, following servants' routes and navigating expertly. All around were chaotic scenes as shark-riding *gyojin* swept the palace in search of the fugitives.

Kakichi came to a stop beside a pearlescent door. "This lead to back of palace," he said. He pushed and pulled, but it wouldn't budge.

"Stand back," Kenny said, cutting a hole in the door with his sword.

"They see hole," Kakichi grumbled. "Know we come this way."

"Then let's make the most of our head start."

Kakichi burst through the high wall surrounding the palace grounds and banked left, heading for the open sea. In the distance, Kenny saw the carcass of the *mukade* and shuddered.

"We've got company," Kiyomi muttered, pointing to a tiny dot ahead of them, growing larger with every thrust of Kakichi's tail.

"You can say that again," Kenny said, glancing back to see a cluster of mako riders discharge from the palace.

As Kakichi drew closer to the gateway, Kenny and Kiyomi saw a huge leatherback turtle circling it. "Me slow them down," Kakichi said, turning towards the pursuing *gyojin*. "You go now."

"Kakichi, thank you. You've been a good friend to us," Kenny said.

"Kuromori spare my life. Me spare his. We now even," Kakichi said and he went to head off the hunters.

The turtle morphed into its human form and Otohime said, "Kuromori-*san*, only I can open the gateway between realms and this I will not do. You have no means of escape."

18 十八

"**K**en-*chan*, let me deal with her," Kiyomi said, her nostrils flaring. "We don't have time for this."

"I am not afraid of you, Harashima-*san*," Otohime said. "I have defied my father in coming here and your anger pales against his."

"Kiyomi, back off," Kenny hissed in her ear. "We need her help or no one's going anywhere."

"Fine." Kiyomi swam out of earshot and watched Kakichi battling the *gyojin*.

Otohime raised her hands towards Kenny in a pleading gesture. "My father forbids you to leave our world."

"Is that with or without the jewel?"

"It matters not. He says you must stay."

"What about you, Princess? What do you say?"

Otohime lowered her eyes. "I say my father's will must be obeyed."

"Then why are you here if he told you not to come?"

"Because . . . I wished to see you again. Alone." She shot a look in Kiyomi's direction. "Do you . . . love the human girl, Kuromori-*san*?"

Kenny blushed. "I, uh, I . . . it's complicated."

"Yet you came here to take the jewel to save her."

"How do you know that?"

"I see many things, Kuromori-*san*. I see a boy who does not know his own heart. I see a man who walks between worlds. I see a rebellious servant. I see honor and courage."

"Your father won't let us leave, but what about you, Princess? You control the gate."

"I . . . do not wish you to leave, Kuromori-*san*. But I can let the girl go."

"Is that the deal you're offering me? To stay here with you, in return for Kiyomi's freedom?"

"Would it be so bad?"

"I have a life – family . . . friends – people who need me back up top. I can't just leave them all behind."

"But I would! I'm willing to let the girl go. If not, you will both be trapped here. What good would that do?"

"Ken-*chan*, hurry it up!" Kiyomi called over her shoulder. "Kakichi's outnumbered and I'm going to go help him if you don't open that gate in the next minute."

"All right," Kenny said to Otohime, lowering his head. "Let her go. I'll stay, but don't ask me to be happy about it. She'll need the jewel."

Otohime stifled a sob with the flowing sleeve of her kimono.

"Now what?" Kenny said, alarmed. "I thought you'd be pleased."

Otohime lashed out, raining punches in Kenny's direction.

"Hey! What have I done?" He caught her wrists.

"You've answered my question! You do love her, whether you know it or not," she spat. "Go! Both of you." She pulled her hands free of Kenny's grip and made a complex gesture. A bright rectangle of sun-dappled water blinked into view against the darker blue of the ocean.

"I don't get it," Kenny said, looking from the gateway to the girl.

"How could I keep you here, like a bird in a cage, knowing you were suffering? You would spend your days pining for the surface world . . . and for that girl." Silvery tears streamed down Otohime's face. "I know how that ends. Your heart would break, I would agree to let you go home to visit and you would never return to me. Go! Get out!"

Kiyomi swam over and reached one hand towards the gate and the other out for Kenny. "She's letting us go?"

"Princess, I . . ." Kenny hesitated, not knowing what else to say. "I will never forget you. Thank you." He clasped Kiyomi's hand and pressed it to the jewel around his neck, saying, "Whatever you do, don't let go of this."

Kiyomi nodded.

"And Kuromori-*san*," Otohime said, "we will meet again."

Emerging from the rectangular arch at the Yonaguni ruins, Kenny was startled by the swirling funnel of hammerhead sharks circling the underwater city in their thousands.

Kicking hard and propelling his free arm, he joined Kiyomi in climbing to the surface, but the weight of their clothing was dragging them down. He quickly summoned an enormous air bubble to surround them both and allowed it to carry them the rest of the way.

Charles Blackwood sat on the cooler, his foot tapping nervously as he fought the urge to check his watch again. Instead, he tried to concentrate on the bobbing float from his fishing line. A lone seagull cruised overhead, hoping for a bite. It squawked and flapped wildly as the water exploded beneath and two teenagers shot upward, like a pair of champagne corks.

Charles swiveled around in time to see Kenny and Kiyomi bomb into the sea, still holding each other tightly.

"Dad!" Kenny gurgled. "Over here!"

"Kenny! Give me a sec!" Starting the engine, Charles chugged the small boat over to where Kiyomi was treading water.

"Charles-*sensei*," she gasped, squinting in the afternoon sunlight. "What day is it? How long have we been gone?"

Charles stretched out his hand to help her into the boat. "It's Wednesday. You two have been gone for . . ."

He paused to check his watch. "Fifty-seven hours. It's four twenty right now."

Kiyomi collapsed on the deck and did the math while Charles hauled Kenny aboard.

"Where'd the other boat go?" Kenny asked, squeezing alongside. "This isn't Captain Mike's."

"It is and it isn't," Charles said, grinning in delight at the two exhausted swimmers. "He gave up waiting and wanted to call the coast guard to report you missing. The best I could do was agree to go back to shore and to borrow this powerboat of his. He's pretty shaken up, but I called Sato to do some damage control. How on earth did you manage –?"

Kiyomi sat bolt upright. "This is day four!" she exclaimed. "Ken-*chan*, we have to get to Matsue by midnight."

"That's not going to happen," Charles said. "We'll be lucky to get back to Kubura by five and the last flight's already gone."

Panic flared in Kiyomi's eyes. "Ken-*chan*, we *have* to get the jewel to you-know-who."

"I know," Kenny said. "I've already worked that out. We just need to get to shore first."

"Jewel? You found it?" Charles's face lit up.

Kenny slipped the *magatama* from his neck and gave it to his father to view. "There you go. From the Dragon King's own treasure chamber."

Charles gave a low whistle. "You'll have to tell me

everything, starting with where you found those clothes." He fired up the engine.

Forty minutes later, Charles guided the boat into the harbor to be met by an anxious Captain Mike. The older man caught the mooring rope and tied it to a post. He straightened up and nearly fainted when he saw Kenny and Kiyomi climb onto the jetty.

"*Shinji rarenai*," he croaked.

"You two, go and get cleaned up," Charles said. "I'll settle up with the captain."

Kiyomi nudged Kenny's shoulder as they trudged uphill towards the *minshuku*.

"I think we need to stop hanging out together," she said.

"What?"

"Well, clearly we're a bad influence on each other. I mean, there I am blowing us up and there you are using your brain."

"Oh, that." Kenny shrugged. "It made sense. You said we couldn't come straight up or the decompression would kill us. Holding on to the stone was the only way. We could've drowned or been eaten by a shark and still be OK."

Kiyomi linked her arm through his as they walked. "I heard what you said to the princess."

Kenny reddened. "That was a private conversation."

"I wasn't *trying* to listen. Sound travels farther in water. Would you really have stayed . . . for me?"

"I'd have worked out a way to escape first chance I got. She knew that."

Kiyomi stopped. "Ken-*chan*. Thank you. For doing all this."

Kenny shook his head. "I'm just trying to put things right. I messed up, but you're the one paying the price."

Kiyomi bit her lip. "Speaking of which, how are we going to get to Matsue? To hand the jewel over?"

"We don't need to go to Matsue," Kenny said. "It's not the *place* we need, it's the person."

"What do you mean?"

"We've only got a few hours left to find Susie, so why bother going to his shrine? Why not cut out the middle part and go straight to Hell?"

"We can do that?" Kiyomi asked, her voice hushed.

"Yeah, I think so. Remember Usa, in the parking lot? Kusanagi opened a doorway straight into *Yomi*. If we can do that now . . ."

"You're serious? Go to him . . . there?"

Kenny nodded. "We should be safe as long as we have the stone. It's the only way."

"Run that by me again," Charles said. They were out on the bed and breakfast terrace with the sun low in the sky.

"We have to take the jewel to *Yomi* and give it to the boss man," Kenny said. "In return, he'll make Kiyomi well again."

"And the sword will take you there," Charles confirmed. "But will it bring you back?"

"It should," Kenny said.

"Should is a big word. What's Plan B, in case it doesn't cooperate?"

"Uh . . ."

"This could be a one-way trip if Susano-wo decides not to play ball. I don't like it."

"Dad, you don't have to like it. We're kind of out of options here. If we don't do this in the next few hours . . ."

"Then I'm done anyway," Kiyomi finished. She put two fingers to her head to make *oni* horns.

"I see." Charles removed his glasses and stood up. "Let's get going then."

Kenny shook his head. "Dad, you're not coming with us. This is the Land of the Dead we're going to and we're expected – you're not."

"Ken-*chan*'s right," Kiyomi said. "And you'll be blind down there because you can't see *yokai* the way we can. We won't be able to protect you and ourselves."

Five minutes later, Charles watched Kenny and Kiyomi climb the hill leading to Cape Irizaki. He waited until they were out of view before taking out his phone.

"This will do," Kenny said, arriving at a clear patch by the path on the headland. The dipping sun painted the sky blood red and black clouds congregated on the horizon like vultures.

"Come here." Kenny held his arms open and Kiyomi reluctantly moved in for a hug. She slipped her arms around Kenny, squeezing him tightly, and clasped her hands behind his back. He gently removed them and placed them on his chest. "Keep your hands on the jewel," he said.

Kusanagi appeared in his hand. "OK, you," Kenny said to the sword. "You know the drill. I need you to open a doorway to *Yomi*, just like you did for the *yurei*. I command you."

"Is this going to work?" Kiyomi asked.

"It has to." He concentrated on the sword, channeling his *ki* into the blade. "Come on. Do this for me. Please." From deep within the metal, a bluish light glowed, and slowly intensified.

A sudden gust of wind leveled the tall grass and ripped at their clothes. The glare from the sword cast long shadows all around and stung Kenny's eyes. He let go, but instead of dropping to the ground, the blade hung in the air and began to spin, slicing at the fabric of reality.

"Hold tight!" Kenny yelled above the roar of the wind and buried his face in Kiyomi's shoulder while her long hair lashed his face.

Crackling coils of energy capered around them, the screaming wind reached its peak and a shaft of lightning speared down to obliterate the ground where they stood, leaving only blackened earth. The ensuing thunderclap rattled the island like an earthquake, causing everyone to stop and look up at the clear sky in wonder.

From where they'd left him, Charles blinked away the lightning after-image printed on his retina. "Kenny, God help you, wherever you are."

Before Kenny could open his eyes, he was assaulted by the stench of a heavy, musky, animal odor – not what he was expecting. The ground swayed and he was doubled over with his weight on his belly; something was carrying him.

"Whoa!" Blinking to clear his vision, he saw the ground scrolling over his head and a trail of clawed footprints in the ash. "Put me down!"

The *oni* who had him slung over its shoulder stopped and shrugged him off. Kenny hit the dirt, rolled and sprang up, sword in hand. The other five *oni* in the welcome party sniggered among themselves. Kiyomi dangled, a limp doll, from one of their huge paws.

Kenny leveled the sword. "Set her down – gently. And then back off, all of you, or –"

"Or what?" challenged the first *oni*. "Kuromori not harm *oni* here."

Kiyomi gave a groan and the *oni* carrying her dumped her, hard.

Incensed, Kenny launched himself forward, brandishing the blade. To his surprise, the *oni* laughed.

"This *Yomi*. Land of Dead," the brute explained.

"Ken-*chan*, he's right," Kiyomi said, catching her breath and swaying on her hands and knees. "What are you going to do? Kill him and send him to Hell? He's already here and so are we."

"Master waiting to see you. Must go now." The *oni* pointed a gnarled claw in the direction of a decaying white Japanese castle, with multiple tiered towers that gouged the blackened sky.

Kiyomi shuddered.

"Is that the place from your dream?" Kenny asked her.

"Yeah. Ken-*chan*, we need to go quickly. I can *feel* the thing inside me." She gasped. "It's much stronger here. It's waking up . . . wanting control. I don't know how long I can fight it." Her fingers raked furrows in the dirt.

"Let's go then," Kenny said. "Lead the way." He helped Kiyomi up and the *oni* escort stamped through the ash towards the bone palace and the waiting Susano-wo.

20　二十

Yomi was a bleak, barren, blasted land of bone, ash and decay. Above, a blanket of black clouds scudded across the sky as if afraid to linger, casting everything in a gray half light. A keening wind carried mournful cries and huge birds soared overhead. The soft stench of rot filled the chill air: a damp, earthy smell like a forest floor. Vermin roamed freely: cockroaches, millipedes, scorpions, dung beetles, spiders, blowflies, slugs, maggots, worms.

"This is not what I was expecting at all," Kenny said to Kiyomi, as they trudged behind the *oni*. "Where are the *yurei*?"

"Oh, they're here all right," Kiyomi answered through clenched teeth. "Probably herded off somewhere. This is an endless desert of ash. Plenty of space."

"*Oni* are devils, right? They torture the dead?"

"Some of them, yes. The ones who deserve it. Those who have lived good lives are left in peace."

A moat, so deep and sheer as to be more like a crevasse, encircled the bone palace, and a single stone bridge spanned the gap from the bank to the colossal front doors. The *oni* marched across and the gang leader pounded the door with his iron club.

The doors swung inward and the group marched through. After the slate-gray, darkened landscape, Kenny squinted against the dull whiteness inside. Pillars of bone supported low ivory ceilings and leathery screen doors sealed off rooms, all illuminated by paper lanterns giving off oily black smoke. Corridors led to stairs that ended in galleries which opened onto hallways. The castle was a maze and all Kenny could tell was that they were climbing higher and higher.

The *oni* finally stopped before two large doors decorated with a fierce-looking, eight-headed dragon. Two of them knelt, one beside each door, and slid it open while the others retreated, their heads held low.

Kenny swallowed hard and was grateful to feel Kiyomi slip her hand into his. Together, they walked into the main hall.

From his dragon-skull throne, Susano-wo beamed with such genuine delight that Kenny was taken aback.

"Well, well, well!" boomed the bearded god, slapping his thigh. "If it isn't my favorite servant, Kumatori. You did it, as I knew you would. There were some who doubted that a pathetic *gaijin* child like you could succeed where others have failed, but I had faith in you, yes I did. Hah! Listen to me – a god having faith in a mortal. It should be the other way around, no?" He tapped a huge hourglass on the table beside his throne. "And here you are, with your precious friend and a few hours to spare too. Bravo, I say. Bravo."

Staring up at the giant, Kenny wished he could turn and run, but he knew he had to see this through for Kiyomi's sake, so he made the effort to hide his fear.

"You know, in some ways you remind me of me," Susano-wo continued. "Same tenacity. Of course, you're younger, smaller, weaker and dumber, but you have *kihaku* – spirit – and I like that about you. You don't give up. And you're so loyal. Just look at all you've done for your little girlfriend."

"She's not my girlfriend," Kenny muttered.

"Ah, but she could be. I can give her to you if you like. I can give you anything your heart desires; after all, you've been such a devoted servant."

"Ken-*chan*," Kiyomi said, her nostrils flaring and breath coming in short gasps. "What . . . is he . . . talking about?"

"Believe me, I have no idea and I'm not sure I want to find out," Kenny said.

"Oh, such modesty," Susano-wo said. "How charming. There's no need to be shy before me, your true master."

"You're no master of mine, you sicko."

"On the contrary, Kutamari, I am master of *Yomi* and you are here in my domain. That puts me in charge."

"Just take your jewel and let's be done."

"Not so fast, Kamatori. I have waited centuries for this

133

moment and I have learned much about patience. Do you know why I, the God of Sea and Storm, am imprisoned down here where there is neither ocean nor sky?"

"Uh, to weaken you?"

"Punishment, Koromuri, for my sins. Yes, my jealous brothers and sisters cast me down, and here I am. Do you know the one thing that has sustained me all these years? Revenge. Revenge upon the living, revenge upon the gods."

"Can . . . we . . . hurry this . . . along?" Kiyomi said through gritted teeth.

"A deal's a deal and I keep my promises," Kenny said.

"And you pay your debts?" Susano-wo leaned forward. "Where is my jewel?"

"Where is the ring?" Kenny countered.

Susano-wo grinned, revealing blackened teeth. "Here. Take it." He wrestled a white jade ring from his finger and tossed it to Kenny. It shrank instantly as it flew through the air, becoming small enough to fit a human hand. Kenny caught it in one palm.

Kiyomi's back arched and she cried out. "Ken-*chan* . . . I . . . can't . . . fight it . . . any . . . longer . . ."

Kenny grabbed her hand and slipped the ring onto her finger, holding her in case she fainted like before. She shuddered, convulsed and drew in a huge breath. When she released it, Kenny felt all the tension drain from her body and she went limp. Setting her down, he stroked the matted hair away from her face and looked into her eyes.

"Ken-*chan*," she breathed, reaching up to touch his

134

cheek. "It's gone. The *oni*'s gone. You did it."

"Jewel," Susano-wo snapped, his hand held open.

Kenny straightened and reached into his T-shirt for the *magatama*. "You know what I don't get?" he said. "What do you need this for anyway? I mean, no one's going to bother you down here. This is your kingdom and you can't die. You're invincible here, so why would you need a protective stone?"

Susano-wo's fingers plucked at the air, beckoning the jewel. "There are many things you do not understand, Karamari. Let this be another one. My stone. Give it to me." He leaned closer, towering over the boy.

"OK." Kenny held the jewel out, dangling it from the gold chain.

Kiyomi stirred and croaked, "Kenny, no!"

Susano-wo's huge hand snatched the stone and he sat back on his throne, a smile of triumph on his face.

"Kuromori, the power of the stone does not interest me," he said.

"Then why go to all this trouble?"

"It is the *meaning* of the stone that matters."

"Ken-*chan*," Kiyomi said, struggling to her knees. "The treasures."

"There, you see?" Susano-wo said. "The girl understands, but then she is *Nihonjin* and you are not."

"Treasures?" Kenny repeated. The answer hovered at the edge of his mind, like a word he knew, but couldn't recall.

Susano-wo shifted his weight and smiled like a kindly uncle. "There are three legendary treasures in these lands, the *sanshu no jingi*. Together, they form the unique symbols of power for the supreme ruler. Over thirteen hundred years ago, they were presented to a human named Ninigi and he was commanded to use them to quell the people and to become the first emperor. Are you still with me?"

"Uh-oh."

"Precisely. Whoever wields the Three Sacred Treasures commands the obedience of every god-fearing being in these lands, be they man, woman, child – or deity."

Kenny felt an icy hand close around his heart.

"The regalia were lost over the centuries. Hidden, some say, scattered to keep them apart."

"And I've gone and found them for you?"

"Ken-*chan*," Kiyomi whispered. "He mustn't get the sword."

Susano-wo continued: "Of course, to truly command obeisance from my divine brethren, I would need all three items: the mirror, the jewel and the sword. Two would not suffice."

Kenny backed away. "There's no way I'm giving you the sword. It's mine. You want it, you'll have to come and take it."

Susano-wo steepled his fingers and smirked. "Why should I do that when it is already mine?"

"What are you talking about? I won it from Hachiman."

"And I won it when I cut it from the tail of the eight-headed dragon Orochi. I am Kusanagi's first and only true owner. It obeys nobody but me."

"That's – You're bluffing!" Kenny staggered back, his mind reeling.

"Have it your way," Susano-wo said. "Call forth the sword and show me how fearless you are."

"You think this is funny," Kenny said. "Let's see who's laughing when I kick your butt."

"Kenny, no!" Kiyomi screamed. "It's what he wants!"

Kenny summoned Kusanagi, his hand ready for the sword, but it did not come. He tried again, but his palm remained empty.

Somewhere, from the depths of his memory, he recalled a mocking voice saying: *A word of caution: don't rely on that sword too much. It won't be there when you need it most.*

"No. Please." Kenny reached down into his core, searching for the familiar place where the sword resided, but only a faint presence remained.

"*Kuromori? My master calls me and I must go,*" said the flat, emotionless voice he knew to be the sword's.

"I thought I was your master," Kenny said, realizing how feeble he sounded.

"*Susano-wo is my one true master. I served him long before I served anyone else. I must heed his summons.*"

"But he's a fruitcake! I thought we were . . . a team."

"*That is true and I would have wished to serve you*

longer, Kuromori, but duty comes before desire. I have no choice."

"There's always a choice," Kenny pleaded. "You can put friendship first, like I did."

"And what has that achieved? Farewell, Kuromori. It was a pleasure to serve you."

"Kusanagi? Kusanagi!"

Where the sword had once rested, there was now nothing, only emptiness.

"Were you looking for this?" Susano-wo said, his voice dripping with malice. In his raised hand was Kusanagi, the celestial Sword of Heaven.

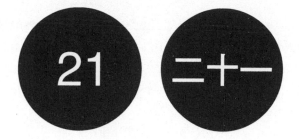

"**K**en-*chan*, what have you done?" Kiyomi said, rising from her knees.

"Uh, I'm not sure, but I think it's bad," Kenny said, the full horror of the situation starting to sink in.

"You . . ." Kiyomi struggled to find the word. "*IDIOT!*"

"Mind how you speak to my servant," Susano-wo said, pointing the sword at her. "Kuromori is not to blame for being fooled in this manner. Better men than he have succumbed to my guile."

"Now what are you talking about?" Kenny asked, irritated. "If you're going to kill us, then kill us. Don't bore us to death with riddles."

"If I wished to kill you, child, then I would have done so as soon as you surrendered the stone. No, I have an offer for you, but before that I wish you to understand why I am showing you mercy."

Kenny scowled. "Go on."

"Let me tell you why I am here, imprisoned as ruler of this dead land. My sister Amaterasu was gifted with the sun and my brother Tsukuyomi with the moon. I was to rule the seas, but my wretched father thought me weak and banished me here, to this wretched domain instead. Do you know why?"

Kenny shook his head and swept the hall with his eyes, searching for an escape route.

"Because I cried for my dead mother."

"What?" That jolted Kenny.

"So all three of us have that in common. Because I grieved – showed what my father thought of as weakness – I was denied my inheritance. Instead, my realm was taken over by that usurping worm Ryujin. Now you know why I slay dragons."

"And all this time, you've been moping down here, dreaming of revenge? Is that it?"

Susano-wo sighed. "Your grandfather would have pieced it together by now. I needed the Three Treasures, but all were hidden, yes?"

"Yeah . . ."

"So I showed the human Akamatsu the resting place of the dragon Namazu and . . . encouraged him to use it as a weapon for revenge."

"Whoa. That was you? I thought Hachiman, being the war god –"

"Oh, please. That simpleton has neither the wit nor the flair to conceive such a plan. I knew this would prompt a search for Kusanagi, to prevent the carnage, and I could find my sword again. This left the other two objects, but then fate lent me a hand, in the shape of you."

Kiyomi struggled to her feet and Kenny ran to help her, holding her close.

"Kuromori, have you learned nothing about me?" Susano-wo asked, his dark eyes glittering. "I am the lord of all *oni*. They do nothing without my permission and that includes the traitor Taro."

"No!" Kiyomi said.

"Oh yes. I commanded him to sacrifice himself, knowing it would give me a tool with which to control you, Kuromori, to turn Inari's champion into my own."

"She warned me about you," Kenny muttered. "Said you were cunning, unpredictable and insane, not to be trusted. *Why* didn't I listen?"

"And it didn't take much prompting to convince my imbecile brother to blot out the sun. I even lent him some of my *oni* to help. All the time he thought he was striking at our sister, when in reality he was merely helping you obtain her mirror for me."

"He used you, Ken-*chan*. And he used me too," Kiyomi said bitterly.

"That left the jewel. Thanks to the mirror, I knew where to find it, so I sent one of my servants along to spy for me."

"The shark-*oni*?" Kenny asked.

"And the *mukade*. In case you hadn't noticed, centipedes are a specialty of *Yomi*. I didn't expect Ryujin to go back on his promise, but I had Kakichi as backup to help you return here, which you did."

141

"You played us. You set this all up just so we could bring you these three objects?" Kenny said. "Why? So you can control the gods?"

"Oh no, Kuromori, it is so much better than that. As supreme ruler of Japan, the gates of *Yomi* are no longer closed to me. You have set me free. I can lead my armies out to the Land of the Living and remake the world as I see fit."

"Hell on Earth, you mean," Kiyomi snarled.

Susano-wo shrugged. "Sometimes you have to wipe away the old to make way for the new." He stood up and stepped off the dais. "And it is you, Kuromori, who has made all of this possible. You have my eternal gratitude. Permit me to reward you."

"Get lost!" Kenny retorted. "You've manipulated me enough. There's nothing you have that I want."

"I can give you the girl. Isn't she why you did this?"

"What do you mean, 'give me'?" Kiyomi said. "I'm not property and I certainly don't belong to you!"

"I can make her compliant," Susano-wo purred. "Break her will so that she lives to serve only you."

"What makes you think I want that?" Kenny said, placing himself between Kiyomi and the god.

"As you wish." Susano-wo sniffed. "How about power? I will give you command of my armies. You have served me well and –"

"Will you stop with that 'serving' guff?" Kenny exploded. "I didn't serve you, not willingly. If I knew what you really wanted, I would never have helped you."

"Yet serve me you did and you were magnificent. Join me and you will have everything you desire. Oppose me and you will have nothing but death and the bitter taste of defeat."

"I made a promise to defend lives and to help people. I would never join you."

"Last chance, Kuromori." The smile vanished and Susano-wo's voice hardened. "You can live and rule nations, or you can die here, with the girl, and feed the roaches." The sword gleamed in his hand. "Use your brain, boy! The gods kneel before me, humans flee in terror and *yokai* do my bidding. No one can stop me. It is over."

"I have a choice," Kenny said, pushing Kiyomi back a step. "I can choose to side with a loser like you, or I can choose to do– this!"

Throwing his hands out, Kenny focused and fired out a force field. The invisible wall slammed into Susano-wo, forcing him to take a step back. His heel caught on the edge of the dais and he tumbled backward, crashing against his dragon-bone throne.

"Run!" Kenny yelled, shoving Kiyomi ahead and charging for the sliding doors at the end of the room. He and Kiyomi hit the doors at the same time, she with a flying kick and he with a shoulder barge.

The two *oni* standing guard outside whirled at the sound of commotion from within the hall and gaped as two humans punched through the brittle doors.

Kiyomi landed on her feet and scanned the anteroom: two *oni*, bone walls, a stairwell leading down and an arched latticework window looking out onto black sky.

Kenny picked himself up from the jumble of splintered bone and stared up at the two *oni*, one red and one white.

"Back off! I'm warning you," he said and positioned his hands ready for the sword.

Shouts and grunts from the stairs signaled more *oni* rushing up in support.

Kenny summoned Kusanagi, blinked at his still empty hands and groaned.

"*RRRRRARGHH!*" yelled the red *oni* and it lashed out with its iron club. Kenny flung himself to one side, feeling the wind whistling through his hair.

The white *oni* lunged at Kiyomi. She vaulted into the air, placed her hands on the back of its head and somersaulted to land beside Kenny. "Come on!" she spat, grabbing a fistful of his T-shirt collar and yanking him backward.

"No escape," the red *oni* said, slapping the club into its palm. Another six *oni* squeezed into the narrow landing from the stairs.

Kiyomi backed up, keeping a firm hold on Kenny. "On the count of three, power punch, got it?" she whispered.

"What? Against these guys?"

"Just do what I do."

Susano-wo's shadow spilled from the throne room and

he strode out, Kusanagi in hand. "You have disappointed me, Kuromori," he said.

Still moving backward, Kiyomi pressed one finger against Kenny's arm.

"So, I have decided to kill the girl slowly while you watch." Susano-wo waved his *oni* aside and glared down at the retreating humans.

Kenny felt the count of two and began to focus his *ki* into his right fist.

"And I will feed her remains to my loyal servants here." Susano-wo paused, his leer wavering. "This is when you beg for mercy, no?"

"No!" Kenny said.

"Three!" Kiyomi roared. She pivoted on her toes, spinning Kenny around, and hammered her fist into the bone latticework covering the window. Kenny did the same on his side and, with a splintering crack, a section of wall erupted, spewing bone down the sides of the castle wall. Wind howled through the yawning gap.

"What's the rest of the plan?" Kenny gurgled, as Susano-wo charged, sword gleaming.

"We jump!" Kiyomi shoved Kenny out through the gaping hole and leapt after him.

As Kenny had feared, Susano-wo's main hall was high up in one of the towers, which meant that not only was it a long way down, but that "down" meant jagged rocks and the bottomless moat.

Falling, he caught sight of a silver ribbon of water

threading its way through the barren landscape before Kiyomi's hand latched on to his T-shirt. Castle walls slid by and Kenny was about to summon a wind to catch them when a cluster of huge black shapes dropped out of the clouds and arrowed towards them.

It was a flock of birds, each one easily the size of a small airplane, with flat, wide wings and long necks, but the snakelike tails and blazing eyes betrayed their demonic heritage. They honed in with horrifying speed, extending their talons.

Kenny realized in a flash that if he stopped the fall they would be easier targets for the creatures to snatch as prey. The ground rushed closer. Screeching in triumph, the demon birds clacked their fanged beaks and stretched out their claws.

As the black shadow of the nearest bird slipped like a shroud over the plummeting Kenny and Kiyomi, a second set of wings came up from behind, furiously beating the air. Kenny felt sharp talons latch on to his shoulder and his world turned inside out.

22 二十二

Evening sunlight stabbed into Kenny's eyes, blinding him after the murky darkness of *Yomi*. His lurching stomach told him he was still falling and the spiky slap of spindly leaves against his face heralded his arrival on fresh earth. He lay winded on the cool ground, grateful to be alive, and felt the jabs and prods of numerous broken branches beneath him.

Before he could open his eyes, a powerful hand hauled him upright and shoved him forward.

"Hey, what's –?" he started to say.

"Ken-*chan*, shut it!" Kiyomi hissed from beside him.

His vision clearing, Kenny glanced backward at his rescuer and his stomach lurched again at the sight of an angry red face with a long nose and a white beard.

"I know," Kiyomi hissed. "Just be quiet before you make things worse."

"After what's just happened, there's a worse?"

The curved gables of the Harashima residence rose above the treetops and Kenny followed the path to the house where Sato, Genkuro and Kiyomi's father stood waiting with scowls of disapproval.

"Inside. Now," Sato ordered.

Once in the main room, another surprise was waiting.

"Grandad!" Kenny said, rushing over to embrace the stern-looking elderly figure.

In spite of his anger, Lawrence Blackwood couldn't help but hug his only grandson. "Kenneth, you're in a lot of trouble right now and I don't know if I can help you."

"It's OK, Grandad," Kenny said into the man's shoulder.

"You're just lucky your father called me when he did."

The room filled up quickly as others entered, including Kenny's tall, stocky, long-nosed rescuer.

"Sojobo-*sama*, how long do we have?" Sato asked the king of the teleporting bird-demons known as *tengu*.

"I have summoned my people," Sojobo answered, "but I will need some time to recover; traveling to *Yomi* is dangerous and difficult enough without having two wayward children to retrieve." He glared at Kenny and Kiyomi.

Harashima lifted Kiyomi's chin and gazed into her eyes, before gently folding his arms around her.

"We shall start with the good news," Genkuro said, in his high, clear voice. "Kiyomi-*chan* is whole once more and the *oni* soul is gone, yes?"

Kiyomi nodded. "Thanks to Ken-*chan*, yeah."

"And you two are still alive, which is also good," continued the aged *sensei*.

"Now for the bad news," Sato said.

Genkuro sighed. "The bad news is that the gates of *Yomi* no longer hold and that Susano-wo rules supreme."

"It can't be as simple as that," Kenny protested. "Doesn't he have to be crowned first or take an oath?"

"He bears the symbols of power that you gave to him," Sojobo rumbled. "That is sufficient to command loyalty."

"I didn't know that would happen," Kenny protested.

"He tricked you," Harashima said. "That is what he does."

"Well, is it so bad if he takes charge?" Kenny tried again. "I mean, who says he's going to mess things up?"

"Ken-*san*, Susano-wo is the God of Storms," Sato said. "It is his nature to destroy. He is violent, unpredictable and cruel, with a long memory and many scores to settle. He will command the sun, the moon and the sea, even without all the armies of Hell. Put it together and you have the end of the world."

"Ken-*chan*, what we saw in *Yomi* is the result of Susan-wo's rule," Kiyomi said, slipping out of her father's arms. "He despises weakness because that's what his father saw in him, and he hates life because he thinks it's weak. Death is stronger to him because it always wins. That's who we're dealing with."

"He's going to kill everything?"

"He rules the dead." Kiyomi held out her hands; what more could she say?

"Oh, crud."

"Yep, and you just set him free."

149

"So, what do we do?" Kenny looked around the room at the grim faces. "There has to be some way to stop him."

"We have to see my mistress, the goddess Inari," Genkuro said. Kenny opened his mouth to protest, but the *sensei* cut him off. "I know you do not wish to do so, but it is necessary."

"OK," Kenny said, letting his shoulders fall. "Time to face the music. Who else is coming?"

"Everyone," Lawrence said. "And by that I do mean everyone."

An hour later, Kenny was fighting down the nausea that always accompanied teleportation. Two of Sojobo's trusted *tengu* lieutenants, Kokibo and Zengubu, had joined them at the house and helped transport the humans to a steep hillside overlooking a valley.

"I smell the sea," Kenny said, taking in his surroundings. City lights glowed to the south. "Where are we?"

"Izumo, in Shimane Prefecture," Lawrence replied. "Near Matsue," he added on seeing the blank expression on Kenny's face. "Where you first came to meet Susano-wo."

"Ohhh."

The path wound down through knee-high grass. Kenny paused to look up and gasped. Lancing high above and blazing across the night sky was a streamer of light, shining like a beacon bridging Earth and the heavens. Its glowing clouds were intertwined with dusty cobwebs, making it resemble the vapor trail from a rocket launch.

"Kiyomi, is that the Milky Way?" Kenny asked. "I've never seen it that bright before."

Kiyomi gazed overhead. "Yeah, that's the side-on view of a spiral galaxy. Pretty cool, huh?"

Kenny rounded another bend and stopped to do a double take. At the bottom of the valley a wide, dry riverbed stretched out before him, but it was awash with points of light, so many in fact that it mirrored the skyward river of stars.

"What is that?" he wondered aloud.

"That's where we're going," his grandfather replied.

Kenny stared. "It's like the stars just flow from the sky and pour into the river."

"Or vice versa," Kiyomi noted. "If you drew a line at the horizon, it'd be symmetry."

Genkuro led the way, with Sato and Harashima, while the *tengu* marched at the back. Drawing closer, it dawned on Kenny that the points of light ahead were moving and some were human shaped.

"Grandad, are those people?" he said.

"Kenneth, you're about to see something that few mortals have ever witnessed."

Kiyomi gasped. "The Divine Assembly?"

"The what?" Kenny asked.

"It's like an AGM – an annual general meeting – for the gods of Japan," Lawrence said.

"They meet every October to swap notes, decide

which wishes to grant, who to help, that sort of thing," Kiyomi said. "It's all very civil."

"Except this time it is a council of war," Sojobo rumbled.

Once on the flat riverbed, Kenny was astounded by the sheer numbers and varieties of the Japanese gods. The softly glowing shapes ranged from rocks and trees to ancient hermits and strapping warriors, all intermingling freely. When they saw the approaching humans they drew back, parting to open a path, their hostile eyes trained on Kenny.

"What's happening?" Sato asked, looking around and seeing nothing but riverbed. "Are they here?"

"They're here," Lawrence answered softly. "All eight million of them. Perhaps it's best if you and Harashima-*san* wait at this spot. It wouldn't help if you offended anyone by walking through them."

Sato flashed an angry look at Kiyomi, but he bowed and stood to one side.

"He's still mad you broke his glasses, huh?" Kenny whispered to her.

"I didn't know they were his only pair," she said.

Genkuro continued to lead. The path inscribed a black line through the pressing crowds of light and ended at a large flat rock which lay half-sunken in the dry mud. On top stood a woman in a kimono of purest white: the goddess Inari.

For once, Kenny didn't have to be told to kneel.

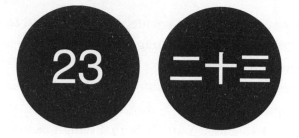

"Arise, Kuromori, so I may see you," Inari commanded.

Kenny and his grandfather both stood up. The goddess dismissed Lawrence with a faint tilt of her head and he gratefully backed away to stand beside a small whirling cloud of dust.

"My brothers and sisters," Inari said, her voice ringing across the valley, "I have called the Assembly early because a grave crisis befalls us, a crisis caused by this human child."

Angry shouts and jeers punctured the silence.

"We are here, at the point where heaven, earth and the underworld meet, to acknowledge our new master."

"No!" shouted an old badger with a walking stick.

"Blasphemy!" cried a skinny man covered in sores.

"Susano-wo possesses the Sacred Regalia," Inari said in a calm, firm voice. "As such, he commands the loyalty of us all. We cannot stand against him. These are the facts."

Inari waited for the chorus of angry shouts which greeted these words to subside.

"Many of you will be wondering how this has come to be. After all, we resolved long ago to hide the treasures, knowing their power."

"That's right! Who has done this?" called out a fat salamander.

Kenny straightened up. "Uh, that would be me."

KLAKK! Genkuro's staff flashed in his hand to deflect a rock thrown at Kenny's head. At Inari's signal, the *tengu* rose to their feet and formed a loose circle around Kenny.

"The child will remain under my protection until we have reached agreement on further action," Inari said. "I chose him, hence his crimes are my crimes."

"I'm sorry," Kenny said. "I didn't know any of this would happen. I wanted to – I tried – I didn't know."

"Did you present Susano-wo with the sword, the mirror and the jewel?" Inari asked.

"I didn't give him the sword," Kenny protested. "He took it, or at least it went with him."

"And you did this even after I warned you?"

"Yes." Kenny stared at his feet, dejected.

"Why?"

Kenny felt thousands of eyes boring into him. His heart slammed against his ribs and his tongue was like paper.

"He did it to help me," Kiyomi said, rising to her feet and standing beside Kenny. She slipped her hand into his and gave it a reassuring squeeze.

Inari softened slightly. "Kuromori, you put your love for this girl before duty to me?"

Kenny cringed. "Well, I wouldn't call it 'love' exactly, more kind of 'like a lot,' but . . . I guess . . . sort of . . ."

"Put him to death!" yelled a clump of bamboo.

"Put them both to death!" spouted a broken water pitcher.

Inari waited for calm. "Susano-wo has yet to march into the light to command our obedience. The gates of *Yomi* weaken with every passing hour, it is true, but they are wide and strong. Nor will he march alone; he will have to gather his armies. There may still be time to stop him."

"How?" grunted a three-legged pig. "He possesses the Three Treasures. Even if we were allowed to resist him, he is invincible."

"That's right," agreed a waterfall. "None of us can oppose him without committing treason."

"Can I say something?" Kenny ventured, raising his hand.

"Haven't you said enough?" protested a white-furred macaque.

Raised voices argued over each other again and Kenny felt Inari's mind touch his. He looked up and saw one of her amber eyes wink at him. Swiveling back around, he was sure that no one had else seen it. Had he imagined it? Did it mean something?

A dazzling pulse of light and heat flared from behind Inari like a miniature supernova, silencing the noise. Stepping up onto the rock was a young woman in a white kimono with a red *obi* sash.

"I wish to hear what the boy has to say," Amaterasu, the Sun Goddess, said. "Let him speak."

Kenny swallowed hard. "Uh, thank you." He turned to address the crowd. "Listen, what you guys are all saying is that no Japanese subject can defy their master, right?"

Heads nodded in agreement.

"Well, I'm not Japanese, remember? I'm just a dumb *gaijin*, which is why I was able to defy Inari and cause this whole mess in the first place. Susano-wo can't command me."

Kokibo perked up. "What are you saying?"

"I can try and stop him."

Lawrence coughed to cover his smile as howls of anger and derision cascaded down from the millions of gods. A flare from Amaterasu brought quiet once more.

"It would be suicide," Kokibo said, his voice dripping with scorn. "He will crush you like an ant."

"Wait, listen," Kenny said. "I'm as good as dead already. You all want to kill me and Susie wants to kill me, so that's already sorted out. I don't care who kills me, so why shouldn't I try?"

"What can you – a mere child – do to stop a god?" sneered a large toad.

"The boy is my champion," Inari declared. "I say he deserves a chance."

"You would say that," countered a large paper lantern. "You are as much to blame for this as he is."

Amaterasu raised her chin. "If not for Kuromori, I would not be here amongst you tonight. He has my support."

"Are there any others?" Inari asked. "We need five more voices to make a count of seven."

"Oh, go on then," grumbled Sojobo. "He deserves a chance."

The myriad deities glanced around and fidgeted, waiting to see if anyone else would speak up.

"*Hai!*" boomed a man's voice. "Mayhap cunning will suffice to best cunning and this pup hath cunning aplenty. Hachiman's banner stands with his." The God of War thumped a fist against his armored chest in salute.

The Dragon King, Ryujin, jostled to the front, his hands tucked into the sleeves of his green robe. "My enemy's enemy is my friend. Do not be fooled by his feeble appearance, my brethren, for this child has vanquished Namazu and a *mukade*."

"That leaves two," Inari said. "Are there two more voices in favor?"

"Hurry up, you sluggard!" snapped a reedy voice. "Is this the best you can do? Out of my way, you imbeciles!"

"I know that voice," Kenny muttered, as a raggedy figure arrived, lashed to the back of a giant tortoise.

"If anyone can stop Susano-wo, it is this boy," said Kuebiko, the scarecrow God of Knowledge. "And I'm never wrong."

"Is there one more?" Inari asked, her eyes searching

the crowd. "This is your chance to choose hope over despair."

"It's treason," said a cat with two tails. "And the master will know who the traitors are. Only a fool would risk his fury."

"Are you calling me a fool?" grated a voice as cold as space itself. Wisps of shadow swirled and coalesced into a cloaked form.

"Tsukuyomi?" Kiyomi breathed and took an involuntary step back.

Shielding his eyes from Amaterasu, the Moon God stepped forth. "This Kuromori is not a normal boy," he said, his white teeth flashing. "Mortal heroes have arisen before. Why should they not do so again?"

"It is agreed then," Inari announced to the crowd. "The rest of you are free of responsibility for this decision. Prepare to greet your lord and master. Those who wish to resist, come with me." She stepped down from the rock and marched away.

"Ken-*chan*," Kiyomi said, gripping Kenny's arm, "are you insane? There's no way you can take Susano-wo in a fight. You are so dead."

Kenny shrugged. "It seemed like a good idea at the time and it stopped them killing me."

"For now," Kiyomi said. "Only for now."

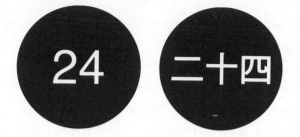

"Take my hands," Inari said, holding out her palms to Kenny and Kiyomi.

Kenny reached out, blinked and immediately felt cool, damp air on his face. He couldn't see a thing in the blackness, but the dripping of water told him that Inari had transported him somewhere, only without the stomach-wrenching, inside-out effect of the *tengu* method.

Yellow light, as soft as a candle, repelled the darkness. It was the oddest thing Kenny had yet seen: Inari, with her perfect white kimono, standing in the murk and squalor of a large cave.

"Underground again," Kiyomi said and shuddered. Kenny curled a warming arm around her.

Moments later the cave was filled with the other six gods, two *tengu* and four humans.

"Is it safe here?" Ryujin said.

"Yes, we can speak freely," Amaterasu answered.

Lawrence peered into the shadows, a smile of recognition creasing his lined face. "Is this . . .?"

"Yes," Amaterasu said. "This is the cave where I took

shelter when I hid myself away from Susano-wo and his cruelty."

"Before the gods tricked you into coming out and restoring sunlight to the world?" Kenny asked, recalling the tale. "So why are we here now?"

"Because it's the only place Susano-wo can't see us using the mirror," Kuebiko said, as if this was the most obvious thing in the world.

"Kuebiko speaks true," Amaterasu said in her soft voice. "The mirror bears some of my essence but it cannot see in here because it knows not the location."

"Ohh, I get it," Kenny said. "It's like with Ryujin's treasure room. The mirror could only show the portal to his realm, but not what lay beyond."

"I couldn't have put it better myself," Kuebiko said.

"First things first," Kenny's grandfather said. "How long do we have?"

"I inspected the gates," Sojobo said. "No more than two days, by my estimate."

"And we know where they're coming from?"

"Yes," Genkuro answered. "The gateway to *Yomi* is in Iya near Matsue. It is a bottleneck that will slow them down."

"We should conduct an inspection of the battlefield at once," Hachiman declared.

"Aren't you are all forgetting something?" Tsukuyomi said, steepling his long fingers. "Kusanagi, the Sword of Heaven."

"I knew that," Kuebiko blurted.

"It matters not who we find to stand against him; so long as Susano-wo possesses the sword, nothing in this world can stop him."

"There's got to be something," Kenny said. "Grandad, you had Kusanagi with you for longer than I did. Does it have a weakness?"

Lawrence scratched his chin. "None that I know of. It was forged to be invincible."

Kenny turned to Ryujin. "Come on. What were you telling us about the *mukade* a few days ago? *Yin yang*. Everything has an equal and opposite. Cosmic balance and harmony."

"Ooh, ooh!" Kuebiko began hopping on his stick. "I know, I know!"

"What is it?" Lawrence asked.

"Ikutachi!"

Genkuro's eyes widened and he raised a brow towards Inari. "My lady, would it work? Could it work?"

"I see no reason why it wouldn't," Inari said slowly. "Although it's never been tried."

"What's Ikutachi?" Kenny asked.

"The Sword of Life," Genkuro answered. "If we allow that in Susano-wo's hands Kusanagi has become a Sword of Death, then in theory Ikutachi may withstand its power."

"I don't like those words 'in theory.' How come no one's ever tried this?"

"Because Ikutachi belongs to Susano-wo."

"What? That's crazy!"

Hachiman sniffed. "There is no dishonor in a warrior wishing to collect weapons. One can never have too many."

"As a symbol of life, it's anathema to him," Lawrence said. "I doubt he's ever held it, let alone used it."

"Where exactly is the sword?" asked Tsukuyomi.

"In Susano-wo's palace," Kuebiko said. "If I had hands I could draw you a map."

"Just describe it to me and I'll write it down," Lawrence said, taking out a notebook and pen.

Kenny groaned. "We have to go *back* to *Yomi* and his palace? While he's there? Why is nothing ever easy?"

"Stop complaining," Kiyomi said. "We wouldn't be doing this if not for you."

"Yeah, yeah, keep reminding me."

"There is one silver lining to this cloud," Genkuro said. "No one will be expecting you."

"Thanks," Kenny said. "Because they'll be too busy massing armies for war? I can get myself in. How do I get out?" He looked to the *tengu* king.

Sojobo shook his head. "I cannot fool Susano-wo twice. He will have defenses ready this time."

"The sword will bring you out, the same way Kusanagi took you in," Inari said.

Lawrence handed Kenny the detailed notes. He squinted at the paper, scowled and glared in the scarecrow's direction. "What if I can't find this sword?"

"Then you're stuck," Kuebiko said.

"Great. OK, let's do this before I change my mind. I'm going to need a lift to–"

"I'm coming with you," Kiyomi said.

"No way. I didn't go to all that trouble to get your soul out of *Yomi* only to have you volunteer to go back."

"Ken-*chan*, I have to. You know that. And anyway you'll need my help."

"The girl is right, Kuromori," Amaterasu said. "You cannot do this alone."

"Of course, some guns would be good right about now," Kiyomi said. "And C-4. Lots of it. Anyone? No?" She sighed.

Lawrence laid his hands on Kenny's shoulders and beamed with pride. "Good luck, Kenneth. Genkuro-*sensei* and I will start rounding up anyone else at this end who can help. I still have a few favors to call in."

Genkuro patted Kenny on the cheek. "You have surprised me before, young Kuromori-*san*. I have no doubt you will surprise me again."

Kenny beckoned Zengubu over and whispered in the *tengu*'s ear. The tall creature nodded, placed a hand on Kenny's back and reached for Kiyomi.

"Kuromori," Hachiman called, "shouldst thou fail us, know that I will kill thee."

"It'll be a bit late by then!" Kenny said and, with a pop of imploding air, he was gone.

25 二十五

"**N**o!" Kiyomi said, folding her arms. "It's bad enough we have to go back to . . . that place, but to do this again?"

"You don't have to come along," Kenny said. "I can do this myself while you head back to Tokyo."

"You won't last five minutes without me."

"Then quit complaining and let's get on with it."

Kenny knelt beside the pond and concentrated, focusing his will on the water, reaching out with his mind to picture a familiar face. Kiyomi stood with her back to the reeds, her arms crossed.

The stars reflecting on the surface shimmered as the water trembled and two bulging eyes displaced a lily pad. "*Nandayo?*" whined the turtle-shelled pond creature.

"Hello, it's us again," Kenny said.

"Me not like you," the *kappa* snapped.

"The feeling's mutual," Kenny said, his nose wrinkling against the fishy smell. "But business is business. I need a favor."

"No favor," the creature said.

"I can pay you. Here's a freebie." Kenny held up a knobbly cucumber.

The *kappa* sniffed the air and wiped drool from its beak before it shook its head to clear it, taking care not to slosh any water from its indented scalp. "No! Not help you," it said.

"Just hear me out and then you can have the cucumber, whatever you decide. Is that fair?"

The water creature squawked and climbed onto the bank where it sat cross-legged like a small child.

"I don't know if you pay any attention to the gods but things have gone horribly wrong," Kenny began.

"Not care," the *kappa* said.

"There's been a change at the top and it's not for the better."

"Not care."

"You're wasting your time," Kiyomi said. "You can't reason with it."

"The gates of the underworld are crumbling and death is coming," Kenny said. "All of your rivers and ponds will fill with bodies. There'll be nowhere for you to hide."

"Not . . . care." The *kappa* blinked its froggy eyes.

"Everything will die, including your people. And these." Kenny held up the cucumber again. "These will die too."

"You lie. Gods will act. Me hear you. Now give me." It stuck out a webbed paw.

"OK. Catch." Kenny tossed the cucumber onto the mud at the *kappa*'s feet. Tracking its path, the creature bent to grab at it – and stiffened when the pond water poured out of the hollow on its head.

"Ack! Me stuck," it wailed.

"Are you ever going to stop falling for that?" Kenny asked. "I tried to be nice and it didn't work. You either help us or you stay like that and watch the world end."

The *kappa* strained every muscle, but it remained locked in place. "Me . . . help . . . you," it croaked.

"Good choice." Kenny tipped it back into the pond and waited for it to swim up again.

"What favor?" the *kappa* asked.

"I need you to take us into *Yomi*."

"Never! Not possible. No water."

"Nice try, but I know there's a river. I saw it last time I was there. All water is connected, so I know you can take us."

The *kappa* wailed, thrashed and beat its fists on the mud. Once its tantrum was over, it stood calmly. "Come. We go now. Way is long and much danger."

Kenny and Kiyomi had traveled using the *kappa*'s unique transportation system once before, so they knew what to expect and had come prepared, but it was still far from pleasant.

After lashing their wrists together, the three travelers waded into the chill water of the pond. Once below the surface, the *kappa* led the way to a circle of lighter-colored water. On entering, a powerful suction propelled them down a swirling tunnel of water at incredible

166

speeds, taking them across miles in seconds. The transit ended in another body of water, this time with a number of glowing portals to choose from. The *kappa* selected its route and another whirlpool carried them away.

His head cocooned in a bubble of air, Kenny lost count of the number of hops, but did notice subtle differences in the water between stops. Temperatures varied as did color and buoyancy. Several times he saw the lights of underwater cities far below, but the *kappa* kept them moving.

Finally, after what seemed like hours, they shot out of another tunnel, but this time the *kappa* held them under the water.

"This Sanzu River," it said. "In *Yomi*. Me go now."

Kenny nodded, cut the cord and handed over the precious cucumber. With a turn and a kick, the *kappa* was gone. Holding Kiyomi's hand, Kenny swam for the nearest bank and flopped onto a slope of dry ash.

A dull, pounding sound, like a giant, distant heartbeat, rolled across the blasted land.

"Ken-*chan*, look at the sky," Kiyomi said, shielding her eyes.

The low black clouds burned with flickering amber hues and smoke carried on the howling winds.

"Maybe the fires of Hell?" Kenny said.

Flocks of shrieking demon birds wheeled below the clouds and a groggy Kenny sat up to see where he was. The bank was steep with black, oily river sludge oozing past.

"Ugh!" Kiyomi said. "To think we were just in that. I hate to imagine what . . ."

Her words died away as a gigantic humped back with spiky dorsal fins broke the surface and sank again.

"That rules out swimming across," Kenny said. Feeling something tickle his hair, he reached up to scratch, touched a rubbery blob and froze. "Kiyomi, please don't tell me that's what I think it is."

She crawled over and knelt to see in the half light. "Eww, a leech. I *hate* these things. Hold still." She held up a finger, closed her eyes and concentrated.

Kenny squinted against the light of the flame that sprang from Kiyomi's fingertip. She leaned in, touched the fire to his scalp and Kenny heard a soft sizzling squeak.

"Great." He wriggled, then peeled off his T-shirt to reveal another five fist-sized bloodsuckers hanging from his torso. "You get me and I'll get you."

Five minutes later, Kenny and Kiyomi crept up the riverbank, leaving twenty-three dead leeches behind.

"Ken-*chan*, you saw the river from Susano-wo's castle, right?" Kiyomi asked.

"Yeah, it was only a glimpse, but it was miles away."

"Do you recognize anything now?"

"I had other things on my mind, like not getting eaten by a giant bird."

"That's what I thought. So we're lost."

At the top of the bank, the black desert of ash stretched away in every direction, ending at distant mountains.

"I don't see any castle," Kenny said.

"That's because we're on the wrong side of the river," Kiyomi said, sounding weary. "Here we go again. We need to cross."

"There are lights that way," Kenny said, pointing along the bank. "Maybe we can ask directions."

"On the banks of Hell?"

"I'm open to any better suggestions. Why are you so negative? I'm trying my best."

"Fine. Let's go tell the demons we're here." Kiyomi stamped off towards the camp.

26 二十六

Kenny hurried to catch up with Kiyomi and fell in step beside her.

"You don't seem very happy," he said.

Kiyomi's eyes narrowed, her fists bunched and she pressed her lips tightly together.

"It could be worse," Kenny tried again. "If you were an *onibaba*, you'd have killed me by now."

"Will you shut up?"

"I'm sorry. I'm just nervous." Kenny managed to be quiet for another ten paces before he said, "You know, I've been thinking."

Kiyomi rolled her eyes. "About what?"

"Is it just me or did Inari not seem to be too mad at me? I mean, she was pretty calm and everything, like she wasn't all that surprised."

"You're telling me she didn't seem surprised that a prime doofus like you managed to mess things up so badly that the whole world is in danger ? Well, knock me down with a feather."

"Hm. Since you put it like that . . ."

Kenny could now make out the rickety outline of a dilapidated shack squatting by the riverbank. Tattered paper lanterns swung in the constant breeze and human shapes were gathered at the front.

"What's with the number seven?" Kenny wondered aloud, still thinking about the goddess. "I mean, I know that four and nine are seen as unlucky but why did Inari need seven voices? If it had gone to a regular vote, we'd have been in trouble."

"It brings good fortune," Kiyomi said, slowing her pace. "We have seven lucky gods, seven herbs for health, lots of things like that. If Inari wants seven votes, no one's going to argue with her."

"Why? Is she like the chief god?"

"No. It's a free-for-all, which is why there's so much squabbling and backbiting. You've seen it yourself. It would be better to have someone in charge, just not Susano-wo."

Approaching the shack, Kenny ducked down and grabbed Kiyomi, pulling her out of sight.

"What is it?" she hissed.

"*Oni*," Kenny said. "They're at the front, like passport control, sorting people out."

"I thought you wanted to find them, to ask directions."

"HAH!" boomed a guttural voice from behind them. "Me thought so! Trying to hide!" The *oni* hefted its iron club.

Kenny summoned Kusanagi to hand before remembering he no longer had the weapon.

"Come. Join others." The demonic creature hauled Kenny to his feet and pushed him down the bank towards the snaking line of people making their way to the shack. "You too," it said to Kiyomi.

A ragged chain of gloomy individuals shuffled forward. Looking back, Kenny estimated the line stretched all the way to the distant mountain range.

The *oni* sentry pushed them into line, then stopped to inspect Kenny. "You in wrong place," it grunted.

"No, it's OK, he's a convert," Kiyomi said quickly. "Full Japanese funeral and everything for him."

"Who you?" the *oni* snarled.

"Stepsister. We both drowned while scuba diving. That's why we're wet and not properly dressed."

Glancing around, Kenny realized that most of the other pilgrims were older, the men dressed in suits and the women in white kimonos. The *oni* looked unconvinced.

"It's true," Kenny said. "I've been to loads of shrines, know my Inari from my Hachiman. I've left *ema* and used the *temizuya*. Go ahead and test me."

The *oni* grunted and stomped away.

Amid the sounds of quiet sobbing and moans from all around, the occasional hair-raising shriek of agony jangled the air from farther ahead.

"Next!" bellowed an *oni* from inside the control hut.

"I'll do the talking," Kiyomi growled, clutching Kenny's arm. "You just act dumb. Be yourself."

"Hey!"

Inside the rotting cabin, a heavyset *oni* sat by a ledger desk, wearing a green eyeshade, thick glasses and holding an ink brush.

"Name and cause of death?" it asked with total disinterest, brush glistening.

"Dwayne and Matt Seale, eaten by sharks," Kiyomi said, elbowing Kenny before he could speak.

The clerk duly noted the details in an enormous book without looking up. "Hm. The names people choose these days. Sounds a bit foreign to me." The *oni* peered up and squinted nearsightedly at Kenny. "Are you a *gaijin*? We've been warned to look out for one. Teenage kid, about so big, looks a bit like you. Seen him anywhere?"

"No, sir. This boy's Japanese," Kiyomi said. "He's my kid brother."

"Can't he speak for himself?"

"No, he's dumb, really dumb. Tragic accident. Cat got his tongue – and half an ear."

"That happened to a cousin of mine. What's with the yellow hair?" the *oni* asked, waving a paw in the general direction of Kenny's head.

"Hair dye," Kiyomi said. "It's trendy."

"Hm. And your parents let you get away with that? No wonder you're dead. Next!"

Kenny jumped as another scream of agony rang out ahead.

"Move!" ordered an *oni* guarding the exit, pointing towards the screams.

To the rear of the hut was a wooden deck with three paths leading away. One wound down the riverbank to a curved footbridge spanning the treacherous waters. The second led to a docking platform and short jetty where a decrepit boat was moored. The last ended at a narrow dirt track running alongside the river. Before the paths stood a spindly willow tree and, on either side of it, an ancient, terrifying and truly hideous couple.

The man reached up to remove a white kimono from the bare branches of the tree where it hung, his sagging, wrinkled skin jiggling with every movement. He was tall and scrawny, naked but for a loincloth. He dumped the white dress into a wooden chest and turned, his fingers twitching in eagerness.

His wife was no better: a wizened hag with cobweb hair, long raking nails on fingers and toes, grayish skin and ribs that resembled banister rails.

"Come, come to Datsue-ba that your sins may be weighed," she said with a voice like a metal spoon scraping a pot.

"Uh, how does this work?" Kenny asked, backing up.

"You gives your clothes to Granny," she said, extending her arms, "and Uncle Keneo here hangs them on the tree."

"Is that it?"

"It depends on your sins. The greater your wickedness, the heavier your clothes and the lower the branch will bend."

"And the purpose of this is . . .?"

"To cross the Sanzu River. The good may use the bridge, the not-so-good take the boat and the wicked have to walk all the way around."

"Ken-*chan*, don't do it," Kiyomi warned.

"What if you don't have any clothes?" Kenny asked. "Like, say, you died in a fire and they all got burned."

The hag's eyes lit up and Keneo rummaged around in the clothes box. "Why, then I gets to weigh your birthday suit!" Datsue-ba cackled in glee while the old man held up what looked like a human-shaped papery gown.

"You *skin* people?"

"Aye, now hurry it up! Granny has quotas to meet." She tottered closer, her claws outstretched.

Kenny sidestepped, closer to the tree, and noticed the boatman unhitching the mooring rope.

"How about I give you my T-shirt?" Kenny said. "My jeans are a lot heavier so that hardly seems fair. And they're wet."

"All of your clothes," Datsue-ba said, clapping her hands impatiently.

"I'm not getting naked out here. I'll catch my death of cold."

"You're already dead!" A hint of suspicion flickered across the hag's face. "Or are you?" Her rheumy eyes widened and she gasped. "Guards!"

"Me here!" grunted the *oni* at the exit and it charged, *kanabo* in hand.

27 二十七

"**S**top!" ordered the *oni*. "Or me will –"

Kiyomi was ready, landing a flurry of kicks and punches to its nerve centers: knee, groin, sternum and throat. She ended with an elbow smash to the nose. "Fall over," she finished.

"Guards!" Datsue-ba shrilled again.

"Will you shut up?" Kenny said, directing a blast of wind. The gust snatched the human skin from Keneo's hand and wrapped it around the hag's head.

"*GMMMFF!*" she yelled, scrabbling to free her face.

Kenny focused again and a mini tornado struck the wooden chest, flinging shirts, trousers, sashes and kimonos into the air. A pair of men's briefs landed on Keneo's head, blinding him.

"Now what?" Kiyomi said.

"The boat! Fast!" Kenny pelted down the path to the jetty. The ferry had already left the wharf and was pulling away into the roiling waters.

"We're not going to make it!" Kiyomi yelled.

"Then jump!" Kenny hit the last board and threw

himself forward, towards the departing vessel. At the same time, the surface of the Sanzu erupted and a cavernous mouth reared up to snatch dinner. Kenny twisted and aimed two blasts: one of flame downward and one of air backward. The river creature bellowed in pain and submerged, trailing smoke, while Kenny landed hard in the stern of the boat, with Kiyomi sprawled on top of him.

"*Rrr yuu ger ror reg rof ry raish?*" Kenny said.

"What?" said Kiyomi, disentangling herself.

"I said, 'Will you get your leg off my face?' Oww!"

Kiyomi sat with her back against the gunwale and laughed. "That was kind of cool. Just like the old days, eh, with me saving your butt?"

Kenny grimaced. "I think you'll find that I –"

"You've never done that before, have you? You just controlled two elements at the same time. Impressive."

Kenny rubbed his bruised backside. "What are you saying? That I'm getting better at this stuff?"

"Just that you seem to be learning faster now that you don't have the sword."

Huddled in the rest of the boat and watching fearfully were naked, shivering people, on their way to judgment. The single tattered square sail harnessed the breeze and drove the ferry across the river.

Kenny looked up at the sound of something clinking and jingling. "Uh-oh."

Making his way down the craft was the ferryman,

a cloaked figure wearing a long hooded robe. He held out an open leather pouch into which passengers dropped coins.

"Do we have any money?" Kenny asked, searching his pockets for change.

"I don't," Kiyomi said.

"What's the worst he can do? Throw us off?" Kenny caught the look on Kiyomi's face. "He'd do that?"

"You'd better think of something fast."

The boatman towered over them and rattled his purse. Kenny gave a weak smile. "Uh, will you take an IOU? Credit card? Season ticket? Bus pass?"

The ferryman gave a low growl that sounded like grating gravestones.

Kenny tried to look inside the shadowed hood, but saw only darkness. He shuddered. "OK, you win. How much to get across?"

"*Rokumonsen*," said the icy voice.

"That's six coins each," Kiyomi said.

"Any particular currency?"

The boatman snarled again.

"OK, OK, calm down." Kenny closed his hands and concentrated. "Here you go." He opened his fists to reveal twelve circular copper coins with square holes in the center. Kiyomi took them, dropped them in the bag and the ferryman returned to the prow.

"How did you do that?" Kiyomi said, sitting beside Kenny. "I mean, even if you just created metal from nothing, which I don't believe, how on earth did you know what an Edo coin looks like?"

"Is that what they are? I thought they were strange." Kenny leaned in close and dropped his voice. "I just summoned them from the bottom of the purse and gave them back to him. Let's hope he doesn't count."

"You –!" Kiyomi punched him on the arm.

"Come on, admit it. I got you there." Kenny's eyes drifted to the huddled ranks of the newly dead. "Where did those guys get their money from, to pay their way across?"

"It's a Japanese funeral custom," Kiyomi answered. "We put six coins in the coffin for that reason."

"This is so weird," Kenny said. "Ever since I arrived in Japan, things have been trying to kill me, to send me here. And now I'm back in the Land of the Dead by my own choice, and I'm not even dead. Talk about cutting out the middleman."

Kiyomi rested her head on his shoulder. "You're a good friend, Ken-*chan*. You've crossed seas, battled gods, fought monsters, all to help me . . ."

Kenny felt his cheeks grow warm. "Well, it was that or watch you turn into an *onibaba*. You'd have done the same for me."

"No, I wouldn't," Kiyomi said, her voice catching. "I'd have left you to die, especially if I'd known this was the cost of saving you. No one's life is worth the fate of my country. Not mine, not yours. Do you have any idea what that feels like, to know that you're responsible?"

"You're feeling guilty that you're alive? Listen to me, Kiyomi, if anyone's to blame for this mess, it's me. I brought you back, I cut a deal with Susie and I freed him. He used me just like he used you. If anyone's behind all this, it's him."

"Ken-*chan*, what are we going to do?"

"I wish I knew."

They pressed closer together against the chill breeze and sat in silence for the remainder of the ride, listening to the slap of waves and the creak of wood.

Four more *oni* waited on the opposite bank as a welcoming committee, in front of another shack.

"Off boat now!" the squad leader barked, cracking a heavy bullwhip. "Make line."

Kenny and Kiyomi followed the passengers up the bank and joined the end of the line leading into the arrivals hut.

"What's happening?" Kenny whispered.

"I don't know," Kiyomi said.

"Stay on path or *onmoraki* eat you," the *oni* warned.

"*Onmoraki?*" Kenny repeated.

The *oni* pointed upward at a passing flock of demonic birds.

Kenny tapped his foot impatiently while the line edged forward at a glacial pace.

"You in hurry for judgment?" the lead *oni* yelled at him. "Stop foot."

"Is this part of the torture?" Kenny complained. "Why is it taking so long?"

The *oni* brandished its whip menacingly. "Staff short," it said. "Now busy time. Maybe you lucky and not tortured much."

"Where do we go next? Susano-wo's palace?"

"No!" The *oni*'s wide brow creased. "How you know about that?"

"Uh, no special reason." A thought occurred to Kenny. "Actually, because I never want to see it."

"Hnh? Or what?"

"Or I'll cry like a baby and maybe even puke. Please, I don't want to see it, or know where it is. Don't make me look at it."

Kiyomi gave him a quizzical look.

A cruel glint flickered in the *oni*'s eye. "You fear master's palace? Hah! You should. Is that way." The demon pointed to the north.

"I'm not looking!" Kenny shut his eyes and twisted away.

"Yes, you look!" The *oni* grabbed his head and forced him to face in that direction.

"I don't see it," Kenny said.

"Is there. Look!"

Kenny followed the *oni*'s finger. "Ah, I see it now. Behind those hills? Ugh! No, it's too scary." He covered his eyes.

"You not sick? No wet self?" The *oni* looked disappointed.

181

"Sorry. Empty stomach. And bladder. Otherwise, I would have. Really."

The *oni* stamped away, muttering to itself.

"Ken-*chan*, that's miles away," Kiyomi whispered, once the *oni* was out of earshot. "It'll take us days to get there, days we don't have."

"I know," Kenny said. "I'm working on it."

Inside the hut, a pimply *oni* with a scraggly beard sat in a booth. It brandished a scroll at Kiyomi and Kenny. "Me have questions," it said. "To offer best torture service, me need know preferences." It pointed its brush at Kenny.

"What sort of preferences?" Kenny asked.

"You have allergies? Make you blow up? Choke?"

"Not that I know of."

The *oni* grunted and made a note with its brush. "Any fear? Spider, snake, height, rat, needle, cockroach, small space?"

"No. And if I did, why would I tell you?"

"Save time. No need to try all."

"Oh, in that case, I'm terrified of candy, especially chocolate. I mustn't ever eat it."

"Me make note to boil you in chocolate." The brush swept across the scroll. "We short staff right now. If we shorten time, take off few centuries, you torture self to help?"

"No, are you nuts?"

"Pull out own fingernails? Cut off toes? What about girl? You torture her?"

"No! I'm not doing your job. Why don't you have enough people? I thought there'd be thousands of you down here."

"Is thousands." The *oni* sat up straight and sniffed. "Get ready for go outside. Ready for much kill."

"And you're stuck here, right? Doing the paperwork?"

"Not fair. Just because me young."

"This army of yours, how ready is it?"

"Ready march now. Need gate fall first. Sign here."

Kenny made an illegible scrawl. "What am I signing for?"

"You sign no blame us if torture not good."

"Really? Do you know how long it is before the gates open?"

"Hah! Master use special sword. Cut quickly. Gate open very soon. Then Hell let loose."

28 二十八

Driven on by their *oni* escort, the bedraggled group of new arrivals slogged along a well-worn trail that snaked across the wasteland towards a low mountain. Kenny kept glancing into the distance, towards the bone palace, afraid that he might lose track of it. Overhead, demon birds wheeled and screeched, keeping watch for stray souls.

"Keep move. Judging waits," the squad leader said, cracking his whip. "After judge comes torture." He threw back his head and roared with glee.

"Ken-*chan*, how's that escape plan coming along?" Kiyomi muttered. "Time's running out and if we get judged it's over. It'll be eternal torment."

"I've got an idea. It isn't great, but it's all I've got."

"A bad plan's better than no plan. Go for it."

"OK, here's what you have to do . . ."

After five more minutes of weary trudging, Kiyomi stumbled and fell, crumpling to roll off the path. High above, sensing a possible meal, one of the *onmoraki* broke off from its flock and circled with interest.

"Up!" the lead *oni* commanded.

"I'm too tired," Kiyomi moaned. "I can't walk any farther."

"You, carry," the *oni* said to his second in command.

"Me? Why not Jiro? He carry good," the vice-leader protested, nodding towards a squat *oni*.

"Jiro carry last one. You turn."

The deputy tramped down the slope towards Kiyomi, muttering under its breath. "Me not carry," it said, taking hold of the girl's long black hair. "Me drag!"

In that instant, Kiyomi placed both hands on the *oni*'s wrist, twisted and rolled, bringing her feet up and locking them around the demon's head. Caught off balance, it only took a little tug for the creature to topple head over heels and crash down the slope.

"Jiro, fetch," the leader said.

The stumpy *oni* lumbered forward, waving its metal club with menace. "Me squash!"

Kenny concentrated for a moment, focusing on the weapon.

"*YEE-OWW!*" Jiro cried, dropping the red-hot club and blowing on its singed paws.

The third *oni* ran down the line to help. As it drew level with Kenny, he stuck out his leg, caught its ankle and shoved, sending it thundering down the embankment.

"*AARRGGHH!* Me kill you again!" the leader threatened, gathering his whip and advancing, with the shadow of the *onmoraki* hovering above.

185

"No, not the whip! Don't beat me!" Kenny wailed, slip-sliding down to cower beside Kiyomi.

"Yes, me whip. You sorry." The *oni* reached back, unspooling the tapered length of braided leather, and lashed out to deliver a brutal blow – but Kenny was ready. He stepped forward as the whip bore down and raised his arm, which was now gleaming metal. The tail struck his wrist and wrapped around it in several coils, at which point Kenny wrenched backward with all his strength.

"Me whip!" the *oni* wailed, watching the handle fly from its grasp.

Kenny scrambled to his feet, grabbed hold of the weapon and swung it in circles over his head. The four *oni* all backed away.

"I thought you guys liked pain," Kenny said, and aimed a blow at the nearest ogre. It yelped and ran, howling, along the path. "You want some too?" Kenny advanced on the remaining *oni* who also turned tail.

"Let's go!" Kiyomi said and began sprinting in the opposite direction, away from the trail. Kenny pelted after her, leaving the abandoned souls to huddle in bewilderment.

Watching keenly, the lone *onmoraki* tucked in its wings and swooped, plummeting towards the two human morsels fleeing from the safety of the path.

"It's working," Kiyomi said between breaths, her eyes flicking upward.

"Tell me when," Kenny said, readying the whip.

Dropping like a silent, deadly arrow, the demon bird closed the distance in a heartbeat.

"Now!" Kiyomi screamed.

The *onmoraki* threw out its wings, spreading the feathers for maximum lift, and lunged with its talons. Kenny spun around and lashed out with the whip. The tip curled around the extended claws and held.

Kiyomi flung herself at Kenny, catching hold of his leg as the fiercely flapping bird squawked and rose into the air. Every beat of its enormous wings took it another thirty feet higher and the ground fell away at a sickening speed.

"It worked!" Kenny yelled, hanging on for grim life. His arms creaked and he felt as if his shoulders would pop from their sockets. To relieve the ache, he summoned a tailwind to lift them both. That was when he realized it wasn't his arms creaking – it was the whip. "This thing's not going to hold our weight!" he shouted to the dangling Kiyomi. "Can you climb up?"

"I'll . . . try . . ." Kiyomi said through clenched teeth. She reached up, grabbed hold of the belt in Kenny's jeans and hauled. Her next grip was around his neck – "*Glkk!*" – and finally she landed a knee on his shoulder, enabling her to stretch up for the bird's claw. Clutching fistfuls of feathers, she climbed up its back to perch behind the head.

Enraged, the *onmoraki* swooped, spun, swirled and shimmied to dislodge its unwanted passengers. Kiyomi dug her fingers into the plumage and clung on while Kenny winced at every creak of the fraying whip in his hands.

Far below, the source of the fiery reflections in the clouds became clear: on one half of the plain sprawled an encampment of tens of thousands of *oni* and other Hellspawn. Fire belched from great gouges in the earth and ranks of one-legged cyclopean blacksmiths labored at forges to turn out weapons. Beyond, straddled across two mountains, was the gate, a wooden dam three miles wide and the same deep. Hundreds of *oni* were wielding giant battering rams, causing the constant pounding sound that Kenny had heard.

The demon bird squawked again and dipped towards the gate. Kenny climbed up the whip, hand over hand, and scrambled to join Kiyomi on the monster's neck.

"Stupid thing's going the wrong way," he said.

"Shouldn't you have thought of that before?" she shot back. "What we need is a way to steer this thing."

Kenny wracked his brains, imagining for one crazy second a bridle and reins on the creature's head. The absurd image gave him an idea. "Wait, I know! Blinkers!" he said. "Look." He focused his will and pictured a black cloud obscuring the bird's left eye. Unable to see in that direction, the *onmoraki* veered to the right and continued until it had completed a U-turn. Kenny dismissed the blind and grinned. "Wow, I'm good!"

"Yeah, so good you caused this mess," Kiyomi said. "Don't get carried away."

KA-RRAKKK! A massive splintering sound reverberated across the land.

"What was *that*?" Kenny said, looking around.

"The gates," Kiyomi answered. "They're starting to fall."

Kenny scanned the blasted, barren landscape far below. Having turned the gigantic bird to a northerly course, they flew steadily towards the fortress of bone. Scattered and half-hidden in hollow pockets were strange, circular walls. Once, Kenny thought he saw a splash of green inside one.

The castle was now about six miles away, looming on the horizon like a jagged tooth. Dozens of *onmoraki* circled the towers, keeping watch.

"We're not going to sneak in past them," Kiyomi said. "There are too many."

"Would they attack one of their own?"

"Do you want to find out?"

"Good point."

Kenny clouded the bird's eyes again, this time leaving the lower halves clear. As he had hoped, only able to see the ground it dipped its wings and began a controlled descent. Claws down, it landed lightly, huge wings whipping up billows of ash. Kiyomi slid off while Kenny cast a dark cloud over the creature's head until they were well away. He then let it see again and it took to the air to rejoin its flock.

Kenny tucked the coiled whip into his belt and followed Kiyomi over the damp dunes. Cockroaches and earthworms wriggled beneath their feet and the keening wind chilled their marrow.

"Did you see that?" Kiyomi said, stopping. "A light. It's gone now."

Kenny watched and waited. The greenish-yellow dot flickered on and off in a soothing and familiar manner. "Wait, isn't that a –"

"Firefly. Yeah." Kiyomi reached out towards the beetle bobbing on the breeze.

"What's that doing here? I thought only scavengers lived in this place."

"Me too," Kiyomi agreed. "This little guy eats pollen, so where's his food coming from?"

"There's another one." Kenny watched a constellation of tiny stars light up the dim grayness. He laughed in delight. "This is so cool."

The cluster of little insects separated into groups which then rearranged themselves to form lines: two parallel, one vertical at the end and two diagonals touching in a point.

Kenny's mouth fell open.

"Yes, it's an arrow," Kiyomi said, "and it's pointing that way. Come on." She started jogging after the glowing shape.

"What if it's a trap?" Kenny asked, trotting alongside.

"Too subtle for this place. It's got to be something else."

Kenny lost his footing and fell, disturbing a mound of maggots. "The ground's shaking," he said from all fours. "An earthquake?"

Kiyomi helped him up. "No, it's more . . . localized, like something moving beneath –"

With an earsplitting shriek, a fountain of dank earth detonated from behind and a bulbous head rose up, its hooked fangs twitching and antennae searching.

Kenny went for his sword and groaned again at its absence. Shaking off the dirt covering him, he sprinted away from the giant centipede in the direction indicated by the fireflies.

Kiyomi overtook him and yelled, "Follow that!" She jabbed a finger towards a bluish ball of fire weaving through the air like a will-o'-the-wisp.

The *mukade* emerged from its burrow, planted its many feet on the soil and scurried after.

Kenny bombed down a slope and saw the curved edge of a circular dry stone wall to the left. The glowing fireball made a sharp turn and vanished into the barrier. Kiyomi tore after it, scrambling around the side, and disappeared from view. With the sharp pain of a stitch in his side and his chest heaving from the effort, Kenny hit the wall and followed the curve, looking for any way in.

The *mukade* was close behind, its antennae sweeping

the dirt, tracking the scent of the fleeing humans.

Kenny pressed his back against the stone and began to focus his *ki*. What he really needed was spit, but his mouth was dry.

"Get in here!" Kiyomi's hand latched on to his collar and pulled him backward through a hidden gap in the wall.

With a deft trip, she dumped him on the ground, threw herself flat by his side and pressed her fingers to his lips. In the dark, the sounds of the centipede outside seemed amplified and Kenny could imagine the drumming of its legs as it turned in circles, wondering where its meal had gone. A scratching sound came from the wall when its antennae brushed against the stone, but after several long minutes it picked up a new trail and skittered away.

Kenny waited for his heart to slow down. "That was way too close. What happens if we die down here?"

"Then you can never leave," answered a woman's voice.

Kenny bolted upright. The blue fireball pulsed in time with the words.

"It's OK," Kiyomi said softly, from beside him. "It's a *hitodama*, a human soul." She knelt and bowed before the flickering light. "Thank you for rescuing us."

The fireball shimmered like heated air and re-formed as an elderly woman, still glowing a muted blue. "We were watching out for you," she said. "Your presence was foretold."

"Not that again," Kenny muttered.

The woman stared intently at him for a moment. "So

you are Kuromori, the child of prophecy. Why does that trouble you?"

Kenny scratched his head. "Uh, because I never asked for it. I don't know what I'm supposed to do."

"But you are already doing it." The woman glided backward, towards the center of the tiny compound. She raised her arms and dozens of tiny *hitodama* swirled up from the ground and danced in the air around her. "Children, we have visitors," she said. "Please adopt a more pleasing form for our guests."

At once, the little fireballs transformed into a luminous crowd of preschool children. They clustered around the visitors, reaching up to touch and stroke living people.

"Who are you? What is this place?" Kiyomi asked, moving forward. The light from the children lit up the center, illuminating a small garden with flowers and fruit trees. Fireflies flitted among the foliage.

"I am Noriko Watanabe and this is a place of sanctuary."

"I don't get it," Kenny said. "I thought everyone got judged on the way in and then it was torture time."

Noriko tucked her hands inside the sleeves of her burial kimono. "That is so for most people, but a few of us – those who are deemed undeserving of eternal torment – are set free to roam these lands."

"Where did the children come from?" Kiyomi asked, reaching down to stroke small heads, but watching her fingers pass through.

"These poor little ones died before they knew right

from wrong, so they could not be judged. They are usually abandoned by the river for the hags and demons to abuse, but we sometimes find them first and bring them to safety."

"This is amazing," Kenny said. "How come the *oni* leave you alone and how can you grow anything here?"

"The creatures of *Yomi* cannot see through stone," Noriko said. "They build with wood, bone, skin, all living things, but not with rock. We search for stones and use them to build these shelters. It isn't much, but it is better than nothing."

"And the flowers?" Kiyomi asked.

"We find seeds sometimes. We plant them, feed them, water them with tears and they grow, like hope, in this desert."

"This is still unbelievable," Kenny said. "You've done so well, to make something good among all this suffering."

"We're in kind of a hurry ..." Kiyomi said apologetically.

"Of course," Noriko said. "But please, before you go, there is someone who wishes to see you. She will arrive at any moment."

Kenny gave Kiyomi a questioning look.

"Here she is," Noriko said as a red ball of ghostly fire slipped in through the wall.

Kenny watched with interest as the red *hitodama* assumed human form: a striking Japanese woman with warm eyes, laughter lines and a regal bearing.

Kiyomi stifled a gasp and clamped her hands over her mouth.

"What's the matter?" Kenny asked.

Kiyomi's eyes brimmed with tears and she said, "*Okaasan*? Mama?"

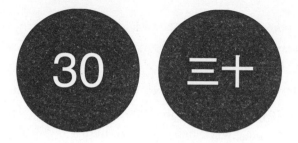

"**K**iyomi-*chan*," the visitor said, opening her arms. "It is true. You *are* here."

Kenny edged nearer to Noriko and whispered, "That's Kiyomi's mother? Mayumi?"

"Yes." Noriko withdrew behind a small peach tree and beckoned for him to follow. "We should allow them some privacy." She motioned for the children to join her. "Kuromori-*san*, why don't you entertain the little ones with tales of your adventures?"

Kenny balked, unsure of where to start. "Oh, gee. It's kind of a long story."

"Perfect."

At the front, Kiyomi wrapped her arms around her mother and felt them slide through her.

"I sensed your presence a while ago, but it was faint, indistinct," Mayumi said. "That's when I began searching for you."

"I was sort of partly here," Kiyomi said, fighting to keep a medley of conflicting emotions in check. "Ken-*chan* – Kuromori – brought me back."

"So I see. It is true then? He defeated death?"

"I wouldn't put it like that. It's not like he knew what he was doing."

Mayumi reached out to stroke Kiyomi's face, her glowing touch lighting up the girl's features. "That boy knows exactly what he is doing in here – " she placed her hand over her heart " – even if he doesn't know in here." She touched a finger to her forehead.

"But he's such a dork!" Kiyomi said. "He's so embarrassing."

"You think your father was any different when he was young? How is he these days?"

Kiyomi chewed her lip, unsure of how much to say. "Papa's never been the same since . . . you know. But he's doing OK."

"Tell him I'm sorry that I can't be with him."

"Mama! It's hardly your fault an *oni* . . ."

"My place is by your father's side. He should not have to raise you on his own."

"We're fine. As you can see, he made sure I can take care of myself."

"At what cost? I remember once, when you were little, your cousins came to play. The boys, they found a frog in the garden and, as boys do, they killed it with a stick. You were so upset, outraged at this act of cruelty. You were so tender."

"I don't remember any of that."

"You were such a gentle, carefree child."

Kiyomi shrugged. "People change. I-I've missed you so much. There've been so many times I've wanted to talk to you, to ask your advice . . ."

"Oh, my poor Kiyomi-*chan*. I am always with you. I hear your voice and I visit every year. You must live your life well, do great things."

"Oh, yeah. Speaking of which, you probably know we have a problem up top. Susano-wo's on the march."

"I know. And, no doubt, there are plans to try and stop him. You cannot win, Kiyomi-*chan*. His army is invincible."

"That's a bit defeatist, isn't it? Surely, we have *some* chance –"

"You do not understand. What happens when you destroy an *oni?*"

"Its soul returns here and it's trapped, imprisoned."

"But if the gates are open?"

Kiyomi's eyes grew wide as she pictured the scene. "You mean they just come right through and rejoin the party?"

"It is an unstoppable, unbeatable army. Everyone you kill comes right back."

"So we'll need to close the gates somehow. Is that even possible?"

"I do not know. Kiyomi-*chan*, why have you come back to *Yomi*? If you die here, you can never return to the world of the living. Your soul will belong to Susano-wo and he will not be merciful."

"We're trying to find something that will help us, but it means going into the palace."

"Then yours is a suicide mission."

"We're in the Land of the Dead, so mission half-accomplished, eh?"

"You must not do this."

"We're out of choices."

"I see. How do you plan to enter the castle?"

"We've no idea. The only route is over the bridge, right? Create a diversion? Maybe smuggle ourselves in?"

Mayumi looked away, deep in thought. "There may be another way. Long ago, before Susano-wo was banished here, the creatures burrowed through the earth and made many tunnels. Some of these still run under his palace."

"You think there might be an underground passage?"

"It is possible. I need to ask. Wait here. I'll be as fast as I can." She condensed back into a red flame and disappeared through the wall.

Kiyomi hugged herself, feeling chilled, and shuffled over to where Kenny was telling stories.

"– so I took her in my arms, like this, but she was already cold. It was horrible, the worst feeling ever. And some little voice deep inside me said, 'No.' I wasn't going to just accept this. I was going to fight for her."

"Ahem." Kiyomi cleared her throat and Kenny spun around, his cheeks flushing.

"How long have you been eavesdropping?" he said.

"A few seconds. Anyway, it's hardly a secret, is it? I was there."

"If you'll excuse me." Kenny stood up to a chorus of disappointed groans.

"Looks like you're a hit," Kiyomi said.

"That's because they're not picky. How did it go with your mum?"

"I don't know. It's not like I was expecting to see her, so it was a bit awkward."

"I can imagine. How do you cram thirteen years into a few minutes?"

"She knows me. She's been watching as best she can."

"Where is she? Can I meet her? I mean, does she know . . . about me?"

"Hah! Everyone knows about you. No, she's gone to find out about a way into the palace."

"A way in? Can we trust her?"

"This is my mother, you idiot."

"Oh, yeah. Sorry." Kenny leaned back against the nearest tree and something hard jostled his elbow. Reaching around, he found a small ripe peach. "Yum. I'd forgotten how hungry I was." He plucked it from the branch and opened his mouth to take a bite.

"*NO!*" Noriko screamed, her hand flying out to slap the fruit away but passing harmlessly through it.

Kenny froze, his teeth grazing the fuzzy skin. "What?"

"This is food only for the dead. If you eat it, you will never be able to leave. You must *never* eat anything in *Yomi*."

"Whoa, thanks for the warning," Kenny said. He set the peach down.

At that moment, the red *hitodama* flitted into the shelter and resumed Mayumi's form. "I have it," she said, eyes bright with excitement. "There is a tunnel, but it is not without danger."

"Let's go," Kenny said.

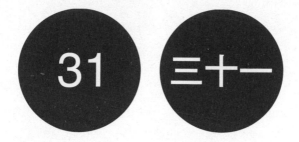

31　三十一

"The entrance is down there." Mayumi indicated the jagged mouth of a cave in a shallow cliff.

"That leads into the palace?" Kenny said, taking Kuebiko's map out of its waterproof pouch. "Do you know where it comes out?"

"I do not. It was a very long time ago that one of the children went in this way."

Kiyomi reached out towards the glowing figure. "Mama, I'll tell Papa that you're not suffering, that you're looking after the little ones. He'll be so happy to know that."

"Tell him he must stop mourning and start living again. Life is too precious to waste a single day. And you, Kuromori-*san*, a word if I may?"

Kenny raised an eyebrow in Kiyomi's direction and went over to Mayumi, running a hand through his dirty hair.

"Yes, ma'am?"

"You know about *yin yang*? That everything has an equal and opposite, for balance and harmony?"

"Yes, I've been hearing that a lot lately."

"Good. You and Kiyomi-*chan* are *yin* and *yang*. That is why you are so strong together. I know you have feelings for her and she for you."

"I wouldn't exactly –"

Mayumi held up her hand. "Please. I am her mother. Together, you each balance the other's strengths and weaknesses. You know this; deep down, you *feel* this – that is why you could not let her die."

"I never thought of it that way before."

"Without Kiyomi-*chan*, you would slowly destroy yourself and the same is true for her without you. You two need each other. Do you understand this?"

"Uh, not really. Sort of, I guess."

"That is good enough." She shrank down to her *hitodama* form and the glowing fireball bobbed in front of her daughter one last time. "Kiyomi-*chan*, I will visit you again next summer if the world remains."

Kiyomi watched the light skip away across the ashen desert until it disappeared from view. A single tear sparkled down her cheek.

"What's all that about next summer?" Kenny asked.

"*Obon*," Kiyomi said, dabbing her eyes on a grubby sleeve. "It's a festival to honor the dead. If we do our part well – clean the graves, say the right prayers, make the correct sacrifices and offerings – then Susano-wo allows some spirits out on day release, sort of a reward for good behavior. There are back routes and secret exits; that's how the *oni* sneak through too."

"They come home once a year? Cool."

"Come on. Let's get this over with." Kiyomi blinked away her tears and they set off down the slope towards the cave.

Kenny ran ahead, sinking ankle-deep into the dust. "Wait a minute," he said. "Let me check something first." He approached the shadowed cavity and unhooked the bullwhip from his belt.

"What are you doing?" Kiyomi said.

"Shh, it might hear you." Kenny uncoiled the whip, reached back and threw his arm forward, lashing the floor of the cave.

"Are you out of your mind?" Kiyomi pushed past him and crouched in the entrance.

"Sorry, last time I dealt with a cave mouth it had teeth."

Kiyomi ran her hand over the dirt. "Look, the ash has been disturbed. There's a big pile of it over there that's damper than the rest. Something's been here and is maybe still digging."

"Great. And we don't have any weapons."

Kenny summoned a small glowing orb to provide light and led the way into the winding burrow, which was wide enough for two people to stand side by side and dipped sharply down. Neither spoke as the tunnel jinked and twisted.

After ninety minutes of walking through the dark, Kiyomi stopped dead in her tracks, eyes wide, her breathing rapid and nostrils flared.

"What is it?" Kenny whispered.

"That . . . smell." Kiyomi forced the words out.

Kenny stopped and sniffed the air, wrinkling his nose at a foul, musky odor. A chill of recognition ran through him as an angry bellow reverberated in the gloom.

"It's behind us," Kiyomi said, gripping Kenny's arm and pulling him along.

As if in answer to the first cry, another guttural roar shook the air, this time from the front. Kenny knew what was coming next: the clicking of spindly legs.

"*Ushi-oni*," he said as a bull's head attached to a bulbous spider body skittered into view. Eerie shadows crept up the wall as the second monster closed in.

"Ken-*chan*, we're trapped," Kiyomi said.

"No, we're not," Kenny said, his voice grim with determination. "But they are."

Transforming his arm into gleaming metal, he charged the nearest creature. It stopped in surprise and, in that second of hesitation, Kenny rammed his fist through its open jaw and ripped his arm back hard. The *ushi-oni*'s eyes bulged, its legs folded and its bulk crashed to the floor as Kenny dropped its still-beating heart and turned to face the second monster, gore dripping from his fingers.

The creature howled with rage. It twisted, aimed its spinnerets and launched a stream of sticky silk at Kenny, who raised his hands. The gluey globs splattered against the air and spread out, yards away from their target.

Kenny lowered his hand, tilting the force field downward, and took a step closer to the monster. Legs scrabbling against the dirt, the *ushi-oni* found itself being driven backward. Kenny held his other hand up and concentrated for a moment. Bright-yellow flames danced from his fingers and reflected in the creature's eyes. It scuttled away, back down the tunnel.

"You show-off!" Kiyomi said, punching Kenny lightly on the arm. "You picked a good time to figure that one out."

"You doubted?"

"Always."

Squeezing past the stricken beast, Kenny and Kiyomi continued along the burrow.

"How far have we come?" Kenny wondered aloud.

"I'd say about five miles," Kiyomi said.

"So we should be near the palace soon."

The tunnel walls widened and stretched away, curving around to form the edges of a large chamber. Kenny stopped. The stench of *ushi-oni* was overpowering and hoarse wheezing sounds in the dark meant the cavern was occupied. Slowly, he increased the brightness of the sphere and sent it towards the middle of the room. Kiyomi's fingers drilled into his shoulder and she breathed into his ear, "It's a nest."

Sure enough, the soft glow illuminated the globular shapes of at least a dozen *ushi-oni* dozing in the gloom.

"The tunnel carries on that way." Kiyomi nodded in

the direction of a black arch on the far side of the den. "We have to go through them." She shuddered.

"I've got a better idea," Kenny said. "Didn't I see your uncle do this?" He clenched his fists, furrowed his brow and channeled his *ki*.

WHOOMPH! Twin walls of flame ignited from the ground. Screeches of alarm, pain and surprise echoed within the chamber as the monsters scurried away from the searing heat.

"Come on." Kenny led the way between the sheets of flame, along the path he had made. On either side, the malevolent creatures glared, but kept their distance.

Once through the cavern the tunnel slanted upward and, after another ten minutes, Kiyomi and Kenny stopped under a circular opening in the roof. It went up another three feet and ended in rough wooden boards.

"What do you reckon?" Kenny whispered. "Is this it or do we carry on with the tunnel?"

Kiyomi shrugged. "Can't hurt to have a look. For all we know, the tunnel might go on for ages and this is the only other exit."

"OK," Kenny said. "Give me a boost and I'll see what's up there."

"How about *you* give *me* a leg up since you're heavier?"

"Who says I'm heavier?"

"Just shut up."

Kenny interlaced his fingers and cupped his hands for

Kiyomi to use like a stirrup. She placed her boot firmly in and hoisted herself up to a standing position with her palms against the curved wall for support. She balanced on Kenny's shoulders before straining to push against the planks. Kenny gritted his teeth and braced himself as the soles of her boots ground into his skin.

A quiet scraping sound, followed by a breath of cold air and streams of dust, signaled the hatch opening above. Kiyomi slid it aside.

"We're in."

32 三十二

Kenny's eyes adjusted quickly to the light as Kiyomi pulled him up from the murk of the tunnel. Coarse planks formed the floor and stone walls stretched from left to right.

Kiyomi slid the trapdoor back into position. "Looks like a cellar or foundation," she said.

"I thought Susie didn't like stone because his pets can't see through it," Kenny muttered, fishing out the map.

"You can only do so much with bone. You still need masonry to build on." Kiyomi moistened her index finger with saliva and raised it to test the air. "There's a breeze coming from that way," she said, feeling the coolness on one side. "Probably a door."

Silently, she crept down the passageway, past darkened recesses. Kenny stopped to explore one of the rectangular hollows and whistled for Kiyomi to stop.

"I know where we are," he said. "Look."

Kiyomi rejoined him and ducked her head into the doorway. Beyond was a tiny stone-walled room. Dangling from a rusty ring sunk into the wall was a short length of chain with two metal cuffs hanging from the ends.

"It's a cell," she said.

"Which means this is the dungeon."

Kenny and Kiyomi continued along the landing until they came to a spiral staircase leading up.

"There's no dungeon marked on this stupid map," Kenny said, consulting Kuebiko's directions. "How are we –?"

"*Nooo* . . . Please . . . no . . ." a deep voice moaned from down the corridor.

Kenny jumped, goose bumps prickling over his skin. "What was *that*?"

Kiyomi inched along the passage, listening intently. "It came from back there." She stopped by a thick wooden door closing off a cell at the far end, past the trapdoor through which they had come. "Locked," she said.

"What do we do? We need to hurry."

"I know that voice," Kiyomi said, resting her hand on the door. "It was a part of me for long enough."

"Huh?"

Kiyomi pressed against the door and traced *kanji* symbols in the air with her other hand. With a sad sigh, the wood crumbled to dust and the metal fixings clanked off the stone floor.

"Harashima-*san*?" rumbled a voice in the dark. "You . . . should not . . . be here!"

"Shh," Kiyomi said. "It's all right. We've come to get you out."

Kenny looked at the hulking shape slumped on the filthy floor, its arms held aloft by the manacles. It was a mess of swellings, bruises and livid scars. Its face was swallowed by the dark, but the outline of a broken horn jutted from its skull.

"Kiyomi . . ." he said. "Is that . . .?"

"Yes, it's Taro."

In a flash, Kiyomi crossed the space, unlatched the shackles and took the *oni*'s face in her hands.

"You poor thing," she said. "They've tortured you, punished you for what you did."

"I knew . . . the price . . . I would pay . . ." The monster raised a fractured finger and stroked Kiyomi's cheek. "But I did it . . . so you . . . would not . . . be here . . ."

Kiyomi dabbed her eyes with her dirty sleeve. "Oh yeah, long story that. We need to get you out of here. Then we can finish this."

"Uh, am I missing something?" Kenny said. "I thought what Taro did was under Susie's orders?"

The *oni* started to laugh, but broke into a coughing fit. "Trust Susano-wo . . . to take a good deed . . . and twist it . . . to his own ends."

"Taro defied him," Kiyomi said. "From the moment he joined my uncle, he proved that *oni* don't have to just follow orders and cause misery, that they can think for themselves."

"I set . . . a bad example," Taro said. "For other *oni* to see."

"So he had it in for you as soon as you showed up down here," Kenny said. "Wow. And, knowing that, you still sacrificed yourself?"

The *oni* shrugged its massive shoulders. "You were ready . . . to do the same . . ."

"There's a trapdoor in the floor that'll get you out," Kiyomi said. "It goes through a nest of *ushi-oni*. Can you handle that?"

"They won't . . . trouble me," Taro said.

"Good. The gates of *Yomi* are almost gone. If you can get to them, you'll be free."

"*What?*" Taro's yellow eyes were wide with shock.

"Yep," Kiyomi said. "Some idiot set Susano-wo free and put him in charge. The gods bow down before him. We're trying to stop him, which is why we're here."

"We're looking for a sword called Ikutachi," Kenny said. "Does that mean anything to you?"

"Of course . . . the Sword of Life. The master keeps it . . . in his personal armory . . . on the fourth floor . . . of the *tenshukaku*."

"*Tenshukaku?*" Kenny repeated.

"The keep, the central tower," Kiyomi explained.

"And this armory? Is it likely to be guarded?" Kenny asked.

"Not now . . . palace is quiet . . . many guards are away . . ." Taro said.

"Yeah, that figures," Kiyomi said. "They're all massing for war."

"Plus, no one's expecting the armory to be attacked. I mean, that'd be nuts," Kenny added. "Here, on this map, can you tell us where we are, where those stairs come up?"

Taro took the paper, squinted at it in the dim light and said, "You come up here . . . Armory is there." He marked the map with a splintered claw. "I will go . . . with you."

Kenny shook his head. "No, we need you to get out and spread the word, tell other *oni* that they have a choice about who they serve. That's the best way you can help us."

Kiyomi and Kenny helped the weakened *oni* down the passage to the escape tunnel, said their farewells and replaced the trapdoor after Taro had squeezed through.

"Do you think he'll make it?" Kenny asked Kiyomi.

"Will *we*?"

They made their way up the winding stairs, which ended at a door leading out into a hallway. Paper lanterns cast sickly pools of pallid yellow light.

"Follow me," Kenny whispered and took off, following Kuebiko's map.

The route wound through empty halls, and the deserted fortress with its ivory ceilings, tattered wall hangings and brittle leather coverings made Kenny think of a gigantic carcass. A sense of decay permeated everything and he felt like it was seeping into his skin.

Long galleries and passageways led to steep stairs

and higher floors. Kenny could see that the *tenshukaku* was designed with defense in mind; any attack would be almost impossible, with invaders having to fight their way up, level by level, in confined spaces.

They came to yet another set of angled stairs and were about to ascend when Kiyomi grabbed Kenny's arm, hauling him backward. Before he could protest, she fastened her hand over his mouth and dragged him into the darkness under the steps. A quiet shuffling sound was coming from above and the sickly-sweet stench of rotting flesh stung his eyes. A scrawny shadow zigzagged down the flight of steps. Kenny saw an outline of straggly hair, a hooked nose and raking talons. The creature stopped to sniff the air before it shambled away.

"What was that?" Kenny whispered.

"*Yomotsu-shikome*," Kiyomi said. "Hellhag. Let's give it a few minutes to shove off."

Once the way was clear, Kenny continued towards the armory. He slid open a door and was surprised to see a polished wooden floor extending before him.

"Don't move," Kiyomi commanded.

Kenny froze, one foot hovering inches above the surface. "But we're almost there. It's across from this . . . dance floor, or whatever it is."

"Ken-*chan*, every floor in this keep has been bone. Why would it suddenly change to wood now?"

Kenny shrugged. "They ran out? Budget cuts?"

Kiyomi rolled her eyes. "It's an *uguisubari*. It has to be."

"Oh yeah. Why didn't I think of that?" Kenny said with undisguised sarcasm.

"A nightingale floor, dummy. Perfect defense against *ninja* or other sneak attacks."

"What, is it a fake floor? Does it collapse or something?"

"No, the planks are fitted with special nails that squeak when you walk on them. Any pressure and they chirp, hence the name, alerting the guards."

"Clever. So how do we cross without setting it off?"

"The trick is to not touch the floor. Here, I'll show you. Watch and learn."

Kiyomi tightened her boots, ran her hands up the wall beside the door and focused, feeling for every minute bump, groove or blemish on the surface. Satisfied she had found a suitable grip, she slid over, fixed her fingers and toes into position and shifted her weight from the floor to the wall.

"Do we have time for this?" Kenny said.

"Shh. I need to concentrate."

Like a free climber clinging to a rock face, she crept her painstaking way along the wall, sweat matting her hair and muscles trembling with the effort. She reached the corner and continued inching her way across the length of the room.

Kenny folded his arms and watched with admiration. One thing he could never deny was that Kiyomi was tougher, gutsier and more determined than he could ever hope to be.

Finally, Kiyomi dropped, landing with feline grace on the far side. She rested on all fours, drenched with perspiration and breathing hard. When her heart rate had slowed and she had caught her breath, she sat up and beckoned to Kenny.

Kenny closed his eyes to channel his *ki*, summoned a mental image of what he wanted . . . and casually strolled across the floor in perfect silence.

Kiyomi's jaw dropped, but then her eyes narrowed and her fists clenched. "You dirty, rotten, cheating –" she began. "How did you do that?"

"Force field. I used it as a bridge and walked across."

"And you let me go to all the trouble of –?"

Kenny shrugged. "You said to watch and learn. I didn't want to interrupt your lesson."

He couldn't help grinning. Kiyomi followed the rules, even when it made things difficult, whereas his talent was to find shortcuts, easier ways.

They hurried along the adjoining passage and stopped outside a heavy wooden door bound with iron strips. An electronic keypad nestled on the wall beside it. "Whoa!" Kenny said. "What's that doing there?"

Kiyomi frowned. "I don't know how to get around it. What say we just blow the door, find the sword and get out fast?"

"OK, but there's something not right about that. It's too out of place."

Elbowing Kenny aside, Kiyomi disintegrated the door

217

and went inside. The armory was extensive and wooden shelves crammed with myriad weapons lined the walls. Suits of traditional *Samurai* armor were neatly stacked, long-bladed weapons stood in racks against the walls and dozens of swords were displayed on tables.

"Wow, Susie doesn't mess around," Kenny said. "This is his personal stash? He gives Hachiman a run for his money."

"Stop drooling and find Ikutachi," Kiyomi said, rifling through the nearest shelves.

"What does it look like?" Kenny asked, picking up a black-handled *katana*.

"How should I know?"

"Well, well, well," boomed a familiar voice from the doorway. "Look who's here. Admit it, Toots, you just can't stay away from me."

The silver *oni*, who they'd last seen burning to a crisp on a space platform high above Earth, flashed a gleaming smile, drew his handgun and waved in six more *oni* guards, all brandishing iron clubs.

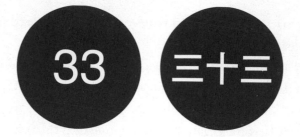

Kiyomi kicked over the nearest counter and dived to the floor. The swords that had been on display flew into the air and she snatched one, rolled and drew the gleaming blade before the tabletop thudded against the floor.

Silver switched aim, swinging the gun barrel away from the now hidden girl to the openmouthed blond boy. He lined up Kenny's head in the sights and pulled the trigger.

BLAMM! The thunderous discharge echoed off the walls. Caught off guard, Kenny flinched, raising his hand. To his complete astonishment, the high-caliber projectile stopped and hung in the air, three feet from his head, still spinning. He didn't have time to admire the trick because two *oni* dived at him, one from each side.

"Ken-*chan*, find the sword. I'll keep these guys busy," Kiyomi said and he heard her scrambling across the floor.

"You'll keep us busy?" Silver growled, moving into the room. "Listen, Toots, your little boyfriend may have a few tricks, but so do I, one of which was setting an intruder alarm on this place."

"What do you want, a medal?" Kiyomi retorted from under the tables. "And he's not my boyfriend."

Silver listened, his pointed ears tilting towards the sound of Kiyomi's voice, and he signaled to the other four *oni*. "Hey, if it looks like a duck and quacks like a duck."

"Speaking of sitting ducks, if you were half as smart as you think you are, you'd never corner me in here," Kiyomi taunted.

Silver grinned and took aim again, lowering the barrel to point through a workbench. He jabbed a finger in that direction, motioning to his fellow *oni*.

"And why's that?" he rumbled.

"Because it's an armory, you dope!" Kiyomi heaved against the rack unit, tipping it forward to come crashing down. A torrent of heavy spiked clubs broke loose from its shelves and battered the *oni* caught underneath. Kiyomi leapt up, drove her sword through the *oni*'s chest and cartwheeled away.

Silver tracked her movements and fired twice, putting two craters in the wall, then yelled as she disappeared again.

Kenny meanwhile had two *oni* bearing down on him fast.

"Me smash!" bellowed the nearest, raising its *kanabo*.

Concentration flickered across Kenny's brow and he thrust out both arms, launching a pulsed force field from each palm. The invisible waves slammed into the onrushing creatures, lifting them off their feet and across the room to smash through the walls, leaving ragged, ogre-shaped holes. A chorus of chirping rose from the adjacent nightingale floor as the stunned *oni* rolled to a stop.

Kenny stared at his hands in awe.

"Stop admiring yourself and find that sword!" Kiyomi yelled, springing up and slinging a handful of *shuriken* at the remaining *oni*.

"Stand still!" Silver barked, throwing tables aside and wading into the room in search of his quarry.

Behind him, one *oni* gurgled and clutched at a *shuriken* in its throat while another scrabbled around the floor looking for its eye.

"I told you, they can't die," Kenny said, picking up sword after sword.

"No, but you can!" Silver said. "And then you're stuck down here with me."

"Perfect!" Kiyomi said and the curved limb of a *yumi* bow rose up from behind a fallen table.

Silver's eyes widened at the sight of the barbed arrowhead. "Down!" he ordered, diving for cover as the arrow sliced through his ear and punched through the forehead of the last uninjured monster.

"Oww! Head hurt!" it wailed, reaching up for the wooden shaft projecting from between its eyes.

"No! Don't pull –" Silver started, but he was too late.

The *oni* tugged at the arrow and the upper half of its head came with it.

"Oh, gross!" Kenny said, looking away. "What was that?"

"A *watakuri* arrowhead," Kiyomi answered. "'Bowel raker' in English. Very effective."

The four wounded *oni* stumbled towards the door, clutching various body parts.

"Get back here, you cowards!" Silver called after them.

Kiyomi stood up, bow primed with another wicked-looking arrow. "OK, big mouth," she said, her eyes skewering the ogre. "You against me. One shot each. What do you say?"

Silver stared at her with hate-filled eyes, but his gaze kept drifting towards the double-barbed arrow pointed at his face. The gun in his hand was slippery with sweat and silver blood dripped from his ear.

"Hurry it up," Kiyomi said. "My hand's getting tired."

Silver turned and bolted for the door. Kiyomi resisted the urge to shoot him in the back and relaxed the bowstring.

"Whoa," Kenny said, approaching with an armful of swords. "Now I get it. They can't die, but you can still mess them up so badly they can't function."

"Exactly." Kiyomi came over, looked through the heap of *katana* in his arms and selected an ivory scabbard with *kanji* lettering on it. "This is it. Ikutachi. Let's hope it can get us out of here."

Kenny looked dubious. "How do you know this is the sword?"

"It's written on the scabbard. Look." Kiyomi traced the brush strokes for him:

生大刀

"There you go. Life. Great. Sword. Ikutachi, the Sword of Life."

Kenny slapped his palm over his face. "You mean, I could have just read it?"

"If you'd learned to read, yes."

A thunderclap exploded so close that the entire fortress rattled and Kenny was almost knocked off his feet.

"Was that an earthquake?" he said.

"*KU-RO-MO-RI!*" a voice raged through the empty halls. "You *dare*?"

"Uh-oh – it's Susie and he sounds really mad," Kenny said, drawing Ikutachi from its scabbard. Engraved on the blade collar was a comma-shaped symbol with a circle in the wide end.

Another shudder rumbled through the palace. "That'd be the front doors," Kiyomi said. "Can you hurry it up?"

Kenny focused on the sword, concentrating his *ki* into the blade to awaken it.

"*You are not Susano-wo*," the sword's voice sounded in his mind. The pitch was female, calm and wise.

"No, I'm –"

"*Kuromori, chosen one of Inari, protector of life. You are late.*"

"I'm sorry?"

"*For what purpose are you claiming me?*"

Kenny reeled in surprise. "Uh, to stop Susano-wo from laying waste to the world. He's got Kusanagi."

"*I see. We should leave. Where do you wish to go?*"

"Huh? Oh, uh, can you take us home?"

"Kenny, he's almost here," Kiyomi said from the doorway, listening to the advancing sounds of destruction.

"There's no place like home," Kenny mumbled.

"You what?"

"Nothing." A soft glow emanated from the blade. "Something's happening. Get over here quick."

Another huge tremor shook the fortress and dust streamed from the ceiling. Kiyomi didn't need telling twice. She wrapped her hands around Kenny's and they both grasped the sword.

"You will not escape me this time!" Susano-wo's voice echoed through the fortress.

The brightness of the sword intensified to a blinding degree and Kenny closed his eyes.

A wild chirping sounded from the nightingale floor in the adjacent hall, warning them that Susano-wo had arrived.

"Enough!"

The enraged god stormed into the armory, Kusanagi in hand, in time to see only a spot of light fading away.

34 三十四

"I still can't believe they let our children go to *Yomi*," Charles said, "without even asking us first."

"I share your concern, but there was no other way," Harashima said.

Both men were seated in the garden behind the Harashima residence, perched on wicker chairs and huddled against the chill autumn evening. Light bled from the shuttered windows of the house, where a war council was under way.

"I don't know. It's my father. Why couldn't he just let Kenny have a normal childhood?" Charles removed his glasses.

"Duty," Harashima said. "You *gaijin* understand so little of this."

Charles reddened. "That's very condescending. I've studied –"

Harashima raised a hand for quiet. "Please, Charles-*sensei*. Do not let your pride speak for you. I mean no slight. Every one of us is born with unique talents, gifts if you like. What should we do with them? Hide them for fear of provoking others, of making them feel jealous or inadequate? Use them to gain power and wealth? Or do we offer those gifts in the service of mankind, to leave the world a better place than we find it? To lead, to inspire, to serve?"

"What, like me teaching or you policing the *yokai*?"

"Or our fathers fighting side by side to keep Japan's heritage where it belongs, in its homeland. They spared us, Charles, knowing that the torch would pass to our children. This is destiny. This is service. This is duty."

"So what are we? Bystanders? You and I just get to count the dead and mourn our losses?"

"We are whatever we choose to be. I will fight alongside your son and my daughter, should they return. What you do is your choice."

Their conversation was rudely interrupted by a crashing from the bushes, accompanied by angry shouts.

"Oww! Ack! Those things are sharp!"

"Kenny?" Charles sprang to his feet and peered into the shrubbery.

"Hi, Professor Blackwood!" Kiyomi said, emerging from the middle of a Japanese quince bush, her hands held high to avoid the thorns, and still clutching the bow.

"You'd think the stupid thing could have brought us inside," Kenny grumbled, unsnagging his T-shirt. "Hi, Dad, and hi, Harashima-*san*."

Harashima threw his arms around Kiyomi and held

her in a fierce embrace. "You made it back! And you, Kuromori-*san*." He beamed. "It is good to see you both. Did you . . .?"

Kenny held up the sword in its ivory scabbard. "Right here. Let's hope it was worth it."

"Welcome back," Charles said, ruffling his son's grubby hair before planting a kiss on the top of his head.

"Mama says hello," Kiyomi said into her father's chest. "We'll tell you all about it."

Half an hour later, in the main room of the house, Lawrence, Sato, Harashima and Charles listened intently while Kenny and Kiyomi finished their tale.

"So, Inari was right," Kenny concluded. "The sword, Ikutachi, did bring us back."

"Let us hope she is also right that it can withstand Kusanagi," Sato said.

With a soft sigh, the door slid aside and Oyama, the mountainous manservant, maneuvered himself into the room to lay a heaped tray of sandwiches on a side table. He bowed and turned to leave, almost tripping over a furry lump scampering past.

"Poyo!" Kiyomi shrieked in delight and stooped to intercept the *tanuki*. She nuzzled her nose against his fur and he gagged, holding his snout. "Fine," she said and plopped him down again. "Be like that. Papa, can we go and get cleaned up? I'm so tired."

"And I'm starving," Kenny added, biting into a corn and mayonnaise sandwich and making a face.

"Soon," Harashima said. His eyes flicked to catch Sato's. "You should tell them."

"Tell us what?" Kiyomi said.

"The gates of *Yomi* . . . they fell an hour ago," Sato said.

"What's the deal with these gates anyway?" Kenny asked. "And what does that mean? What's Susie going to do when he gets out?"

"His name is Susano-wo," Sato corrected, a steely edge in his voice. "But let's start with the gates."

Lawrence cleared his throat. "This all begins with two of the oldest, most powerful of the gods, Izanagi and Izanami. Together, as husband and wife, they created all the islands of Japan and most of the current generation of gods."

"But tragedy struck when Izanami gave birth to Fire and she was burned to death during the delivery," Sato said.

"In his grief, Izanagi decided he would go to *Yomi* to find his wife and bring her back to the Land of the Living," Lawrence said. "So he made the journey and came to a grand palace guarded by terrible demons. He sneaked around the back, found Izanami as beautiful as ever and begged her to return with him."

"But it was too late," Charles said. "Having eaten food from *Yomi*, it was now impossible for her to leave."

"So it was a wasted trip?" Kenny asked, sampling a fried pork cutlet sandwich.

"I suppose," Lawrence continued, "but Izanagi didn't give up that easily. He persuaded Izanami to go and ask if there was any way she could leave, but she made him promise to wait outside while she did so. After a full day's waiting he suspected the worst and broke into the palace."

Kiyomi shuddered, knowing what was coming next.

"There he found Izanami, but she was asleep in her true form, that of a hideous, rotting corpse," Lawrence said. "Heartbroken, Izanagi ran in terror, but Izanami awoke and swore revenge on him for breaking his promise and for seeing her in her true state."

"Harsh," Kenny said.

"So she sent a horde of demons and hags after him," Charles said, picking up the tale. "Izanagi slowed them down and fought them off, but then Izanami herself came after him. He managed to reach the pass of *Yomi* – a gap between the mountains that encircle the Land of the Dead – and rolled an enormous rock over the entrance, sealing it off forever."

"And that rock is the only thing left holding Susano-wo back," Kiyomi said.

"But that's just a fable, right?" Kenny's smirk faded at the sight of the stern faces around him. "No?"

"Iya Shrine in Higashi Izumo was built to mark the site," Sato said. "It honors Izanami and the dead."

"There's a huge boulder marking the point in our world where the pass leads out from *Yomi*," Lawrence said. "It even has a name: *Yomido ni sayarimasu okami*. The gods built an enormous wooden fortification on the *Yomi* side and protected it with powerful wards to prevent any *Yomi* creature from approaching it."

"But once Susie – sorry, Susano-wo – became ruler, those spells were broken?" Kenny said.

"That's right. And now that the barrier is destroyed it's only a matter of time before the boulder is moved and the legions of Hell are loose," Kenny's grandfather said.

"You asked what comes next." Sato reached for the remote control and clicked to open a bank of TV screens covering a wall. "It isn't pretty. Here's the shrine."

The screens blinked into life, displaying a map of Honshu, the main island. Sato zoomed in to a coastal area with the Sea of Japan to the north. A city straddled the gap between two vast lakes and Sato pointed to a patch of green sandwiched between a railway line and a water channel.

"The city is Matsue, home to two hundred thousand people," he said. "As you can see, it's mountainous away from the coast, but there's a lot of farming here, on reclaimed land, thanks to a series of small dams."

Lawrence paced slowly while he spoke. "Susano-wo will take Matsue as his base. His armies will march, reinstating an old practice known as *Hyakki Yagyo*, the Night Parade of One Hundred Demons, to cause mass hysteria, panic and insanity. Spirits will take possession of the populace, enslaving them as human puppets, and travel freely to other cities. Gradually, they will take control of the government and the armed forces. Martial law will be declared to control the insanity pandemic and the borders will be closed, sealing Japan off from the outside world once again."

"It will be a second Dark Age," Sato said. "Susano-wo will turn back the clock and instigate a new era of death. Wars, bloodshed, purges to cull the weak, all in the name of making Japan strong again. When he's done, he'll expand his empire."

"We can't let that happen," Kenny said. "We have to stop him."

"Yes, but *how*?" Harashima said. "Susano-wo commands an unstoppable army. He has invincible weapons and the gods bow down before him."

"Not to mention he can watch our every move and stop anything we might try," Lawrence added.

"Defeating him is impossible," Sato concluded.

"Impossible or not," Kenny said, "we're the only ones standing between him and millions of defenseless people. We have to try."

"Or die in the attempt?" Lawrence asked.

"So what do we do?" Charles said.

"I don't know, Dad, but there has to be a way. There has to be."

"And if there isn't?"

"Then we're all dead."

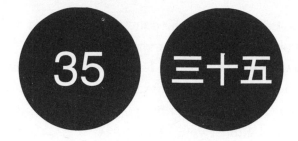

An hour later, Kenny exited the bathroom in a cloud of steam. His skin was pink, scrubbed clean of the dust of *Yomi*. He had washed his hair five times to lose the rank stench of death and, dressed in a cotton *yukata*, he felt much better.

"And they say girls take forever to get ready," Kiyomi said. She was sitting on the floor of the hallway, her legs tucked up, also wearing a bathrobe.

"How long have you been there?" Kenny asked.

"About half an hour." She patted the floor at her side. "I wanted to talk to you about something," she said.

Kenny ran a hand through his damp hair and plonked himself down.

"I've been thinking," Kiyomi said. "About choice. We don't have to do this, you know. We don't have to fight Susano-wo."

"What, we just surrender?"

Kiyomi lowered her voice and put her hand over Kenny's. "We could run away. There's still time. We could get to the airport, leave before . . ."

Kenny peered into the shining almond eyes. "I can't tell if you're kidding me or not. Is this a test?"

Kiyomi sighed. "I don't know. I thought I'd ask. He's going to kill you; that's for sure. I don't care how much you think you know or what you can do, but Susano-wo will totally murder you."

"Yeah, I kind of worked that out myself. Only my death will satisfy him."

"Ken-*chan*, I . . . am not going to watch you die." A single tear escaped and rolled down her cheek.

Kenny lifted Kiyomi's chin. "You know, we have a saying in English: 'No good deed goes unpunished.' I'm responsible for all this. It's me Susie wants. I cheated him to save you. You should get away, leave now. That way you won't have to watch."

Kiyomi sniffed. "No. You need me. *Yin yang*, remember? You're useless without me."

Kenny smiled and touched his forehead against hers. "I guess that settles it then."

"*A-hurm.*" Kenny jumped at the sound and saw the bulk of Oyama behind him. The servant made a beckoning gesture and led the way.

"How can someone that big move so quietly?" Kenny grumbled to Kiyomi as he got up.

Back in the main room, Harashima, Lawrence, Sato and Charles were engaged in a heated discussion, but fell silent when Oyama entered.

"Kenneth," his grandfather said, "I know it's late and

you're tired, but there's something you should know."

"Susano-wo's moved the rock?"

"Yes. How did you know?"

"Lucky guess. How long have we got?"

"He sent word," Sato answered. "Noon tomorrow. He wants this settled quickly. He's massing his army on that farmland I showed you. He wants all the gods there too, to swear allegiance to him. And then he marches on Matsue."

"Surely he knows there'll be some who oppose him?" Kiyomi said.

"That's why we meet on a battlefield."

"I have a question," Kenny said. "What if he orders the gods to destroy us for him?"

"He won't," Lawrence said. "He has too much pride for that. And he would lose face having others do his dirty work. No, one thing you've done, young Kenneth, is to rile him like no one else has done for a thousand years. You've cheated him, you've mocked him and you've rejected him. Believe you me, it doesn't get more personal than that."

Kenny nodded. "I seem to have a knack for hacking off these guys. Maybe I can use that against him."

"Get some rest if you can," Sato said. "Tomorrow we travel to Matsue."

*

Kenny was asleep the instant his head touched the

pillow. Discordant images of undersea dragons and space centipedes haunted his dreams, before a soothing glow intensified to chase them away.

In his sleepwear, Kenny saw himself standing alone in an endless white void. He sensed Inari's presence before he saw her and the goddess gazed at him with her vulpine eyes.

"Kuromori," she said, "the journey started by your father's father comes to an end. Tomorrow, Susano-wo will rule Japan and he will have you to thank."

"I'm sorry," Kenny said. "I know now why you tried to stop me, to warn me."

"I do not fault you, Kuromori. You are but a child and a willful one at that. It is both your greatest strength and greatest weakness. If anyone is to blame it is I for placing such a burden on young shoulders."

Kenny shook his head. "No, I let you down. I see that now. I put my own needs first, thinking only of what I wanted and not about others, or the bigger picture."

"You acted because of love, as I had asked of you. Once you said you would give your life to save the girl's."

"That's right."

"Tomorrow you will have your chance. Susano-wo's hatred stands opposed only by your love. We shall see which is stronger."

"I know how this ends," Kenny said. "There's a debt to be paid. He won't rest until that happens."

"Would it help if I told you this was foretold?"

Kenny rolled his eyes. "Oh, man. Another prophecy? Whose is it this time?"

"Mine, foreseen long ago. I proclaimed:

"The gates of Yomi open wide
And Hellspawn surge in unchecked tide,
Their freedom bought by willful child
Whose actions leave the earth defiled.

For one who sought to outwit death
Stole life to restart final breath,
Not knowing the cost is Treasures Three
With which to set the dread god free.

And now the debt must be repaid:
Life for life, the bargain made.
To contain the Hellborn flood
The price will be a hero's blood."

"You didn't tell me that when I first signed up."

"I asked you to put your life before the lives of strangers and to this you agreed."

"I didn't think it was literal." Kenny sighed. "Can you promise me something?"

Inari lowered her eyes. "I see your thoughts."

"Then you know. Will you do it? Will you keep Kiyomi safe . . . when I'm gone? Otherwise, what's the point?"

"Kuromori, the girl has her own destiny. It is not

for me –"

"Promise me! Lie if you have to, but don't tell me this will all be for nothing!" Kenny pleaded, fighting back tears.

Inari nodded slowly. "She will be safe. I shall see you tomorrow, when the old world comes to an end."

The light faded away until Kenny found himself alone once more, this time in darkness.

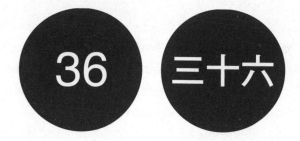

At 6:00 the next morning, an extraordinary collection of people crammed into the main room at the Harashima residence. At the front, beside the wall of TV screens, stood Harashima, Sato, Lawrence and Genkuro. Standing across from them were Sojobo, Zengubu, Kokibo, Oyama, Charles, Kenny and Kiyomi holding Poyo.

"We're like the Dirty Dozen," Kenny whispered to Kiyomi.

"Wasn't that a suicide mission?" she said. "Great example."

Harashima bowed to signal he was ready to begin the briefing. "Today, my friends, we face a threat like no other." The monitors behind him showed an aerial photograph of the Matsue area. "The portal from *Yomi* is here, by the Iya Shrine. Susano-wo has taken his forces north and massed them half a mile away, on this flat land here, to the east of the city. Our objective is to stop him marching west."

"As you know, we cannot rely on the gods or any of

their followers for help," Kenny's grandfather said, "so we have had to rally support from unaligned beings, giving us around seven hundred and fifty troops. These comprise three hundred *tengu* under the command of Sojobo, two hundred *kitsune* that Genkuro-*sensei* has rounded up, one hundred *tanuki* related to Poyo, a hundred *mujina* and *itachi* loyal to Sato-*san* – that's badgers and weasels – and fifty of Harashima-*san*'s people including us."

"Our *tengu* allies have been keeping watch on the enemy's camp," Sato said. "Their numbers are in excess of ten thousand with hundreds more crossing over every hour."

"Our only hope is to destroy as many of the enemy as possible, in the hope that we can drive them back and keep them from the city," Genkuro said. "If we thin their ranks enough, it might be possible to contain them."

"It's not going to work," Kenny said, squeezing his way to the front. "As soon as you send one of them back to *Yomi*, it'll return to the battlefield through the open gate. Susano-wo isn't going to sit there while we destroy his soldiers. He's got Kusanagi and the stone, so he's invincible. He's bound to wade in."

"Hm." Genkuro stroked his chin. "Kuromori-*san*, what is it you suggest?"

"Inari chose me to be her champion because I think differently, right?"

"Go on," Sato encouraged.

"I've got a plan. It's pretty nuts and probably won't

work, but he won't be expecting it."

"What is this plan of yours?" Sojobo rumbled, his deep, resonant voice like distant thunder.

"I can't tell you."

Lawrence scowled. "Kenneth, this is not the time for –"

"No, think about it . . . Susie could be watching us right now with the mirror. He'll hear everything. Genkuro-*sensei*, could you . . . erase my mind, blank out memories, if you wanted to?"

"I could. It is a simple trick for *kitsune*."

"Good. Do you guys know what a double blind is?"

The *tengu* looked at each other and shrugged.

"If any of us knows the whole plan and gets too close to Susano-wo, he'll read our thoughts and the game is up, right?" Kenny said. "So what I've done is write down small parts of the plan and given you each your own part in it. Since no one knows all of it, it can't be given away."

"What about you?" Kokibo asked. "You'll know the plan and if you get too near to Susano-wo he will know it too."

"Not after Genkuro-*sensei* does a mind-wipe on me. Not even I will know my own plan."

"Isn't that terribly risky?" Charles said.

"It's the only way, Dad. Kiyomi?"

She took a handful of white envelopes from her pocket and moved through the room, handing them out. "Here's what we prepared earlier," she said.

Kenny waited until each person had read their own instructions.

"This is a bad plan," Sojobo declared.

"Are you serious?" asked Harashima.

"You haven't left me much time to make arrangements," Sato grumbled.

"If you have any better ideas, now's a good time to speak up," Kenny said. He looked at the grim faces. "No? OK, let's get ready – and no discussing your part with anyone else."

When everyone had gone, Kiyomi rounded on Kenny. "Good job fooling them, but you can't fool me. Susano-wo is the God of Storms, but he's also a loon. It'll be like you going up against Thor and Loki in one. He'll kill you."

"Yeah, he will," Kenny agreed. "But it's my choice."

An hour later, the crunch of tires on gravel was followed by the chime of the doorbell and everyone reassembled in the main room.

Oyama went to the door and returned with two American naval officers wearing service dress uniforms. The senior officer had a wide gold stripe on each cuff surmounted by a single star and six rows of ribbons on his chest.

"Professor Blackwood?" he asked, looking around the room.

"Yes?" Charles and Lawrence answered together. Kenny's grandfather raised a wrinkled hand.

"There's over a dozen warrants still out for your arrest," the officer said, before grinning and extending his hand. "I've heard a lot about you, sir. You worked with my father during the Occupation."

"Thank you, Rear Admiral . . .?"

"Clark, sir. And this is my aide, Captain Myers." Once the introductions were over, Clark got down to business. "Your request was relayed from the Pentagon to COMPACFLT and I was directed to assist you – as far as we can without causing a major incident."

"I fully understand, Admiral, but we are already in the midst of a major incident," Lawrence said "What can you give us?"

"I'm liaising with my SDF counterparts, who I believe your Mr. Sato has put on alert. We might be able to get you something out of Sasebo, but what you're asking for is a pretty tall order."

"Believe me, Admiral, I wouldn't be asking this if it wasn't a national emergency."

"Understood." Clark saluted. "I'll do my best, sir."

Kenny knelt on the floor of his room in a nest of maps, reference books and notepads, covered in scrawl.

After tapping lightly on the half-open door, Kiyomi entered, carrying a steaming mug.

"Tea break," she said.

Kenny yawned, stretched and got up, grateful for the interruption.

"How are you feeling?" Kiyomi handed over the drink.

"Absolutely terrified. I should have kept one of those

astronaut diapers for when I meet Susie." He took a sip of tea and put the mug down.

"Have you checked out the sword yet?" Kiyomi nodded towards Ikutachi, propped against the wall.

"Nah. What's the point? Either it'll work against Kusanagi or it won't. There isn't much middle ground."

"Ever the optimist." Kiyomi took Kenny's hands in hers and leaned closer, locking eyes with him. "Look, Ken-*chan*, if this all goes wrong . . . I want you to know that I . . ."

BING-BONG! The doorbell sounded again.

"We'd better go see who it is," Kiyomi said, turning away quickly to hide her blush.

"Wait. You were about to say?"

"It'll keep. Come on, we're needed."

Kenny rolled his eyes and muttered, "Duty, duty, duty."

Another American visitor stood in the front room. He was tall, tanned and slim with a dazzling smile and a firm handshake.

"Allow me to introduce my US counterpart," Sato said. "Cal Turner is CIA station chief based out of the embassy in Tokyo. Needless to say, that's classified information, not to go outside this room. It's good of you to come at such short notice, Cal-*san*."

"Not at all," the visitor said. "To be honest, I was expecting a call sooner. Looks like you guys are in real trouble. It finally happened, huh?"

"How much do you know?" Lawrence asked, viewing him with suspicion.

"That's not for me to say –"

"Spit it out, Cal, before I pull what you know out of your head!" Sato exploded. "Now isn't the time for spy versus spy."

Cal removed his frameless glasses and gave them a polish. "We know everything of course. Believe it or not, we're trying to help, behind the scenes. It doesn't serve our interests to see Japan go under. Mass hysteria and insanity have a habit of spreading."

"I told you," Lawrence said, a sour look on his face. "They've known about *yokai* since the war and they've been keeping tabs. Probably tried recruiting them too."

"What interests me most right now," Cal said, "is your secret weapon."

"What are you talking about?" Sato said.

"Him." Cal aimed his finger at Kenny like a pistol. "You're hanging everything on a fifteen-year-old kid. I guess it helps that he can see your monsters and has a history of stopping them."

"How do you know about my son?" Charles said, stepping in between Kenny and Cal.

In answer, Cal called out: "Come on in, sweetheart."

The door slid open and in walked the last person on Earth that Kenny expected to see.

"I brought doughnuts," Stacey said, holding up a paper bag.

37　三十七

"Ken-*san*, you *know* this girl?" Sato said.

"She's my classmate," Kenny said, "or so I thought."

"And you never mentioned this to me?"

"Since when do you care who I hang out with?"

"It matters when she's the daughter of the CIA head in Tokyo."

"I didn't know that part."

"Boys, chill," Stacey said. "Dad does his job, and I do mine." She beamed at her father and hoisted the doughnuts out of Poyo's reach.

"So you've given your dad the full rundown on me, is that it?" Kenny fumed.

"Uh-huh. It's not my fault you were so careless at the observatory, getting caught on camera."

"Part of my brief is to watch out for any individuals with unique talents," Cal said, "so when a boy rescues people from a burning building, I ask questions."

"But why involve her?" Kenny asked, glaring at Stacey.

"Show them, sweetie," Cal said.

Stacey took a slow, measured look around the room, counting heads. "Dad, guess what? *Tengu*. Three of them, at the back. And a nine-tailed *kitsune* judging from the old man's shadow."

Kenny's head spun. "You can see *yokai*? All this time and you never said anything?"

Stacey shrugged. "I told you my mom was Japanese. Yes, I can see them, but only since I met you."

"So now you understand why I brought her along," Cal said. "You're going up against an invisible army that won't die. You'll need every pair of eyes you've got."

"What about you, Cal-*san*? What are you going to do?" Sato asked, his voice heavy with suspicion.

"I'll meet you there. But first I'm going to get you as much satellite data and enemy intel as I can. I'm also going to coordinate with Admiral Clark to get you what you need. Fair enough?" He held out his bronzed hand.

"Fair enough." Sato bowed, ignoring the proffered handshake.

"Hurry it up. We leave at oh nine hundred hours," Harashima's voice barked through the halls of the house.

Everywhere people scurried around, some packing bags and gathering equipment, others saying prayers and writing farewell messages.

Stacey watched Kenny throw a few items into a backpack and blew a pink bubble. "So you get to be Pandora?" she said.

"Huh?" Kenny paused in annoyance.

"From the Greek myth. Pandora opened the box and let out all the demons."

"She also released hope into the world," Kiyomi said, appearing in the doorway. She had changed into her leathers and held the *yumi* bow in one hand and her *katana* in the other. "Ken-*chan*, are you ready?"

He nodded, zipped up the leather jumpsuit she had put out for him and grabbed Ikutachi, the Sword of Life.

Minutes later, a sharp sea breeze whipped salt into Kenny's face and he found himself standing on a low ridge overlooking a flat plain of fields. Behind him, several trucks had parked and Harashima's men were busy checking weapons and loading ammunition clips.

Kokibo vanished and returned a minute later with Stacey and Genkuro. Before long, the *tengu* had brought everyone from the house.

"Whoa. That was rough," Stacey said, clutching her stomach. "Some kind of folding of space? A mini wormhole?"

Sato handed Kenny a pair of binoculars. "Tell me what you see."

Kenny put the field glasses to his eyes and scanned the acres of grass and lettuce. "They're camped over there, behind that line of trees." He paused to count, his lips moving. "There's thousands of them."

"One good thing," Kiyomi said. "This area is mostly uninhabited."

"I asked my people to evacuate the farms," Harashima said. "We told them there was a chemical spill."

Kenny read through his handwritten notes again, then beckoned to Genkuro. "*Sensei*, take these and destroy them, please," he said, handing over the papers. "And can you wipe my memory of the last few hours?"

Genkuro nodded. "Let us hope I don't do too good a job, otherwise you may forget that you yourself have instructions to follow." The old teacher placed two fingers to each of Kenny's temples and closed his eyes in concentration, muttering under his breath. Light glowed briefly from his fingertips and he withdrew his touch.

Kenny blinked. "We're here? In Matsue?"

"Yes," Sato said.

"And Susie's armies are waiting?" Kenny took a deep breath. "OK, let's get this started."

The rebel forces organized themselves into companies: Sojobo gathered his three hundred *tengu*; Genkuro spoke to the two hundred *kitsune*; Poyo handed out doughnuts to the hundred *tanuki*; Sato commanded his contingent of badgers and weasels; Harashima gave directions to his company, including Oyama.

Lawrence took Charles by the elbow and said, "Time for you to leave, son. We can take it from here. I'll get one of the *tengu* to –"

"No, Dad, I'm not going."

"Charles, don't be absurd. You know nothing about –"

"I know Kenny needs all of us. You've both tried protecting me and it hasn't worked. I'm a part of this; it's our family business, right?"

Lawrence's watery eyes searched his son's face.

"Dad, if not for me, Kenny wouldn't be alive now. I've earned the right to make my own choice. I stand and fight with my son – and my father."

Lawrence gave a thin-lipped smile. "I guess Kenneth isn't the only chip off the old block, eh?" He took Charles in his arms and held him close.

Kiyomi drew Kenny to one side. "Ken-*chan*, we've all got our tasks to carry out, including you."

"Really? OK. What do you need me to do?"

"This is for you." She handed Kenny a white envelope, which he tore open and read the note inside.

"I have to do what? Which crazy idiot came up with this idea?"

"You did. It's your plan. Here." Kiyomi grabbed him by the collar and smashed her lips against his. "That's for luck."

The low, mournful drone of a horn carried into the gray sky.

"Come," Genkuro called. "Destiny awaits."

"Uh, what are we doing now?" Stacey asked, as the troops made ready to march.

"We take our sides on the field of battle," Sato said. "There will be a formal challenge and then – war."

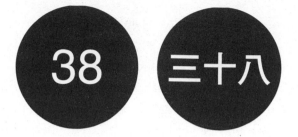

"Oh wow," Stacey said when she saw the vast extent of Susano-wo's assembled forces. A quick march across the fields and through the bordering trees had brought them to a wide expanse of grassland with black plastic-wrapped hay bales piled in one corner.

Half a mile away stood the massed ranks of *Yomi*, in lines two hundred across and fifty deep. At their front stood Susano-wo. He had exchanged his customary white smock and red *hakama* for a suit of black *o-yoroi Samurai* armor. On his left arm hung a shield.

"Come forth, my divine brethren, I command you!" he roared in a voice of thunder. "Your new ruler demands tribute."

"What is happening?" Harashima asked, looking at an empty field of gently rippling grass.

"Susano-wo's calling out the gods," Kiyomi said. "I'll give you a commentary."

On each side of the field, the air vibrated and hundreds of gods appeared, many in their finest garb. Power radiated from the throng.

"Greetings, my most loyal subjects," Susano-wo said, his upper lip curled into a sneer. "Many of you will not remember me, since I was banished long ago, so permit me to introduce myself. I am Susano-wo, son of Izanagi, brother to Amaterasu and Tsukuyomi. I command the sky, the sea and the storm." He raised his arms and lightning lanced across the sky.

"Where did that come from?" Charles said, squinting up at the iron sky.

"I'll say this for him," Kenny muttered. "He may be a fruitcake, but he knows how to make an entrance." He slipped away from the others and began the long walk across the grass towards the opposing army.

Susano-wo continued: "Lest any doubt my sovereign right to rule, know that I bear the Three Sacred Treasures and with these signs of divine authority I command you all to submit to my will."

Hachiman stepped forward from the hushed crowd. "Let me see these regalia," he said. "Otherwise, how dost we know this is not another of thy famous lies?"

"Mark how you speak to me, whelp," Susano-wo growled. "I know of your treachery and will reward you for it at a more fitting time. But, for any of you who doubt, here is the mirror." He held up his circular shield and twisted his arm to expose the polished, reflective inside.

"So he keeps the mirror on him at all times," Kiyomi said. "And it doubles as a shield."

Susano-wo raised his right hand. "And here – behold!

– Kusanagi, the Sword of Heaven."

Kenny felt a pang of regret as he watched the sword materialize in his enemy's grasp.

"And, finally, the precious Jewel of Life itself." Susano-wo reached into his breastplate and drew out the comma-shaped stone hanging from his neck by a leather thong looped through the hole.

"Now that I have proven my claim, you will acknowledge it by kneeling before me," Susano-wo said. "Kneel!"

One by one, slowly at first, but then gathering pace, the gods fell to their knees. All except for six.

"I know who has been plotting against me," Susano-wo said, glaring at the rebels. "You cannot escape the scrying eye of the mirror. Now *kneel*."

A fiery glow burned from within the Three Sacred Objects and Kenny saw the same light flare around Inari, Amaterasu, Kuebiko, Ryujin, Tsukuyomi and Hachiman. The gods' faces contorted in pain and agonized cries escaped from their throats. Each dropped to the earth.

"*AAAGH!* Stop it! I can't kneel even if I wanted to!" Kuebiko shrieked.

"That's better," Susano-wo declared. Behind him, his thousands of *oni* pounded their iron clubs against the ground and roared in approval.

"The ground is shaking," Sato said, looking at the empty field. "What's happening?"

"The hairy dude's got everyone kneeling before him

and his army is celebrating," Stacey said. "It looks bad."

"All of Japan trembles before me," Susano-wo said, "and with good cause. Mortals have despoiled this beautiful land, poisoned it with their machines and greed. But I will –"

"Learn to shut your mouth and stop counting chickens?" Kenny said, looking up at the giant figure.

"Kuromori! You dare to show your face?"

"Come on, admit it. You were expecting me. We *gaijin* have no sense of decorum. It's typical of us to mess up your little coming-out party."

"Silence!" raged Susano-wo.

"You don't scare me." Kenny prayed that his jelly legs wouldn't give out on him. "If not for me, you'd still be rotting in your hole. I made you king and I can unmake you too."

"You are but one insolent boy."

"Uh-uh. I've got an army behind me, as you know, but why have more bloodshed? Violence never solved anything. How about just you versus me, loser goes home and we call it a day?"

"Are you insane?"

"Yes or no? Or are you too scared?"

Kenny felt Susano-wo's mind press against his and the god rummaged through his thoughts. "This is a trick!" he spat. "Your feeble mind is even emptier than usual. Never try to deceive a deceiver. I will not be taken in by it. No. Go back and ready your warriors. We fight – and you . . ."

he pointed an accusing finger at the assembled gods, ". . . will stay out of this."

Kenny returned to the ridge where his friends were waiting.

"And?" Lawrence asked. "Did he go for it?"

"Hook, line and sinker," Kenny said. "Time for phase two."

"You girls, with me," Sato said, taking out keys and heading towards one of the trucks.

Kiyomi and Stacey climbed into the cab while Genkuro, Lawrence, Charles and Sato hopped into the back.

Kenny watched the truck rumble away before shouting, "Everyone, take up positions!"

The squad of *kitsune* formed the front rank, armed mostly with staves. Behind them, the badgers, weasels and *tanuki* made up the second line. Harashima's squad filled the gaps as best they could. Finally, Sojobo's *tengu* comprised the third tier.

Three rows of woodland creatures versus fifty columns of Hellspawn. Kenny knew it wasn't even a contest. They were outnumbered fourteen to one and the enemy's numbers were growing with each passing minute.

"Let's move it out," Kenny said to the company leaders and his troops began the long march across the field.

Half a mile away, the truck skidded to a stop in a deserted parking lot and Sato jumped out, phone in hand.

"Everybody get behind the truck," he said, while speed-dialing and putting the phone to his mouth. "Cal, where are you?"

"There," Stacey said, listening to a low drumming sound coming in from the west and pointing up at two dots in the sky. The helicopter engines grew louder and a squat Black Hawk chopper touched down while the second, a fully armed Apache gunship, completed a circuit before landing.

Cal Turner slid open the side door of the Black Hawk and jumped out. He ran towards Sato.

"Both pilots have been briefed to do exactly as they're told and not to ask any questions," he shouted above the pounding noise of the rotors.

"What about the other bird?" Sato yelled.

"Give me a break! Do you know how many strings I've had to pull to get you these two?"

"I don't care! Go straight to Admiral Clark, you hear me? We need that one or it's game over."

"I hope you know what you're doing," Cal grumbled.

"That makes two of us," Sato said under his breath and he waved Kiyomi, Lawrence, Charles and Genkuro towards the waiting Black Hawk.

Cal put an arm around Stacey's shoulders and guided her to the Apache. He helped her up to the cockpit and she slid into the copilot's seat.

"Make me proud, sweetie," he said, "and come back safe."

Stacey gave a thumbs-up sign and Cal slammed the cockpit closed, dropped to the asphalt and ran for the truck.

Kenny's smart watch buzzed and he checked the message from Kiyomi: IN THE AIR AND EN ROUTE. WAITING FOR YOUR SIGNAL.

Five hundred yards away, Susano-wo's forces were stamping the ground, howling obscene challenges and stoking their bloodlust. Thousands of *oni* formed the bulk of the ranks, but vile hags moved among them and shambling corpses in various stages of decomposition hovered behind the legions of skeletal warriors who made up the front lines.

Kenny took a deep breath and looked across at the watching gods, still on their knees. Inari caught his eye and she nodded once: it was time.

Susano-wo strode out in front of his troops. "Kuromori, on this, my day of enthronement, I am moved to be generous. My offer still stands. Join me, lead my armies and you shall be richly rewarded. Refuse and I promise you will die this day."

Kenny shrugged. "Everyone has to die sometime. Why not today?"

"So be it." Susano-wo raised Kusanagi to point to the heavens. His slavering troops coiled their muscles, ready to spring. The sword sliced the air and pointed to Hell.

With a blood-chilling roar, the forces of *Yomi* charged.

39 三十九

Kiyomi watched from the window of the Black Hawk as vegetable fields flashed past below. These were bordered to the south by a channel of Lake Nakaumi and, on the opposite bank, the suburbs of Higashi Izumo. A snaking line of *oni* marched along the back roads, heading towards the battleground.

In a matter of minutes, the helicopter soared above a thickly wooded area and began to circle. Sato clambered over and yelled to be heard over the roar of the engines.

"We're above Yomotsu Hirasaka – the Japan side of the portal," he said. "Are we ready?"

"Not yet!" Kiyomi shouted back. "I'm waiting on Ken-*chan*'s signal."

The ground shook under the weight of thousands of pounding feet and Kenny wanted nothing more than to turn and run at the sight of the stampeding hordes, but he knew that was not an option. This was his fight; he had started it and he had to finish it.

"Not yet!" he called to the rank of eager *kitsune*.

"Hold your line." The fox soldiers snarled and their ears twitched, but they waited.

Skeleton warriors seated astride skeletal horses led the enemy charge, lances and spears lowered. Behind them lumbered the *oni*.

"Wait for it," Kenny ordered. "Wait till you see the, uh, dark of their sockets!"

Lightning scarred the heavens and the stench of death rolled across the grass. The skeleton cavalry was mere feet away.

"Now!" Kenny called, drawing Ikutachi with his right hand and projecting a force field with his left. The invisible wall smashed into the onrushing skeletons with devastating effect: spines shattered, rib cages blew apart, skulls soared skyward and limbs were sundered.

Directly behind the mounting piles of fractured bones, the *oni* tried to stop before impaling themselves, but their sheer numbers made this impossible. Some were pushed to the ground and trampled whereas others were pitched forward onto the broken shards of bone.

The *kitsune* leapt into the air, vaulting the fallen bodies, and landed amid the *oni*, staves firmly in hands. Kenny watched in admiration as the foxes seemed to dance their way through with strength, precision and grace. A jab to the knee dropped one *oni*, bringing its head into range for a smash to the ear with the other end of the staff. Continuing the same move, the staff pivoted into the back of the *oni*'s neck, allowing the bearer to vault over the tumbling body and launch himself, feetfirst, to land a two-footed kick to the head of a second ogre.

"*RRRARRGGH!*" The shadow of a huge amber-colored *oni* raising its iron club fell over Kenny. Ikutachi, the Sword of Life, sprang into a parrying position and sliced the club in two as it hammered down. Kenny dived to the side and swung the blade, severing the *oni*'s left leg. It went down in a heap and he finished it with a single blow. The body crumbled to dust and disappeared on the breeze.

The *kitsune* continued to waltz their way through with balletic grace, but the vast numbers of *oni* made them impossible to contain and hundreds surged past. Waiting for them, and armed with stout cudgels, stood a band of plucky *tanuki*, weasels and badgers, led by Poyo. Many were in humanlike transitional forms; the remainder were ready with tooth and claw.

An *oni* stumbled through the bone pile and was immediately set upon by a gang of *tanuki*, which scrambled up and over the demon, pummeling it on all sides until it collapsed in a stunned heap.

The weasels were armed with short curved swords. Seeing an *oni* advance, three of them sprang into the air and spun like miniature whirlwinds. They hit the *oni* from three sides, with blades whirling. The effect was like walking into a lawnmower and the hapless *oni* was shredded in a matter of seconds.

Harashima waited with his men, watching in wonder

as *kitsune* danced through an empty field, as if performing t'ai chi, and *tanuki* climbed into the air. When Harashima saw the grass flattening in an advancing series of circles he leveled his assault rifle, letting loose a blast of automatic fire. Splashes of green *oni* blood blossomed in the air and the falling body of the monster materialized before it hit the ground in a cloud of ash.

As hundreds of bloodthirsty *oni* marched towards the edge of the battlefield and the ridge leading to the town of Matsue, three hundred *tengu* warriors shimmered into view.

"Turn back now if you value your lives," rumbled Sojobo, "for this is a line you will not cross."

The *oni* forces bellowed their defiance and stampeded uphill – just as the *tengu* forces took to the air and landed behind them. Blades bit deeply into flesh and the *oni* crumbled to dust.

Kenny, meanwhile, was in the midst of so many monsters that he couldn't even see the sky. His sword, Ikutachi, flashed and twisted with a life of its own, hewing limbs and dispatching *oni* by the dozen, but it was no use: for every demon Kenny felled, another three took its place.

Hacking away, he stumbled backward, felt thick fingers close around his ankle and was pulled to the ground beside a wounded ogre, which reached out to grab his sword hand. Another *oni* closed in and raised its club.

Before Kenny could react, the *oni* stopped, coughed once and fell to its knees, dead. Behind it, with hands slick from demon blood, crouched a pile of black rags with spindly, clawed limbs. The Hellhag leered at Kenny, licked its bloodied fingers and moved in for the kill. It vanished into an oily black shadow and one moment it was crouched in the dust of the *oni* it had killed, the next its claws were around Kenny's throat and its fangs were bearing down.

A brick-red figure crashed down beside Kenny, laid a steadying hand on his shoulder and directed a hurricane-force blast of wind to scatter hundreds of *oni*, including the hag, like bowling pins. Sojobo lowered his seven-feathered fan and helped Kenny to his feet.

"Now," he said.

Kenny nodded and jabbed a message into his smart watch.

Kiyomi was glued to the helicopter window, watching in horror as throngs of *oni* surged from a hole in the ground once marked by a huge boulder, which now lay in pebble-sized fragments.

"How bad is it?" Sato called to her.

"Bad," she said. "There are hundreds coming across all of a sudden." Her smart watch buzzed. "It's Ken-*chan*," she said. "Time to go!"

Sato grabbed his phone. "Stacey, you're up!"

Seated in the nose of the Apache attack helicopter,

Stacey gave a thumbs-up, which she hoped would be seen in the Black Hawk hovering behind.

"Light it up," she said into her helmet mike. "Give it everything you've got."

"Roger that," the pilot said, arming all the weapon systems.

Charles and Lawrence joined Kiyomi at the window of the Black Hawk and watched in awe as the Apache unloaded its terrifying payload of thirty-eight precision-guided Hydra rockets and eight Hellfire missiles.

On the ground, the *oni* spilling out from the portal had no idea what hit them. Rocket after rocket ripped into the hole marking the entrance to *Yomi* and detonated, blasting the escaping ogres to pieces.

In *Yomi*, on the other side of the gateway, missiles streaked down the pass and smashed huge chunks of rock off the mountainsides. Blinded, deafened and disorientated, the *oni* reinforcements ran for cover, fleeing from the devastating onslaught.

"The path is clear," Stacey said. "It's all yours."

Kiyomi slid open the Black Hawk cargo door, tossed out a rope ladder and began the long climb down, followed by Sato.

Charles reached for the rope and felt Lawrence place a firm hand on his son's arm. "This isn't your fight, Charles. You don't have to do this."

"Dad, let it go. Kenny needs all of our help," Charles said and twisted to place his feet on the ladder.

"Then take this." Lawrence handed him a 9mm semi-automatic pistol. "Just in case."

Kiyomi hit the ground and steadied the rope ladder for Sato and Charles. Genkuro and Lawrence simply jumped, dropping the hundred feet to land softly on the damp earth. The two *tengu*, Zengubu and Kokibo, blinked into existence and joined the group.

"Let's go," Kiyomi said. "Fast as we can, before they regroup. Once they figure out what we're up to, it's going to get really bad."

"One moment," Sato said. "Charles-*sensei*, you'll need this." He reached into his suit pocket and withdrew a shattered pair of sunglasses, patched together with superglue and sticky tape. Snapping the bridge, he handed one half of the frame to Charles. "Use it as a monocle," he said, holding it over one eye to demonstrate. "It will allow you to see *yokai*." He followed Kiyomi towards the bombed-out rupture in the ground.

"This is it," Kiyomi said, crouching down to peer into the blackness beyond. "Looks like I'll see you in Hell." She sat on the edge, dangled her legs a moment and then vanished into the hole.

Sojobo guided Kenny back across the field, past dozens of broken bodies and mounds of ash. A cohort of *tengu* formed a defensive circle around them and both sides fell back to regroup and to count their losses.

Susano-wo swaggered to the center and spread his arms to encompass the combat zone.

"I have tested your forces, Kuromori, and they have been found wanting. You have lost a third of your followers whereas I have only gained numbers. Look!"

Kenny glanced back to see hundreds of *oni* filing along the road from the portal and taking their places at the back of Susano-wo's army.

"This is hopeless," he muttered. "There's no way we can win if they never lose anyone."

"That is so," Sojobo agreed. "Nonetheless, duty commands us. As long as any of us lives, they will not have won."

"Kuromori-*san*, you fought like a man possessed," Harashima said, limping over with a water bottle in his hand.

"Sir, you're hurt." Kenny saw that Harashima's right leg was slick with blood.

"It's just a scratch," Harashima said. His eyes flicked away. "I've completed a count. It's not good."

Kenny let his head drop. "How bad?"

"The *tengu* have fared well." Harashima chuckled. "It's hard to kill something you cannot catch. The *kitsune* less so; we have a hundred and twelve left of their number. The smaller creatures have been hit hard."

"What about your people?" Kenny asked, dreading the answer.

Harashima stared out towards the lake. "We can't fight what we can't see. Any *oni* breaking through has the edge. I've lost twenty-three good fighters."

"This is all my fault," Kenny said, hot tears blurring his eyes. "I should face Susano-wo on my own, spare anyone else."

"No, Kuromori-*san*," Harashima said. "Be patient, your chance will come."

Kenny felt a weight bump against his leg and looked down. A bloodied Poyo stood with his paws clasped around Kenny's calf.

"Hey, you made it!" Kenny said, reaching down to pick up the fat *tanuki*. "How many did you get?"

Poyo held up three stubby fingers.

"Three? Way to go."

The dull bass of the *oni* horn reverberated around the field.

"Break's over," Kenny muttered. "Time for round two."

BEEP-BEEP! The returning truck slid to a stop and Cal Turner leapt from the cab. "I stopped to get a couple of rocket-propelled grenades on the way," he said. "Any use?"

"I'll let you know," Kenny said, turning back towards the battlefield.

"Kuromori!" Susano-wo bellowed. "Behold! I have a new adversary for you."

At first Kenny thought it was the wind blowing scraps of paper into heaps, but as he stared in horror, he realized it was piles of bone clumping together. Shards and splinters flew through the air like iron filings drawn to a magnet; larger bones turned end over end and amassed into columns. Slowly, steadily, the bony remains were combining to form one gigantic skeleton.

"You've got to be kidding me," Kenny said to himself.

"What is it?" Harashima and Cal both said at the same time.

"You don't want to know."

Kiyomi dropped into a pile of gray ash. Behind her, the portal to Japan shimmered and undulated like the surface of a swimming pool. The blue glow darkened momentarily and Charles landed beside her in a puff of dust.

"This is *Yomi*?" he asked, eyes wide with fascination. "I wonder where the light is coming from?"

"Who cares?" Kiyomi grumbled. "This isn't a sightseeing trip."

Her uncle came through the doorway next. His eyes swept the terrain, making a swift assessment. They were at the top of a scree slope, at the base of a narrow chasm. Sheer rock walls rose up on either side and farther down the pass lay the broken beams of the thick wooden barricade among which lurked hundreds of *oni*, having sought shelter from the explosive onslaught.

Sato put the cracked lens to his eye. "Kiyomi-*chan*, they've seen us and they're coming."

Lawrence, Genkuro and the two *tengu* all crossed over into *Yomi*.

"It worked," Lawrence said. "The Apache cleared the way."

"Yep, but we've lost the element of surprise," Kiyomi said, eyeing the onrushing *oni*. "Charles-*sensei*, come with me and Zengubu-*san*. *Oji*, you know what to do? Take Kokibo-*san* with you." Sato nodded.

"Dad, what about you?" Charles said.

Lawrence bowed to Genkuro. "It's been a long road, *sensei*. It's fitting we take the last steps together."

"Indeed, my young *oshiego*. Everything we have ever done has led us to this."

"Dad! Where are you going?" Charles called, watching the two elderly figures pick their way down the slope.

"They're buying us time," Kiyomi said. "Let's not waste it." She scrambled up the rock face until she reached a narrow ledge on which Zengubu was waiting for her with Charles.

"What's the plan?" Charles asked, nervously looking over the edge at his father.

Kiyomi opened her pack to reveal dozens of blocks of C-4 plastic explosive. "We use this to close the pass, seal the portal long enough for Kenny to do his bit."

"And how do we get out?"

"That isn't part of the plan." Kiyomi turned to Zengubu. "We need to pack this deep into the rock. If we don't, it'll just bounce off. How can we get under the surface?"

Zengubu placed his palms against the mountainside and swept his fingertips lightly over the stone. "Everything has weaknesses," he said. "Imperfections, flaws, stress fractures – the key is to know where to find them." He stopped, his index finger resting on a chip of shale. "This will do."

Charles leaned closer to inspect the outcrop. "I'm not sure I see –"

WHA-BAMM! Zengubu's fist hammered down onto the rock and – *KA-RAKKK!* – a horizontal fissure split along a seam. "Is this acceptable?" he asked.

"I need something deeper, more of a tunnel," Kiyomi said. "Can you do that?"

"It will take some time." Zengubu took a deep breath before launching his fist against the rock in a rapid series of blows, each with the speed and power of a jackhammer.

Stone crumbled and fell in a fine rain of granules, while the pounding echoed through the pass.

Charles peeped through the broken eyeglass and was startled to see scores of huge, lumbering, demon-like creatures making their way up the slope towards the portal. The only thing standing in their way was his father and Genkuro.

On the battlefield, the gigantic skeleton towered like a colossus. It was at least a hundred feet tall. Behind it, the army of *oni* assembled in lines and beat their clubs against the ground.

As Kenny watched, a dull-yellow glow lit up the cavernous eye sockets and the skeleton shuddered into life with jerky, spasmodic movements. Its lower jaw opened and it brayed its name, "*Gashadokuro!*" With that, it moved, lifting one giant bony foot off the ground to slam down with earthshaking force.

Kenny's troops all took an involuntary stop backward.

"Is that an earthquake?" Cal asked, holding on to the truck for balance. As far as he could see, the field was empty.

Susano-wo motioned for his army to follow and they marched behind the *gashadokuro* in their thousands.

Kenny glanced around, hoping against hope for a sight of Kiyomi or Genkuro, anyone who could tell him what to do against this monstrous creation. Instead, he found only hundreds of allies, all looking to him for leadership.

"We cannot fight this," Sojobo declared and, at his signal, the entire contingent of *tengu* vanished as one.

"They've . . . gone?" Kenny said in disbelief. "They ran away?"

Fear gripped his heart like an icy hand. He had just lost half of his warriors, but he had no time to dwell on it as the giant foot came bearing down to crush him.

41 四十一

Genkuro and Lawrence had chosen their position well. Not only did it provide the advantage of higher ground, but also the narrowing of the trail created a natural bottleneck which only allowed two *oni* through at a time.

The first was a coal-black brute with three eyes. It slammed its iron club down to crush Genkuro, but the old *sensei* flicked a finger to parry the blow. The club rebounded upward, smashing the *oni*'s head down into its neck. The second ogre was slate gray with dreadlocks and it rushed at Lawrence. Stepping forward, the elderly man caught its heel with his to trip it, spun to administer a swift kick and sent the beast flying headfirst into the mountainside.

Two more *oni* took their places and the sound of combat filled the pass.

On the ledge, Zengubu paused, breathless, with blood staining his knuckles. He had excavated a channel about three inches wide and fifteen deep.

"That'll have to do," Kiyomi said. "Nice work." She

began to pack the hole with C-4, ramming the blocks in with her fist for good measure.

Charles continued to watch the fight taking place below, using the broken eyeglass. He could see that his father and Genkuro were hopelessly outnumbered and would eventually be overrun. Something glinted in front of him and a large shape blocked his view.

"Hah! I knew it," crowed the silver *oni*. "That's why I volunteered to stay back. I knew Toots here couldn't keep away." Its huge paw swung around and swatted Charles aside and off the precipice.

"*Chikara!*" Kenny launched himself to the side with a power jump, hitting the dirt and rolling as the giant bony foot slammed into the earth, crushing a dozen unfortunate *tanuki*. Following close behind was a tidal wave of baying *oni*.

"No!" he yelled, thrusting out a force field to stop the advance with immediate effect. While *oni* crashed into the energy barrier and piled up, Kenny centered his *ki*, summoned a powerful gust and soared into the air.

He came down on the back of the giant skeleton, balancing his feet on the first rib and leaning against the neck bones. It was like being on board a ship, with the dips and swells of the *gashadokuro*'s gait.

Kenny looked past the skull to see the low industrial buildings of eastern Matsue barely a mile away. With its giant strides, the colossal skeleton would be there in minutes.

Drawing his *katana*, he stabbed it into the groove where two vertebrae joined, driving the blade all the way in. Using both hands he pulled, slicing, sawing and grinding as he cut across the width of the column. In a shower of splinters, the sword came free and Kenny fell backward, sprawling onto the rib.

The *gashadokuro* took another step. Its bone heel slammed into the ground; the impact reverberated up its leg, its spine juddered and the recoil reached its neck. A series of loud cracks split the air and shards of bone flew as the enormous composite skull wobbled, like a heavyweight boxer who had received a knockout punch.

Kenny ducked as the head teetered towards him before it rolled forward again and broke loose. Skeletal arms curved inward and the *gashadokuro* literally had its head in its hands. After a moment of confusion, it turned the skull around to face the front and resumed its onward march.

Reeling from the silver *oni*'s blow, Charles felt the ledge slip away from under his feet and knew that a sheer drop awaited him. Twisting in the air, he stretched out desperate fingers while Silver charged towards Kiyomi and Zengubu.

The sting of sharp rock beneath his fingertips and a painful jarring in his left shoulder told Charles that he had somehow latched on to an outcrop. He dangled for a second by one arm, legs kicking to find a grip on the cliff wall, before he managed to scramble his right hand onto the ridge.

"You've nowhere to run this time," Silver said to Kiyomi, as she backed away. "Just think, after I kill you, we'll be together forever. Ain't that sweet?"

Zengubu appeared, positioning himself between Silver and Kiyomi. He moved with liquid speed and grace, landing a combination of kicks and punches on the approaching *oni*.

"Gah! Stay still!" Silver roared as the *tengu* materialized and dematerialized, teleporting in and out, while raining down blows. A kick to the back of his knee dropped the *oni* to all fours and an elbow smash to the head brought a yelp of pain. "OK, OK, enough!" Silver raised his hands in defeat.

Zengubu stood over the *oni*, fists clenched. "I accept your honorable surrender."

"No!" Kiyomi yelled.

"Sucker!" Silver charged forward, burying his head in the *tengu*'s chest, slamming his back against the rock wall. Zengubu gasped, his eyes wide. The *oni* drew back, his demon horns dripping with blood which ran down his shiny skull and into his open mouth.

"You guys should know you can't take me on my own turf," he said. "Down here, I can't die, no matter what you do. You, on the other hand . . ."

Kiyomi drew two *tanto* blades and set her feet in a defensive stance. "Can mess you up so badly, you'll wish you were dead."

Harashima and Cal crouched on top of the truck, watching the bizarre sight of Kenny bobbing through the air forty yards above their heads, while the ground shook under the marching *oni* army.

"What is that thing? Some kind of walking tank?" Cal said. "Can he bring it down before it hits the city?"

Harashima scowled. "If anyone can, he can."

Up on top of the *gashadokuro*, Kenny had a brain wave. Using the ribs like a giant climbing frame, he clambered down the back until he reached the bottom ribs. From here he had a clear view of the legs swinging from the pelvic girdle, each stride eating up the ground.

The monster was trampling its way across a field of lettuce. Kenny leaned over and concentrated, focusing his will, channeling his spirit. The consistency of the soil changed from firm to slushy. The giant bony foot squelched down and sank in past the ankle – at which point Kenny hardened the ground to concrete, encasing it.

The skeleton gave a yelp of surprise and toppled forward before arresting the fall with its other leg. As it struggled to regain its balance, Kenny repeated the trick to trap both feet. Howls and groans of dismay arose from the following army.

Kenny cupped his hands around his mouth and yelled, "Shoot me!" towards the truck.

"Did he just say to shoot him?" Cal repeated to Harashima.

"Yes, he did," Harashima said. "I think I know what he means." Kiyomi's father slid down from the roof, hopped into the back of the vehicle and emerged with a three-foot-long metal tube. He aimed the RPG launcher at the space directly below Kenny's floating feet and pulled the trigger.

FA-WHOOSH! The booster ignited, launching the grenade out of the tube at over three hundred feet per second. The rocket-propulsion system fired, boosting the acceleration threefold, and the warhead arrowed in on the invisible monster.

Seeing the flash of light and discharge of white smoke, Kenny took his cue to leap from the ribs of the *gashadokuro*. The grenade blazed below him, hit the skeleton's spine and the high-explosive warhead detonated.

Carried by the wind, Kenny watched a fireball mushroom out of the monster's rib cage, blasting apart its pelvis and spine. The upper half teetered and fell backward, crashing onto the *oni* below and squashing hundreds of them. A split second later, the massive skull dropped like a bomb and shattered, the pieces ripping through Susano-wo's army.

Kenny landed by the truck and smiled grimly at the

sight of two giant skeletal legs sticking up and thousands of *oni* retreating to their camp.

"Enough!" Susano-wo screamed in rage. "Kuromori, it's just you and me!"

High up on the ridge, Kiyomi slashed and thrust at the silver *oni* with her short swords. The ledge was narrow, limiting her movements. Silver ducked and feinted, staying out of Kiyomi's sword range. Charles, meanwhile, had braced his feet against a protruding rock and was inching his way higher, the eyeglass pressed to his face like a monocle.

"Give it up and I'll go easy on you, I promise," Silver said.

"Never!" Kiyomi spat and she swept a blade around, slashing the *oni*'s knee.

"Ow! Why you little –" Silver kicked at the pile of gravel that Zengubu had excavated, spraying a face-full of grit into Kiyomi's eyes. She ducked her head and Silver piled in, clamped a paw around her throat and began to squeeze. Unable to breathe, Kiyomi felt blood pound in her head and the edges of her vision began to dim.

"I've got you now," Silver exulted, leaning in. "It's over."

Not trusting his aim, Charles rested one elbow on the ridge and pointed his automatic pistol at the nearest target–Silver's foot. He opened fire, emptying the magazine.

The *oni* roared in pain as its right foot turned to pulp and it released its choke hold, arms spinning like a windmill to retain balance on the ledge.

Kiyomi struck without mercy or hesitation, stabbing one blade through the *oni*'s ears and plunging the second through its left eye. With her back braced against the cliff, she hammered a two-footed kick into Silver's midriff, propelling the ogre off the shelf and towards the rocks below.

"I could use a hand, please," Charles said, still dangling.

Kiyomi breathed in harsh gulps of air and hauled Kenny's father to safety beside the injured *tengu*.

The falling Silver smashed into a boulder, bounced and rolled to a stop at the base of the ravine. "Oww." Opening his remaining eye he strained his neck to see his fellow *oni* fighting to reach the portal.

Standing in their way and fighting shoulder to shoulder, Lawrence and Genkuro continued to repel the advancing *oni*, but the numbers surging towards the pass were growing by the second.

"There are too many of them," Lawrence said, firing a bolt of lightning through one *oni* and into another close behind.

"That is because your grandson is doing his job," Genkuro said, changing an *oni* into stone and then shattering it with a punch. "The more he kills, the more we face."

"*RRARGH!* Got you," bellowed a hoarse voice from behind and a silver paw clamped around Lawrence's leg, twisted and snapped the limb.

The elderly man cried out and fell, allowing a slavering amber *oni* to step into the breach.

Genkuro whirled to see a twisted, broken, half-blind Silver crushing his friend's leg. "No!" he said, and hurled his staff like a spear. In midflight, the end sharpened to a point and tore through the stricken monster, impaling it.

Another *oni* reared up beside Genkuro. With their defensive line breached, it was over.

"Form up!" Kenny commanded and his ragtag band of humans and woodland creatures assembled in a line.

"We have two hundred and fifteen soldiers," Harashima reported. "Barely a single rank."

"Do we know how many Susie has lost?" Kenny asked, wiping a tired hand over his grubby brow.

"Maybe a couple of thousand."

"OK." Kenny stopped to consult his notes again. "Any word from Kiyomi?"

Harashima shook his head.

"Then they'll need more time," Kenny said. He drew Ikutachi and marched out again onto the battlefield. Seeing him, the kneeling gods raised their heads in surprise.

"I knew it!" Kuebiko's shrill voice rang out. "I told you he wasn't dead. I told you."

Susano-wo strode ahead of his waiting army. "Kuromori, it has been many a year since I last encountered a mortal as irritating and burdensome as you."

"I do my best," Kenny said. He felt the god's mind probe his once again.

"Hnh? You wish to die at my hand?" declared the bearded warrior, quizzically. "Very well." Susano-wo turned on his heel. "Prepare to attack!" he commanded.

"Kiyomi, wherever you are, can you hurry it up?" Kenny muttered to himself as he returned to his troops.

Kokibo materialized on Kiyomi's ledge with Sato. "Our work is done," he reported.

"Explosives all rigged on our side and detonators in place," Sato said. His gaze fell upon the bleeding Zengubu, propped up by Charles, and the silver blood staining the ground. "What happened here?"

"Tell you later," Kiyomi said, tying off a length of electrical cord leading from the hole Zengubu had made. "We're all set."

"There is a problem," Kokibo said, perching on the rock edge and pointing down.

Kiyomi looked, gasped, and covered her mouth with her hands. Far below, dozens of *oni* were battling with Genkuro and the wounded Lawrence.

"We have to help them!" she said. "Get them out of there."

"We're in no shape to help anyone," Sato said. "Look at us."

Genkuro chopped the ground with the side of his palm and a shock wave exploded outward, scattering *oni* like skittles. He helped Lawrence to stand and looked upward. "Close the pass," he commanded. "Now."

Groaning, the stunned *oni* rolled to their feet, spurred on by more numbers coming up the pass.

"No, *sensei!*" Kiyomi said. "We can't let you die here. You'll never leave."

"That's our choice," Lawrence said, his face creased with pain. "Charles? Are you there?"

"Yes, Dad, I'm here," Charles said.

"Be the father to Kenny that I should have been to you. Promise me that."

Charles nodded, his eyes filling with tears. "I promise, Dad. I –"

"No!" Kiyomi shouted. "I'm not going to do it. I won't . . ."

Genkuro sighed. "Then I will." He raised his hand.

The *oni* forces charged through the narrow gap. All that stood between them and the portal to Earth were two elderly humans.

"*Noooo!*" Kiyomi screamed.

With one arm supporting Lawrence, Genkuro snapped his fingers. A double explosion cannoned through the mountain pass, shredding the cliff walls. Fissures opened and giant slabs peeled away from bedrock.

The silver *oni* raised his one good eye to see the mother of all avalanches plummeting towards him. He swallowed hard before thousands of tons of ancient rock buried him and sealed the pass forever.

43 四十三

"Hold your line!" Kenny ordered, as the ground shook under the thundering feet of thousands of stampeding *oni*. "Wait for it!"

"This is crazy," Cal muttered to Harashima, standing by the truck and watching the grass of the field flatten as if beaten down by a heavy gale. "There's no way that line can hold."

"Wait!" Kenny said, and realized his knees were shaking. The charging ranks of *oni* closed the gap. Fifty yards . . . forty yards . . . thirty . . . "Wh–?"

Sudden darkness shrouded the battlefield, like a thick cloud passing over the sun. Spinning around, Kenny stared upward – and screamed.

Rippling out of the sky was a thousand-ton mass of black serpentine muscle, over a mile long. Spines ran along its back, long horns crowned its head and whiskers hung from its mouth. Its one good eye burned with hate.

Clinging to the dragon like a swarm of lice were the three hundred *tengu* commanded by Sojobo, and Kenny immediately realized what had happened. The *tengu* had not retreated; they had gone in search of help – help in the shape of Namazu, the earthquake dragon, sworn enemy of Kusanagi, the Sword of Heaven, current owner: Susano-wo.

The *oni* army stopped mid charge and terrified cries filled the air as the dragon streaked out of the sky towards them like a cruise missile.

"No!" Susano-wo said in disbelief, just before Namazu smashed into him, tearing up the earth, shaking the ground and crushing hundreds of *oni* under its mountainous bulk.

"What just happened?" Cal shouted, picking himself up off the ground.

"The cavalry just arrived," Kenny said, watching the *tengu* take up position on the front line.

"I can see them!" Stacey yelped from the front seat of the hovering Apache. "They did it! They did it!"

Kokibo carried Zengubu from the opening, with Charles, Kiyomi and Sato traipsing behind. The Black Hawk touched down long enough to allow the ground team to board.

"Take us to Iucho, across the water," Sato said to the pilot.

Kiyomi slid open the door and seated herself behind the six-barreled mini gun mounted by the hatch.

Kenny had glimpsed Susano-wo for a fraction of a second before the dragon's jaws fell on him like a collapsing building. Kusanagi, glowing brightly, was in his hand and he seemed to leap into Namazu's throat.

The dragon writhed and undulated over the ground like a dog trying to dislodge a flea. Its gargantuan tail swept back and forth, grinding *oni* into dust, and its raking claws swept demons into the air by the hundred. Tense moments ticked by while Susano-wo's forces ran in all directions. Those who came too close to the *tengu* line were picked off easily.

Namazu finally rolled onto its front, settled its four taloned feet on the ground and roared in triumph.

Sojobo bowed before Kenny. "It worked. Namazu has defeated his ancient enemy and the sword is now gone."

Kenny whooped and punched the air. "That's brilliant! Whose idea was it to drop a dragon on his head?"

"That was you," Sojobo said. "It pushed all of us *tengu* to our limit to teleport something so large."

"But it worked!" Kenny said. "And it wiped out maybe half of his army too. Nice job. Now how do we get him home again . . . ?" Kenny's voice trailed away as he sensed something was wrong.

The dragon shook its massive head then rolled its shoulders. It turned in a circle, a perplexed look on its face, then crashed to the ground as its legs gave way. It uttered a low groan and its head hit the earth. Kenny ran forward, instantly on the alert.

Namazu's tail twitched and a sliver of light emerged from the tip, accompanied by a tearing sound like a sheet of paper being slowly ripped in half.

"Oh no," Kenny said.

The dragon's scales turned from black to gray and it crumbled into ash. Dusting himself off and strutting from the tail was Susano-wo. "A nice trick," he said, "but I told you before, I am the slayer of dragons."

"It isn't over yet," Kenny said, trying to sound more confident than he was. He whispered to Sojobo, "What else did I come up with?"

The *tengu* king shrugged. "I did as you asked. I know not what you said to the others."

"Wait, something is wrong," Susano-wo said, looking around at his decimated troops. "Why are there no replacements?" His eyes widened and he pivoted to level an accusing finger at Kenny. "A ruse! Kuromori, you have been toying with me to allow others to close the door to *Yomi*."

"I knew it!" screeched Kuebiko from the side.

"Which means anyone who gets wasted now isn't coming back," Kenny said, directing his words at the demoralized *oni*. "And that includes you."

Fury blazed in Susano-wo's eyes and his fingers tightened on Kusanagi. "I sense your strange desire to die at my hand and that is the only reason why I am not granting your wish, but know that my patience wears thin."

"Hey, what's that sound?" Kenny paused, hearing a distant thrumming noise.

"Spare me your deceit," Susano-wo snapped. He addressed his troops. "This world is ours for the taking. I am supreme ruler and no one – not the gods, not mortals and certainly not this boy – can stand in my way. Stiffen your spines and strike. One more attack and we end this."

Kenny's head swiveled around, trying to identify the drumming sound. And then he saw it: two helicopters roared in, skimming the tree line. In front was an Apache which opened fire with its nose-mounted chain gun, spewing a deadly hail of high-explosive rounds at a rate of over six hundred per minute.

BRRRRRRRRRRRRRRR! Scores of *oni* burst into dust as Stacey rained death upon them. Right behind her was Kiyomi, manning the Gatling gun in the Black Hawk. The barrels spun, churning a storm of high-velocity projectiles with deadly accuracy.

Susano-wo bristled with rage and coils of electricity rippled across his knuckles. "Enough defiance!" he screamed, pointing at the gunships. An arc of lightning leapt from each hand and lanced through the aircraft, frying the electrical systems.

Sojobo vanished and Kenny watched in horror as the two helicopters fell spinning from the sky to come crashing down on the *oni* below. Rotor blades chewed the ground, snapped and rebounded away, slicing through flesh, before each chopper exploded, ripping apart any *oni* within range.

"Dad! Kiyomi!" Kenny called in shock, the flames

reflecting in his watering eyes.

"Right here," Kiyomi said from behind his shoulder. "Miss me?"

Sojobo had a hand on Charles and Kiyomi, while the injured Zengubu gripped the arms of Stacey and Sato for support. Kokibo had both pilots in hand.

"That was too close," Sato said.

"Is that it, Kuromori?" frothed a wild-eyed Susano-wo, standing amid the wreckage. "Any more tricks before I flay you?"

Kenny nudged Sato. "*Is* that it?"

Sato winked and cocked an eyebrow at Cal who was wrapping an arm around his daughter. "Admiral Clark came through. The bird's on its way. Just keep him talking," Cal said.

"Over to you, Kuromori-*san*," Sato said, patting Kenny on the back.

Kenny nodded and strode over to face the Storm God. "Last chance," he said. "Surrender now, hand me back the treasures I found and we'll shake hands and go our separate ways."

"What? You dare? You insolent whelp! You have no respect."

Kenny shrugged. "Yeah, sorry. *Gaijin* and all that." He looked across at the perturbed faces of the gods before returning his gaze to Susano-wo. "So? Do you want to stop this madness?"

"Or what?"

Kenny swallowed hard and said, with as much conviction as he could muster, "Or I'm going to have to kick your stupid butt."

Kiyomi's mouth dropped open.

"Hey, what's that noise?" Stacey whispered in Kiyomi's ear. "Is that Susie?"

Kiyomi cocked her head and listened: a sound like distant thunder was rolling in fast.

"Now, we end this!" Susano-wo roared, signaling for what remained of his troops to gather for a final charge. "But leave Kuromori for me. You wish to die, boy? Consider your wish granted."

Kiyomi ran forward and tugged Kenny's shoulder. "What's he on about? He's read your mind and . . . you want to die?"

"It's the only way," Kenny said.

"Are you insane?"

"I started this. I have to finish it. Once and for all."

"And that means he kills you?"

"Trust me." Kenny took Kiyomi's face in his hands and pulled her close, pressing his lips to hers.

Kiyomi pulled away, fighting back tears, and thumped her fists against his chest. "No, I'm not losing you as well. You need me. *Yin* and *yang*, remember? Separately, we're a mess, but together we can do anything."

"I know," Kenny said, pressing a tattered white envelope into Kiyomi's hands. "That's why I wrote this. Just don't wait until I'm dead to read it." He turned and signaled to his waiting forces of animals, *tengu* and humans. "Are we ready?" They roared in reply. "Then let's give it to them!"

The drone of the *oni* horn signaled the final assault. Susano-wo lowered his sword and the forces of Hell raced across the battlefield for the last time.

Kenny took a deep breath and went to meet his death.

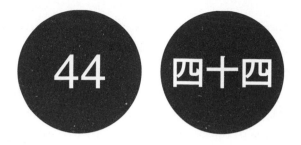

44 四十四

engu formed the front line, with *kitsune*, *tanuki*, weasels and badgers behind them. On the far side of the churned-up battlefield, Susano-wo's troops numbered some four thousand. Their losses had been considerable, but their force was still overwhelming. They stampeded in their droves, ready to sweep aside all opposition.

"Hold the line," Kenny said. Something grabbed his leg and he looked down to see a fat, bloodied *tanuki*. "Poyo! *What are you doing here?* Go find Kiyomi. She needs you."

The *oni* closed the distance, screaming and howling.

Poyo shook his head and pointed to his cousins, armed with cudgels.

"You're not a fighter," Kenny hissed. "Go on, get out of here."

The ground shook and thunder rumbled in the air.

"I mean it. Go! That's an order." Kenny shook the furry creature off his leg.

Poyo whined and slunk away as the wave of *oni* arrived, slamming into the waiting *tengu*. Up close, Kenny saw why the bird-demons were among the most feared warriors in Japan. They were fast, strong, superbly trained, and their power of teleportation meant they could blink in and out of sight to attack from every angle in seconds. Blades flashed, limbs flew, bones cracked and, somewhere in the middle of the storm, was a fifteen-year-old boy from England with a sword that fought on his behalf.

Ikutachi stabbed, blocked, parried, swept, slashed, punched and deflected everything that came in Kenny's direction. *Oni* after *oni* fell under the enchanted blade as Kenny carved his way through to Susano-wo.

The Storm God had the same trajectory, but from the opposite direction. Kusanagi sliced through bone, bronze, steel, wood and flesh without distinction, zeroing in on its sworn enemy.

Just as Kenny glimpsed Susano-wo towering above his *oni* soldiers, hurling bodies aside, thunder split the sky and a US Air Force F-22 Raptor from Kadena Air Base streaked low over the battle zone. From the corner of his eye, Kenny saw it release a guided penetration bomb. "What the –?"

The "bunker buster" honed in on its target: a fifty-foot-high earthfill dam built on the edge of Lake Nakaumi to hold back the waters and enable land reclamation. Over two hundred pounds of TNT punched downward and obliterated the dam, heaving a dome of rock into the sky.

Susano-wo paused as the earth trembled underfoot, his heightened senses jangling–and then he saw the wave. Freed by the dam's destruction, the waters of Lake Nakaumi surged forward to reclaim their old territory.

Oni, *kitsune*, hag and *tanuki* alike were swept aside by the flood and the battlefield was cleared in less than a minute. *Oni* rolled in the three-foot-deep tide and struggled to stand, ribbons of chill water streaming off their bodies.

"*YAAAGH!*" One of the *oni* vanished under the water, then another and another. As the *tengu* pulled their allies to safety, Susano-wo's legions were dragged down into the lake and drowned by an underwater army.

Kenny spluttered to his feet and gaped at the desolation all around. Susano-wo's army of thousands was all but gone, with a few bedraggled *oni* splashing away from the deadly waters.

"We did good?" a whiny voice called from behind Kenny.

He whirled around to see a familiar frog-eyed face with a beak and ring of black hair encircling a concave skull.

"Yes! You did great!" Kenny said to the *kappa*. "I knew you'd come."

"Yes," the *kappa* agreed. "We help needed." Hundreds of other *kappa* popped up from the water and waved.

"You!" bellowed Susano-wo, wading across the shallow lake water, his eyes fixed on Kenny. "Now, you die!"

Splashing towards the ridge, Kiyomi read the soggy note a second time.

"You have got to be kidding me," she muttered. "He's crazy. This is the stupidest idea ever." She glanced at the returning warriors, looking for one small one in particular.

Sato paddled past. "*Oji*," she said, "can you get the RPG?"

Kusanagi sliced through the air, aimed at Kenny's skull. Ikutachi sprang upward, parrying the blow, and to Kenny's relief the blade held firm.

"So, you have a weapon to counter Kusanagi?" Susano-wo said, circling. "And you rely on it to fight for you? How pathetic. You should know that it is the warrior who controls the weapon, not the other way around." He lunged again and Kenny's sword flicked to the side, deflecting the jab.

Kenny's mind worked quickly; there was no way he could beat Susano-wo based on strength and the god towered several feet above him, so his only hope would be to use speed and turn the height difference to his advantage.

Susano-wo came at him with a combination of blows and thrusts, his sword tip weaving intricate patterns in the damp air. Like his partner in some kind of deadly dance, Ikutachi swooped and countered, blocking each strike. The air rang with the clatter and clang of steel against steel and everyone stopped – human, animal, ogre and god alike – to watch.

Everyone except Kiyomi. With Poyo sitting on her shoulders, she took up position beside the cab of the truck. Sato, at her side with a half spectacle over his eye, rested the grenade launcher on the hood and took aim.

WHANG! CLANG! TING! The flurry of hefty smacks forced Kenny back and his sword was little more than a blur. Kenny knew he had to take the initiative and he dived forward, into the lake, and kicked out, swimming between Susano-wo's legs. The giant roared and stabbed downward into the water. Kenny sprang up behind him and jabbed his sword into the god's calf, attempting to sever the Achilles tendon.

"*ARGH!*" Susano-wo yelled and stamped both feet to squash his opponent.

Kenny dived again and resurfaced to see the wound close itself up. He struck again, this time going for the foot, but Susano-wo anticipated the move and smashed Kenny with his shield.

Thirty feet away, Kenny splashed down, his head ringing and he saw two of Susano-wo rushing at him. The twin images merged into one as the Storm God stood over him, sword in hand, and drove the blade down towards his chest. Ikutachi leapt into action to block, but Susano-wo leaned in with all his strength and weight, driving the point inexorably towards Kenny's heart.

And then it stopped. Kusanagi froze in midair.

"Hnh? What treachery is this?" Susano-wo roared, with face red and muscles straining.

"It's ... fighting you," Kenny said, scrabbling backward. "Kusanagi . . . it's resisting. Making a choice."

"No! There is no choice. There is no freedom. There is only my will."

"Now!" Kiyomi said and Sato fired the rocket launcher.

FWHOOSH! The grenade streaked across the flooded field and caught Susano-wo just below the throat, where it detonated.

Susano-wo flailed, managing to stay on his feet, but his armored breastplate hung loosely in shattered halves and the bones of his neck were exposed, stark white against the red of flesh.

"*GLKKK!*" he said, reaching for his ruined throat, but the tissues were already knitting together.

"Get him now!" Kiyomi screamed, nocking an arrow into her *yumi* longbow.

Kenny sprang up and plunged his sword deep into the exposed wound, driving the blade down into Susano-wo's chest. The god's eyes bulged, before narrowing with raw hate.

Unarmed, Kenny took a step back – and Susano-wo ran him through with Kusanagi.

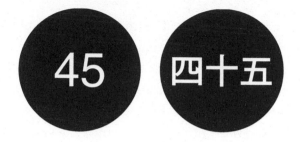

Kenny gasped, his legs buckled and he sat down in the water, staring down at the sword handle protruding from his chest. Blood bubbled into his lungs, making it impossible for him to even scream out in pain.

Her lips curled in concentration, Kiyomi fired the arrow. It soared across the battlefield. From the edge of his vision, Susano-wo saw the missile flying in towards his throat and twisted. A warped bronze plate of broken armor swung upward and the arrowhead punched harmlessly through it.

Susano-wo smiled in triumph and reached for the sword handle sticking up from his chest. That was when he felt the tickle of small furry feet scampering across the back of his neck, heard the snap of sharp little teeth and felt the jade stone slip from around his collar.

Kenny raised a hand weakly, but Poyo's aim was perfect, landing the stone in his palm as he keeled over into the rank waters.

Susano-wo reared up, his eyes wide with panic, and thrashed around, searching for the stone. He dropped to his knees and splashed in the water, until his hands closed on Kenny's leg. Lurching to his feet with Kenny dangling upside down from his fist, Susano-wo formed the words, "Give . . . me . . . my . . . stone . . . before . . . I . . . take . . . it . . ."

Kenny wrapped both hands around the stone, but he knew it was hopeless. Susano-wo could rip his arms off to get it.

"I think not," a deep voice rumbled. "The stone is with its rightful owner." Hachiman, the God of War, placed one armored hand on Susano-wo's chest and his other on the storm god's wrist. "Release the boy, lest I break thine arm."

"You . . . have . . . no . . . authority . . . over . . . me . . . lackey . . ." Susano-wo wheezed. "I . . . am . . . your . . . ruler . . ."

"'Tis true," Hachiman concurred, "so long as thou bearest the Three Sacred Treasures."

Realization dawned in Susano-wo's eyes.

"But whence I stand, I count only two. Which means I can do – this!" Hachiman spun and landed a crunching uppercut to Susano-wo's jaw, lifting the Storm God off the ground and dumping him a hundred yards away.

Kiyomi splashed her way across to Kenny, scooping up a sopping Poyo along the way.

"We did it, Ken-*chan*!" she said, beaming. "We did it."

"Whose idea was it to shoot Poyo on an arrow?" Kenny asked.

"Some idiot I know came up with that," Kiyomi said. "Pretty clever though, taking out Susano-wo at the same time."

"Did I really plan all that?" Kenny said. "Wow, I had no idea I was that good."

"Don't get carried away. Even a broken clock is right twice a day. Besides, it wouldn't have worked without me."

Kenny reached out and drew Kiyomi close, feeing the warmth of her body against his cold wet skin.

"Have I earned a kiss?" he said, blushing.

"OK, go on then," Kiyomi said and she squished Poyo's furry muzzle against Kenny's puckered lips.

"Hey!" he spluttered.

"Kenny! Thank goodness you're safe," Charles said, wading across. "I . . . I love you, son, and I'm so very proud of you. So is your grandfather." His voice caught.

"Where is Grandad anyway? I don't see him," Kenny said, scanning faces. Kiyomi looked away.

"Dad didn't make it," Charles said. "Nor did Genkuro."

"No!" Kenny gasped. "That can't be."

"They sacrificed themselves so we could get away. And close the gate."

"You mean they died in *Yomi*? So they can't leave? And Susie now has their souls?" Kenny's voice rose with each question. "That is so wrong! We have to go back."

"I'm sorry," Charles said, sounding numb. "It was their choice."

"Do not fear for them." Kenny instantly knew Inari's voice and looked up to see the goddess standing a little way off. "Their spirits are both safe with me." She was as beautiful and inscrutable as ever. "I would never abandon such brave and loyal servants. Come with me, please, Kuromori." She walked away from the crowd, her feet never touching the water.

"Uh, sure," Kenny said. "Be right back," he said to Kiyomi and his father.

"Kuromori," Inari said, "when you agreed to serve me, I imparted a fraction of my essence to you."

"You did?" Kenny said.

"When I touched you on the forehead. This enabled me to be with you always, to see what you see, to feel what you feel. I have been with you every step of this journey."

"Whoa, does that mean you've been controlling my actions, like some kind of puppet? Is that why I've been able to do weird things?"

"I have no power to control you, Kuromori. Everything you did, you did by yourself." Inari paused. "You have served exceptionally well, better than I had dared hope."

"Really?" Kenny said. "I thought I messed everything up big time by not listening to you."

"And you thought I did not know that would happen? When I chose you, Kuromori, I knew that your love for the girl would lead you astray, that you would deliver the regalia to our enemy."

"You did? And you never tried to stop me?"

"Look at what has come about," Inari said. "For the first time, the gods are united. We have stood together against a common foe and all of our squabbles have been set aside."

"You mean to say you let this happen? To bring about peace?"

"You yourself have seen what our quarrels can do. Now, with the Three Sacred Treasures under my control, I can usher in a new age."

"That was one huge gamble," Kenny said. "I mean, what if I'd failed and Susano-wo had ended up in charge?"

For the first time, Inari smiled. "Even the gods can have faith in a mortal."

With thousands of deities on hand, the cleanup took no time at all. They moved freely among the vestiges of battle, stopping to heal the injured. Hachiman personally escorted Susano-wo back to *Yomi* to await punishment. Amaterasu burned through the clouds, allowing sunshine to dry the earth. Ryujin drove the waters back to the lake, while others repaired the dam.

"How are you going to explain this away?" Kenny asked Sato.

The government agent scratched his head. "Oh, I'll think of something. Probably a live fire training drill went wrong and a helicopter crashed on maneuvers."

Kiyomi drew Kenny aside. "So, Inari's in charge now

and it's thanks to you."

"What do you think?" Kenny asked. "Does this mean a new era of peace?"

"We'll see," Kiyomi said.

Tsukuyomi swept past, carrying Kuebiko on his shoulder. He saw Kenny, paused and lowered his head. "Kuromori, you did well today. Not bad for a *gaijin*."

"I told you he would do it, didn't I?" Kuebiko said. "I knew it."

Amaterasu held out her hands to Kenny and Kiyomi. "Kuromori, we must reward you for what you have done. Name your prize."

"Oh, no. Not after last time," Kiyomi groaned.

"Relax," Kenny said. "I've learned my lesson." He scrunched his forehead and then smiled. "You know, there is one thing. I still haven't tried that peach-flavored milkshake we talked about."

Kiyomi slapped a palm over her forehead. "Ken-*chan*, you are such a dork."

"Sorry, that was kind of stupid, wasn't it?" Kenny said. "I'll get you one as well."

"No," Amaterasu gently chided. "A true hero deserves a true reward. You may have anything your heart desires."

Kenny grinned and pulled Kiyomi closer.

"I already have that."

GLOSSARY

hakayaro *(hah-kah-yah-roh)* – idiot, fool, moron

-chan – term of affection appended to a name
chikara *(chee-kah-rah)* – power

ema *(emma)* – small wooden plaque on which Shinto
worshippers write their prayers or wishes

futon *(foo-ton)* – a thin padded mattress

gaijin *(guy-jean)* – foreigner, outsider
gashadokuro *(gah-sha-doh-koo-roh)* – a gigantic
composite skeleton
gyojin *(gi-yoh-jean)* – a fish with humanoid
characteristics; a variety of merman

hai *(high)* – yes
haiku *(high-koo)* – a poem of seventeen syllables in
three lines of five, seven and five

hakama *(hah-kah-mah)* – traditional pleated trouser skirt

hitodama *(hee-toh-dah-mah)* – a human soul in the form of a glowing fiery ball

Hyakki Yagyo *(hee-yah-kee-yag-yoh)* – the Night Parade of One Hundred Demons

itachi *(ee-tah-chee)* – a weasel

itadakimasu *(eat-a-dakky-mass-oo)* – bon appétit; enjoy your meal

kamishimo *(kammy-shee-mo)* – traditional Japanese outfit comprising a kimono, loose pleated trousers and a sleeveless jacket

kanabo *(kah-nah-boh)* – a spiked metal club

kanji *(kan-jee)* – a system of Japanese writing using Chinese characters

kappa *(kap-pah)* – water demon

katana *(kah-tah-nah)* – a long single-edged Samurai sword

ki *(kee)* – energy, spirit, life force

ki-aii! *(kee-eye)* – a short shout or yell uttered before making an attacking move in martial arts

kihaku *(kee-hah-koo)* – spirit, guts

kijimunaa *(kee-jee-moo-nah)* – a type of wood sprite resembling a child-sized human with bright-red hair

kitsune *(kee-tsoo-neh)* – a fox

magatama *(mah-gah-tah-mah)* – a comma-shaped jewel

minshuku *(min-shoo-koo)* – a Japanese-style bed and breakfast

mujina *(moo-jee-nah)* – a badger

mukade *(moo-kah-deh)* – a giant venomous centipede

nandayo? *(nan-dah-yoh)* – what is it now?

Nihonjin *(nee-hon-jean)* – Japanese person

ninja – person skilled in martial arts and stealth, hired for sabotage, assassination or spying

okaasan *(oh-kah-san)* – mother

obi *(oh-bee)* – a wide sash for a kimono

Obon *(oh-bon)* – Festival of the Dead, held every summer

oji *(oh-jee)* – uncle

oni *(oh-nee)* – demon, devil, ogre or troll

onibaba *(oh-nee-bah-bah)* – demon hag

onmoraki *(on-more-ak-kee)* – a demon bird

oshiego *(osh-ee-ay-goh)* – a disciple

o-yoroi *(oh-yoh-roy-ee)* – traditional Samurai heavy armor

rokumonsen *(rok-koo-mon-sen)* – six coins of old Japanese money

ryu *(ree-yoo)* – jewel, dragon

Ryugu-jo *(ree-yoo-goh-joh)* – palace of the dragon god

sakura *(sah-koo-rah)* – cherry blossom

-sama *(sah-mah)* – term of great respect appended to a name

Samurai *(sah-moo-rye)* – a member of the Japanese warrior class

-san – term of respect appended to a name

sanshu no jingi *(san-shoo-noh-jing-gi)* – the Three Sacred Treasures of Japan, the Imperial Regalia

sashimi *(sah-she-mee)* – bite-sized pieces of raw fish eaten with soy sauce or horseradish

sensei *(sen-say)* – teacher; master

shinji rarenai *(shin-jee-rah-reh-nigh)* – I don't believe it

shuriken *(shoo-ree-ken)* – concealed bladed weapon; metal throwing star

sono bakayaro wa dokoda? *(son-noh-bah-kah-yah-roh-wa-doh-koh-dah)* – where is that idiot?

tanto *(tan-toh)* – short sword, between 6 and 12 in. long

tanuki *(tah-noo-kee)* – Japanese raccoon dog

temizuya *(teh-mee-zoo-yah)* – cleansing place at a shrine

tengu *(ten-goo)* – long-nosed bird-demon

tenshukaku *(ten-shoo-kah-koo)* – the main keep of a Japanese castle, the central tower

uguisubari *(ooh-goo-ee-soo-bah-ree)* – a wooden floor with special nails that squeak when walked upon

ushi-oni *(oo-shee-oh-nee)* – a monster with the head of a bull and the body of a spider or crab

wagyu *(wah-gyoo)* – a premium brand of Japanese beef
watakuri *(wah-tah-koo-ree)* – bowel raker; a barbed arrowhead

Yasakani no Magatama *(yah-sah-kah-nee-noh-mah-gah-tah-mah)* – the Jewel of Life, one of the Three Sacred Treasures
yatta! *(yah-tah)* – I did it; yes!
yin yang – Chinese philosophical concept of opposite forces acting in harmony
yokai *(yoh-kigh)* – supernatural creature such as oni and kappa
Yomi *(yoh-mee)* – the underworld; Land of the Dead; Hell
Yomido ni sayarimasu okami *(yoh-mee-doh-nee-sah-yah-ree-mass-oh-kah-mee)* – the name of the huge rock at the Iya Shrine blocking the entrance to Yomi
yomotsu-shikome *(yoh-mott-soo-she-koh-mee)* – a Hellhag
yukata *(yoo-kah-tah)* – a light cotton kimono
yumi *(yoo-mee)* – an asymmetrical longbow
yurei *(yoo-ray)* – ghost, spirit of the dead

J